THE SORCERER'S CURSE

THE SORCERER'S CURSE

THE STORY OF THE FIRST ARCHIMAGE

BOOK 4

MICHAELA RILEY KARR

Rye Meadow Press

Published by Rye Meadow Press, based in Emporia, KS.
ryemeadowpress@gmail.com

ISBN (paperback): 978-0-9986065-7-6
ISBN (hardback): 978-0-9986065-8-3
Library of Congress Control Number: 2020911135

Cover Design © 2020: Magpie Designs, ltd.
Photo Credit: Pixabay
Texture Credit: Sascha Duensing
Author Photo Credit: Jordan Storrer Photography
Interior Map © 2020: L. N. Weldon

Printed in the United States of America.
First Edition, 2020.

DEDICATION

To Hannah Robinson: my favorite roomie, my forever Taco Bell date, my writing-partner-in-crime, my best friend.

NERAHDIS

TREDENO

JOSHUUA'S TREE

RHYDIN
PALAC

LEONAR

THE KINGDOM OF
MINERALTIR

CADI

MINERALTIR CASTLE

★
DEMORA

TRANINI

THE
GREAT DESERT

★
IONDRIA

N

IVANN'S DELTA

★ CAPITAL
● CITY
■ CASTLE

FAMILY TREES

———⸰⟲⟳⸰———

(contains spoilers)

♦ denotes marriage
◊ denotes an affair/relationship
[denotes siblings
* denotes sovereign king/queen
↓ denotes the second time a person is listed
Year 1 = Humans arrived in Nerahdis with Emperor Caden.
B.N. = "Before Nerahdis"
A.N. = "After Nerahdis"
    - dates without a suffix should be considered "A.N."

Book 1: *The Allyen* = Year 344
Book 2: *The War of the Three Kingdoms* = Year 346
Book 3: *Reign of Darkness* = Year 348
Book 4: *The Sorcerer's Curse* = Year 359

LINEAGES OF OLD

Emperor Caden Gornan (18 B.N. – 30 A.N.)
♦Empress Melodi Heid (18 B.N. – 8 A.N.)

  Joshuua*, *the First King of Mineraltir* (4 – 58)
  ♦Emma Rollins (4 – 64)
    Minndosia, *the Second Archimage* (22 – 63)
    Cilla (25 – 86)
    Levi* (29 – 89)
      (see Mineraltin Lineage)
    Drina (32 – 72)
    Grace (33 – 82)
  Ivann*, *the First King of Auklia* (5 – 62)
  ♦Abigayle Cedal (6 – 35)
    Felicity* (31 – 90)
      (see Auklian Lineage)
    Dathian (33 – 88)
    Leah (35 – 91)
    Hyllary (37 – 82)
  Spenser*, *the First King of Lunaka* (6 – 70)
  ♦Laurenn Tané (7 – 63)
    Marya (31-92)
    Jeremie* (37 – 97)
    Alora (42 – 101)
      (see Lunakan Lineage)

Lord Anders Soreta (32 B.N. – 28 A.N.)
♦Lady Mae (24 B.N. – 15 A.N.)
  – **Nora Soreta**, *the First Allyen* (7 – 59)
  ♦Charles Rodgers (4 – 59)
    – Myron Rodgers, *an Allyen* (36 – 92)
      (see Allyen Lineage)

MINERALTIN/RANGUVARIIAN LINEAGE

—————————⟨𝕠⟩—————————

-9 Generations Between King Levi and King Camerron-

Camerron Rollins* (279 – 325)

♦Popuri (285 – 340)

    ⌐ Josip Rollins* (265 – 311)

         – Morris Rollins* (298 – 344)

           ♦Lyla (309 – 325)

             – **Xavier Rollins*** (325)

             ♦**Mira Tané** *of Lunaka* (326)

               ⌐ **Taisyn Rollins** (346)

               ⌊ **Lyla Rollins** (348)

           ♦**Jasmine*** (304 – 348)

             – **Ren Rollins** (330 – 348)

    ├ Andromeda Rollins, *an Archimage* (268 – 319)

    ⌊ Emily Rollins (270 – 307)

     ♦**Clariion Arii Buiikan,** *a Ranguvariian* (19)

        ⌐ Istrii Buiikan (295 – 295)

        ├ Laveniia Buiikan (300 – 339)

        ♦Viincen Owiins (297 – 333)

           ⌐ **Rachel Owens** (324)

           ♦**Jaspen Coralii** (320)

             – **Mathiian Coralii** (347)

           ├ **Luke Owens** (326 – 348)

           ⌊ **James Owens** (329)

        ├ Siirella Buiikan (301 – 301)

        ├ Siimeon Buiikan (305 – 333)

        ◊Tiril, *an Aatarilec* (305 – 331)

          – **Conriin Buiikan** (331)

        ⌊ Friid Buiikan (307 – 307)

—————————⟨𝕠⟩—————————

Chieftess Doona (267)

       ⌐ **Chieftess Jaana** (300)

         – **Onna/Chelsea** (329)

       ⌊ ↓Tiril (see above)

AUKLIAN LINEAGE

-9 Generations Between Queen Felicity and King Harold-
Harold Cedal* (274 – 319)
Marissa (276 – 303)

    Maria Cedal* (299 – 344)
    ♦Walter Hester (300 – 331)
        – Daniel Cedal* (322 – 346)
        ♦Lily (322)
            – Unnamed Son (344 – 344)
    Dathian Cedal, *an Archimage* (303 – 346)
    ♦Anne (305 – 338)
        – Sabine Cedal* (325)
            Chretien Cedal, *adopted* (341)
            Willian Cedal, *adopted* (341)

LUNAKAN LINEAGE

-10 Generations Between King Jeremie and King Adam-
Adam Tané* (295 – 348)
♦Gloria (305 – 348)

    Frederick Tané* (324)
    ♦Cassandra Gale (323 – 346)
        Nathia, *a Rounan/adopted* (343)
        Dominick Tané (345)
        Rayna, *removed magically* (346)
            (see Allyen Lineage)
    Mira Tané (326)
        (see Mineraltin Lineage)
    Cornflower (333)

ALLYEN LINEAGE

-9 Generations Between Allyen Myron and Allyen Saarah-
Saarah Rodgers, *an Allyen* (283 – 344)
♦Orren Harvey (280 – 325)
   ⌐ **Robert Harvey**, *an Allyen* (305 – 348)
    ♦Elaine Garnett (306 – 341)
       ⌐ **Linaria Harvey**, *an Allyen* (324)
       ♦**Samton Greene**, *a Rounan Kidek* (323)
          ⌐ **Kylar Greene**, *a Rounan* (345)
          └ **Rayna Greene**, *an Allyen/adopted* (346)
       └ **Evanarion Harvey**, *an Allyen* (324)
       ♦**Cayce Dale**, *a Rounan* (325)
         – **Aron Harvey**, *a Rounan* (347)
   └ Jedidiah Harvey (307 – 337)
    ♦Marie Smith (309 – 341)
       ⌐ ↓Evanarion Harvey, *adopted* (see above)
       └ **Keera Harvey** (332 – 344)

    ↓Elaine Garnett Harvey (see above)
    ♦Liam Sanders (303 – 341)
       ⌐ ↓Linaria Harvey, *adopted* (see above)
       └ **Rosetta Harvey** (328)
       ♦**Mikael North** (327)
         – **Erikin North** (345)

CHAPTER ONE

RAYNA

M y island was like a living creature. Its heart beat along with the waves that eternally crashed against its shores. It breathed in through the leaves of every palm tree, shrub, and particle of moss and breathed out in salty, humid breezes.

To some, my island was a paradise. A slightly overpopulated refuge from the dark empire just a boat ride away. It was warm and summer all the time aside from the occasional ocean storm. I spent many of my childhood days sketching the scenery. All of this didn't change the fact that my old friends at school thought I was crazy for wanting to leave. To me, the Republic of Caark was a prison. A beautiful prison, but a prison nonetheless.

I guess that's what happened when your parents leave you behind to save the world a little over ten years ago.

"Rayna, this is the third time this week you've gotten into a fight with the other kids," my brother chided as we slowly walked home from our sagging schoolhouse. He was just a bit taller than me with a long face and tousled brown hair. "You've got to stop bringing attention to yourself."

"Or what?" I huffed, adjusting the strap of my bookbag angrily. "You'll tell Aunt Rachel on me? If they knew who I am, they wouldn't dare messing with me."

Ky rolled his eyes, hard. "If they knew who you are, who we *all* are, we wouldn't be able to go to school. Caark itself wouldn't even be safe!"

"Oh, shut up. It's not like arithmetic is that important anyway," I grumbled, fighting the desire to just pitch my bookbag into the ocean. "Someday, Mama and Papa will come back for us, and none of it will matter anymore."

"Pretty sure our parents can read and do math. You can't *draw* for a living. Look out, keep this up, and you'll be the only person in this family who's magic-less *and* illiterate!" Ky chortled, trotting faster down the sandy path out of the small town of Aemita, where our school was since Aunt Rachel didn't want us in the big, bustling city of Calitia.

To add insult to injury, Ky summoned his Rounan powers to lift a flattened coconut from the ground and chuck it nearly a half-mile into the ocean, skipping it four times. It didn't matter if he was seen using his magic. Nearly three-quarters of the kids in Caark were Rounans since it was the only place in Nerahdis they wouldn't be hanged. The Rounans were a minority group within the human population, and their magic manifested as an invisible force that could manipulate about anything. While any magic that wasn't Emperor Rhydin's was illegal, his laws were pretty much nonexistent here, far from the mainland. The only thing Ky had to hide was that our father was the Kidek. Leader of the Rounans. Someday, Ky would be too.

If he can tie Papa's faded bandana around his big head, that is. I laughed in my mind.

"Are you two about done? I swear, I have to listen to the same argument every single day," groaned Aron, our cousin, as he lugged his pile of books home. Aron was a year younger than me, yet he was doing the same work Ky was doing, a year older. My little cousin was a *massive* bookworm.

2

On cue, he withdrew a heavy volume from his bag and stuck his nose into it, using his Rounan powers to gently nudge any tripping hazards out of the path so he could walk and read at the same time. He was a full head shorter than me with close-cropped lavender hair, so it didn't stand out so much or curl up into a frizz. I'd been told he looked just like his mother, Aunt Cayce.

"Oh, rub it in then," I moaned, furiously trudging in front of the boys so I didn't have to look at them for the rest of the way home.

Ky's voice softened behind me, "Rayna, you know it'll happen eventually. Don't worry about it."

"Just you wait," I swore angrily, "my magic will awaken any day now, and I'll be more powerful than the two of you combined."

Before Ky could respond, I quickened my pace, leaving him and my cousin in the sandy dust, trotting down the path as it bent toward the west to give a view of the coastline. There was a new, large piece of salmon-colored coral that had washed up onto the shore, and my eyes soaked in an opportunity to draw something I hadn't already done a thousand times.

The beaches in the southern regions of Caark were actually somewhat nice unlike the busy, dirty ones closer to Calitia. We weren't allowed to be near them without Chelsea or Sonya though, the two Aatarilecs – mythical water creatures – who lived near us. Just like we weren't allowed to go anywhere near the city of Calitia.

Too many rules. This place was suffocating.

I dreamed of leaving Caark. I'd dreamt the same dream for as long as I could remember and tried to imagine what the coast on the other side of the ocean looked like. What my parents' homeland of Lunaka looked like. But I knew there was no chance of leaving. I was useless to my parents right now; I couldn't help them. What was an Allyen, a mage of light, whose magic hadn't awakened yet?

Worthless.

Just as Ky and Aron were catching up, I took off to run the last mile to the hodge-podge shanty we called home. The original room our parents had constructed had been added onto multiple times as us kids grew up. Each addition was made out of a different building material, whichever one happened to be cheaper at the time. I never got to go with Aunt Rachel on her shopping trips – another rule – but from what I understood, prices and inventory seemed to fluctuate a *lot* on the island. It all depended on whatever new tariffs and restrictions Emperor Rhydin imposed, seemingly at random.

The center of the shack, what our parents built before they left us, was made of Mineraltin lumber and consisted of a living area and a small, back room where Aunt Rachel, or one of the other Ranguvariians, slept whenever she made a trip to the Continent. The addition Ky and Aron shared was constructed of large, light-colored sea stone from Auklia after lumber vanished. All too soon, imports from Auklia started becoming scarce too, so the smaller addition which housed my room was cobbled together with dark, dried-out coral from just below Caark's shores.

Altogether, you could definitely say it was a unique shack. It had served as great practice for drawing different textures. Sometimes, I wondered if my parents would even recognize it. If they ever came back.

I darted through the door just as the sunny heavens were beginning to sprinkle Caark with a surprise rain that the native Caarkians called "sun tears." Over my shoulder, I could see Ky and Aron pick up their pace, and the latter began to whine that his book was now wet. Dark thoughts plagued my mind as I shut the door behind me to impede them and get them back for all their magic usage.

"What is wrong, small fry?" a squeaky yet smooth, accented voice resounded from behind me. For a Ranguvariian, he had the best Gornish I'd ever heard. "You look like someone threw your sketchbook into the ocean or something."

"Nothing, Mathiian," I whined, rolling my eyes. "Mind your own bee's wax."

"Heh, my mother would be disappointed if I did that," Mathiian laughed.

I turned to face him. The young Ranguvariian boy was lounging at the table with the kitchen chair tilted so far back it looked to be millimeters from falling. He was the same age as Aron, twelve, but he was already nearly six feet tall – and likely not done growing since adult Ranguvariians were like seven feet. Ranguvariians were another mythical race that lived in the extreme regions of Lunaka. They were very tall with pointed ears, leathery skin, and eyes that changed color based on their mood.

Aunt Rachel had left her son here with us when she went to Nerahdis on a short trip last week, saying he was ready to watch us on his own this time since Chelsea and Sonya were next door. After all, we're apparently incapable of being without supervision at *any* time. Plus, Mathiian supposedly needed practice with his already impeccable Gornish.

"I know what's bothering you. Mother told me before she left," Mathiian responded arrogantly. "Just relax. Mother said Allyen Linaria's magic didn't awaken until she was nineteen. You're thirteen. It's not like it's abnormal or anything."

"Uncle Evan was thirteen when his awakened," I huffed as I flung my backpack through the open doorway to my room without a care for any of its contents. I'd left my one, prized possession, my sketchbook, at home today. "I need it *now*, Mathiian."

Mathiian snorted. "The only reason Allyen Evanarion's magic awakened that young is because his family was attacked and his uncle killed by Rhydin's Followers. His life was in immediate danger. So no, you do not *need* it now."

I paused on my way to tip his chair the rest of the way over. That was new information. Aunt Rachel had never told me how either of my mother or my uncle gained use of their magics. I stuttered a bit as I asked, "R-Really? Then how did my mother's come alive?"

"She was falling off a cliff. She was running for her life from Rhydin's Followers with King Frederick at some festival when she was nineteen." Mathiian shrugged like it was the most obvious thing ever, his shoulders brushing the long, brown braid hanging behind his pointed ear. "It takes danger, small fry. You don't need magic when you're safe."

"Danger, huh?" I mused.

The words had barely left my lips before Mathiian leapt out of his chair faster than lightning and waved a tanned finger in my face. "Don't. Even. *Think* about it! Mother would *murder* me, Rayna!"

"Oh, come on, Mathiian," I crooned as I walked around him in a half circle. "Aren't you *bored* on the island? Don't you want some adventure like a *real* Ranguvariian warrior?"

The son of Rachel and Jaspen, the future Clariion of the Ranguvariians, drooped so much I swear his long ears lowered. He muttered, "Just…forget I said anything. We're too young, and you know it. If it was a good time for you to rejoin your parents with the rebellion, they would come get you."

Whatever fire that had sparked inside of me was suddenly smothered. I glared at the Ranguvariian boy, insulted. "Great. Thanks for the obvious."

"Rayna," Mathiian whined, but I didn't stick around to hear what he had to say. The door burst open to reveal Ky and Aron, both sopping wet, but I didn't even care anymore. I hopped over to my bedroom and flung the rickety door shut behind me. The door was cracked in so many places that it really didn't function like a true door, but it was better than nothing.

I kicked my bookbag that I had thrown earlier farther under the blanket that still lay strewn on the floor from the morning. My straw tick and pillow sat haphazardly in the corner on the floor, utterly neglected at all times since I never bothered to make it up. The room was pretty much empty otherwise aside from several random piles of clothing and other small treasures I'd kept from when I was little, having no place to store them. Being the child of the Allyen and the Kidek sure was glamorous.

I angrily slammed my heel into a worn floorboard, causing the opposite end to shoot up and reveal the only thing that truly made me happy. My sketchbook was a thick binding of parchment, the cover smeared with charcoal smudges and grimy from years of my sweaty hands gripping it. I clutched it to my chest as I sunk to my tick on the floor like it was a life raft keeping me afloat. I had meant to take it out and draw my feelings away, but I found myself immobilized. Drawing couldn't solve this problem.

Could anything solve this problem?

My parents didn't want us with them because they're constantly in danger. They wanted to protect us, and no matter how much it made me angry, I couldn't totally fault them for that. My heart stirred in my chest. I probably just said that to make me sound less like a whiny teenager, but at the end of the day, I couldn't help but be sure that if they *truly* wanted us with them, they would have found a way by now.

And, perhaps, they couldn't find a way because I didn't have my magic and was a total sitting duck. Ky and Aron, too, didn't know how to do anything of substance, just random tricks they'd picked up from their friends at school. Nobody was training us because all the adults kept us so safe, danger couldn't even smell us.

I flipped through my sketchbook toward a page somewhere in the middle that I'd had earmarked for as long as I could remember. Two people came into view, people without faces. One of them was very tall with a bandana on his head while the other was a short woman with shoulder-length hair. I had written the colors off to the side since we couldn't afford colored utensils. Brown hair for the woman;

reddish-brown for the man. There was a locket around the woman's neck, and a scar that reached from the temple to the jaw of the man.

They were my parents. Lina and Sam Greene. Cobbled together from all the random descriptions I had ever heard of them from Aunt Rachel. It killed me that I couldn't see their faces. It wasn't like Aunt Rachel ever said, "your mother had big eyes," or "your father had a pronounced nose." She would sometimes say that Ky or I favored one of them in a certain way, but I never really knew how to transcribe that to my drawing. So, they remained faceless. In my sketchbook and in my mind.

I slapped the book shut. But now, I knew there was something I could do about it. As the muffled voices of the boys complained about the weather in the other room, I threw a bunch of clothes under my blanket to make it look like I was sleeping and donned my heavy cloak, my sketchbook in its big pocket. Then, I slipped through my window with nothing but my wits and followed the worn path in a direction I'd never gone before. North. To the city of Calitia.

I tried to jog most of the way there, knowing that the clock was ticking toward Mathiian's discovery of my absence, but it was still a good two hours before the lights of the port town broached the jungle-lined horizon. Beads of sweat collected on my brow, the humidity crushing and the air choked with the noises of insects. I had never run so far in my life, and I had to stop to walk many times. However, once I reached the outer limits of Calitia, I began to wonder how in Nerahdis I was going to go about putting myself in danger to get my magic to awaken.

Raising the hood of my cloak, I began to walk into the city. Aunt Rachel had told me once that the outer rim of the city pretty much popped up over night when Rhydin became emperor, and I believed her seeing it now. There was no real boardwalk, only a slim area between the ramshackle buildings and a narrow, dirt road which absolutely stank of waste. I was wondering where this had come from when, on the other side of the road, a woman flung the brown contents of a pot out of the upper window of a shanty. I walked faster as I tried not to gag.

I waded deeper and deeper into the swollen, overpopulated city and tried not to think about the fact that I was more than likely lost. None of the roads made sense; they intersected at strange angles and overlapped in places, which was evidence of a city that had definitely not been planned out. All I knew was that the more congested the city became, I was likely getting closer to the docks.

A screaming bellow cracked my ears and made me jump against the nearest wall. A creature I'd only seen in books snorted and kicked as it rushed down the road. My eyes soaked up the creature's long, muscular legs and beautifully-braided mane. This was a horse. There were so few of them that had made the journey to Caark. I could hardly believe my eyes. I had seen illustrations and been taught what one was of course in school, but...it was simply *huge*. I had never imagined them so large in my life.

Without realizing it, I had tip-toed into the middle of the road, staring after the amazing, russet beast in awe as it trotted away from me with its wealthy owner astride it. What would it be like to ride such an animal, I wondered?

I was jolted from my reverie by a bunch of screaming and yelling, and I turned just in time to see a small buggy led by yet another horse coming my way. Lightning dashed through me, which broke me from my frozen fear, as I stepped backward just enough that I was pushed to the side by the horse rather than trampled beneath it. I lost my balance and fell, the hard, dirt road jarring my tailbone. My trousers slowly became wet as they soaked up the puddle I'd landed in, of who knows what, and I gasped for breath as all the people around me began to stare.

"Are ye alright, lass?" a man with a scraggly beard across the road asked.

"Where are your parents?" a woman with a muddy dress asked as she stepped closer to me.

I backed away from her in fear, terrified she would see my face. Which, looking back, is ridiculous because it wasn't like my face was known or anything. But I had always been taught that my presence in Caark had to be a secret, and that habit took a long time to die.

"Child, let me help you!" the woman whined as she reached for my hood. She repeated, "Where are your parents?"

I stuttered and stumbled to my feet, "I-I'm fine, thank you, I'm going to them now, good bye!"

My shoulder roared with pain as I tripped into the nearest alleyway and ran until I couldn't breathe any longer. If I wasn't lost before, I was truly lost now. I eyed the tall buildings on either side of the alley, dark shapes crouched around their roofs. A cat rubbed against my leg and scared me into another run. I almost couldn't believe it when the city buildings suddenly gave way to an empty, dark horizon.

I collapsed on the beach, hunkered down behind a damp rock and far from the city now. I fought the urge to cry before I suddenly sat upright. My life had been in danger! Could my magic have come, and I was so afraid and distracted that I didn't realize it?

"Okay," I breathed, my eyes fluttering closed. "I can do this. I can do this."

My hands outstretched in front of me, I tried to move them how I saw Ky and Aron do whenever they used their Rounan powers. I focused on a shell a few feet from me and attempted to grab it and throw it into the ocean.

After maybe ten minutes of trying to move the shell, I foolishly remembered that Allyen magic didn't work that way. Only Rounan magic was an invisible power that could move things like that. Allyen magic was technically Gornish magic; it was elemental. Light magic. Aunt Rachel had at least taught me that much. But how did Gornish magic work? She had never said.

Unwilling to give up, sure that my magic was right at my fingertips just waiting to be used, I tried the Ranguvariian way that Aunt Rachel and Mathiian used: music. After a quick glance up and down the long, empty shore for any people, I hummed a few notes that I'd heard so many times they were ingrained in my head. Yet, no beautiful streamers of neon-colored magic appeared at my fingertips.

I deflated. I'd nearly been run over, my life had been in danger, but my magic was nowhere to be seen. Why didn't it work? *Was* I an Allyen or not?

Was it because I had stepped slightly out of the way? That I had been able to barely move myself to the side where I would just be pushed instead of trampled? Maybe, it wasn't a true life-or-death situation because there had been something I could do to save myself. My mother couldn't do anything to stop herself from falling off a cliff. Uncle Evan was unable to escape Rhydin's Follower who had already killed his father figure. Perhaps, I needed to be in such a dangerous situation that there was nothing I could do to remove myself from it.

My gaze slowly tilted to my left where the dark, murky waters lay. The thought had barely arisen before I tossed it out. I doubted trying to drown myself would work either since it was me putting myself in that situation.

How the heck was an Allyen supposed to get some magic around here?

"*Rayna!*" a squeaky male voice called.

I jumped out of my skin and dove back behind my sandy rock. When I peeked out from behind it, I could see three figures: one taller than most adults and the other two not fully grown yet. Well, this completed my failure.

"Rayna, what are you doing out here?" Ky scolded in a tizzy, his long face screwed up. "We were all worried sick!"

"Sorry, Mama," I mocked him, my arms locking over my chest. "How did you guys even figure out where I went?"

"It wasn't that hard," Mathiian groaned, his long hands finding his narrow hips. "You seem to forget that as a Ranguvariian, I can sense that feather around your neck!"

My skin prickled as I remembered. I'd worn a Ranguvariian feather every hour of my entire life, so I often forgot it was there. The lime-green shard could have been embedded in my chest for all I knew. It was supposedly hiding my presence from Rhydin, although they didn't work as well as they used to. Rhydin had cracked most of the Ranguvariians' secrets after the death of Aunt Rachel's brother, Luke. The feathers didn't work within a few miles anymore, but the distance of Caark kept our three in commission. Of course, seeing as Ranguvariians gave up their feathers for this cause, they *would* be able to sense them anywhere anytime.

I groaned, fighting the desire to rip the necklace off. "You guys just couldn't give me a night to myself, could you?"

"Give you a chance to try and get yourself killed just to activate your magic?" Ky chided, crossing his arms. "I think not."

Ugh, Mathiian told him. The disapproving looks on all three of their faces was too much. My anger boiled over, and I shouted, "How are you three not sick of this life? Our parents are heroes, amazing mages and warriors, and we can't talk about them, much less meet them! Are we supposed to just stay here until they die, Rhydin dies, or we do?!"

"Rayna, Caark is the only place that's safe," Aron responded firmly, his lavender brow knitted together. "And-..."

"And it's so *safe* that I'll never be able to prove myself as an Allyen!" I argued. For a moment, I measured each of the boys' expressions and upon seeing the slight waver in Mathiian's, I turned to address him. "How can we show our parents that we can help, that we deserve the titles we are inheriting, if we just keep hiding here? If we don't take this chance, we could be stuck waiting here forever."

"What chance?" Ky asked, his voice beginning to turn as well.

"Aunt Rachel is off on a trip and won't be back for a few days. Chelsea and Sonya are back at the shacks. Here we all are in Calitia, right next to the port. Let's go. Let's go help our parents," I explained, and my smile began to grow. I wanted this so badly it hurt.

"And once we reach the mainland, I can try to sense their feathers and lead us straight to our parents," Mathiian continued my train of thought, his eyes sparkling green now. "I could see my father again for the first time in years. Prove to him and my mother that I'm worthy of being Clariion and a Ranguvariian warrior."

"Yes!" I nodded enthusiastically, and turned to Ky, somewhat open, and Aron, who looked utterly against the whole idea. "Please, Ky. Please, Aron. We have to do this. We could be together with our parents by the end of the week! I have some money for the ship, all we have to do is go."

Ky thought for a moment, then bobbed his head hesitantly. Aron wasn't so easy, but after a few more eager sentiments about becoming families again and aiding our parents in the fight against Rhydin, he slowly came around. Mathiian, ever the hotshot, was already as fervent about the idea as I was.

Before I knew it, we were boarding the next ship for the mainland, which would dock in Canis, Lunaka. We each had our feathers and the hoods of our cloaks pulled close. Mathiian easily looked like a parent with three children because of his height. I couldn't believe my eyes when the ship unfurled its sails and pulled away from the only world I knew. The dim lights of Caark sank away into the fog rapidly, and as we descended into nothing but darkness and ocean, my heart shone bright with hope.

CHAPTER TWO

LINA

I sensed the arrow coming before it had even been fired. I threw myself to the side just as the arrow whizzed past my ear, then I rolled along the loose sand and cut Rhydin's soldier down with my sword. Its sand joined the stuff at my feet as the magic holding it together disintegrated. All of his soldiers that we encountered anymore were Einanhis, magically-created humanoids made up of sand that were far from human.

I liked that. I'd seen enough blood to last two lifetimes.

"James!" I bellowed as I smacked another Einanhi with a punch of light magic and slashed yet another as I sensed it trying to impale me from behind. "Get these people out of here, now!"

"I know, I know, I'm trying!" James roared back as he snatched a teenage, Rounan girl out from the clutches of yet another Einanhi. He disappeared in a flash of bright light and reappeared less than a minute later, his arms empty. "We should have brought more backup; I'm the only one here who can transport!"

There was no time to groan and wish the situation was different. It was true, only Ranguvariians and Rhydin had the power to transport.

I felled two more Einanhis, their sands spilling forth, as I crouched in front of the middle-aged, Auklian noblewoman who had called us here. Our mission was supposed to only be collecting intel, as it often was. She had neglected to tell us that she had a large family of Rounans hiding in her cellar or that Rhydin's forces were after her for the same information. I'd brought three people on what I thought was a two-person mission when it was actually more like a six-person fight, leaving all our usual crew-members, including June my second, at home. One of the ones I'd brought, James, was a human-looking Ranguvariian, which helped but definitely wasn't enough.

The noblewoman summoned a puny wave of water magic to try and protect our rear, her emerald tresses falling into her face. As she did, I stopped another Einanhi in its tracks and began pushing the noblewoman backward toward the wall of her home. There were just too many enemies coming from too many directions with too much darkness disguising them. When my shoulder blades hit stone, I realized too late that we were being pinned down instead of gaining cover.

I glanced around desperately. James was still busy trying to save the last couple of members of the Rounan refugees, the father and the eldest son, who were also pretty limited with their magical abilities. Sam was even farther away, juggling so many of Rhydin's soldiers that I could barely see him. My heart lurched at the sight, but there was absolutely nothing I could do to help.

My gaze faltered too long. As I slid my sword against one Einanhi's blade, the next thing I knew, I was on the ground with exploding pain in the back of my skull. Through a hazy cloud, in what seemed like slow-motion, an Einanhi leapt off the roof of the house and landed behind us, sinking its sword into the noblewoman's chest.

Anger ripped through me. I failed; she had only been able to give me part of her information before the Einanhis arrived! That feeling was quickly replaced by fear when the Einanhi rotated its head on its thin, unnatural neck toward me, its perfectly white eyes wide in the darkness.

"No!" I heard Sam call from what seemed like a million miles away.

Balls of light burst into my hands, and I flung all of the power I had left at this being and the two behind it. They dissolved into nothing, but five more rapidly took their places. I lifted my sword across my chest, ready to do whatever I could to delay the inevitable. My children's infant faces rapidly flicked through my mind. Was I going to die without ever seeing them again?

Just as all the Einanhis surrounding me lifted their blades, they suddenly were wrenched up into the air, their feet dangling. Then, they were catapulted away from me, landing hard and melting away, indistinguishable from the rest of the Auklian sand.

My breath came out in shaky, ragged puffs, and my sword fell from my limp hand. The world grew silent as the rest of the Einanhis were dealt with, and I found it hard to focus my eyes on the sandy dunes or the noblewoman's empty house. I heard a thud as someone rushed over and dropped on the ground next to me.

Sam's voice lilted in. "Lina? Lina, can you hear me? You're going to be okay, alright? I promise, you're going to be okay."

"We need to go. Right now." James said firmly, coming out of nowhere. "Before more come."

"Take Lina first. Get her healing started," Sam responded as my consciousness spiraled. "Looks like she took a sword butt to the head. No cut."

"But you're injured too…"

"Take her, James. That's an order!"

As the world around me rocked, faded away, and swayed back into existence, I thought I was going to lose my dinner. But, when the familiar, musty scent of the Dome entered my nostrils, it strangely grounded me and helped my consciousness begin to limp back. James was yelling for a Ranguvariian medic, and as soon as a warm, magical touch barely caressed the back of my skull, James was gone again. As my pain faded, my vision cleared to where I could make out the face of a Ranguvariian man I didn't recognize, a long strip of brown hair braided down the center of his head. He must be a new guy from the Ranguvariian Camp.

"Much swollen, your head," he murmured in one of the lowest registers I'd ever heard, "but is whole. Nice egg, no cracks."

Well, I guess I can add a goose egg to the list of injuries Rhydin has inflicted upon me over the years.

Just as my pain reduced to a dull throb, there was another burst of light. Sam and James materialized out of nowhere, both of them utterly exhausted. James's shining, Ranguvariian wings of glass shards hung to the ground before they vanished, and Sam's appearance gave me a brief flashback to the War of the Three Kingdoms. His all-black clothing was torn, sweat streaming down his face, his fingers dirtied and limp.

I leapt to my feet, thanked the Ranguvariian healer, and rushed over to Sam. He immediately hugged me, sighing with relief, his fingers threading through my hair for my wound. "Ouch!" I yelped when he found it. "Hey, that's still fresh!"

"Sorry," Sam chuckled, his expression lighter now. He removed his hand and absentmindedly put it to his ribs. "We were in way over our heads back there. You're lucky I love you, or I'd never follow you on a mission again."

"Ugh, it's not my fault that noblewoman left some details out!" I groaned, and then tried to peel his hand away from his ribs, "What are you hiding? James said you were injured."

Sam released his hand, revealing a thin, red line that traced perfectly over four or five of his lower ribs. "Eh, it's not that bad. Hurts worse than it looks," Sam responded

"Hmm," I mused, studying it. It was like the Einanhi wasn't even trying, although it seemed like Rhydin's unnatural forces had been going down in quality recently. Quantity over quality, perhaps. "You're right, it doesn't look bad at all, but I still think you should go visit my friend over there." I gestured to my new favorite Ranguvariian healer, dressed in bright green robes.

"I will later," Sam said quietly, his voice getting lower by the second. "I want to go with you to report to Rachel. I want to hear what information we just about died for."

Well, I couldn't argue with that. Plus, it would sure help to have him there for another topic I needed to discuss with Rachel.

James had transported us into the Dome, the secret underground base of our rebellion, at the back entrance, to the south. This entryway was much smaller than the larger opening to the west, which led to a series of complicated tunnels before letting out just a short jaunt from Caden's Plain. The back entrance was a larger secret, only known to those of us who conducted missions of questionable legality and the Royals of course.

While most of the people in the Dome, our huge, hollowed-out mountain, hadn't once left it in over a decade, I left it pretty frequently. Over the last several years – what is it now, eleven? Twelve? – I'd run too many missions to count. Keeping track of Rhydin's newest measures to oppress Nerahdis, meeting with nobles or others who happened to have gleaned what Rhydin could be doing next from his inner circle, acquiring supplies for the now thousands of people living in the Dome, and sometimes getting people out of sticky situations or delivering my own version of justice whenever possible.

THE SORCERER'S CURSE

The problem was that nearly every Nerahdian was in some sort of danger anymore. Rhydin's whole "Liberator" charade that he spun during the war to get the people on his side was utterly dead. We tried to help as many as we could. Rounans on the run from Rhydin's hangings, the poor who could not afford the ever-increasing taxes of the land, extended Royal family members who had long been in hiding to save their own necks after the Royals in charge were executed during the Crushing of the Thrones over a decade ago. A lot of the time, whomever we saved often came back to the Dome with us in order to survive. This was both good and bad.

As Sam and I picked our way through the clogged arteries and alleyways sandwiched between ramshackle homes and shops, it felt like we could barely get where we were going without rubbing elbows with people or buildings on either side. The Dome was a cacophony of noises, the sounds having nowhere to go. It was deafening, and everything inside the Dome was bathed in aquamarine light due to the cluster of crystallized Ranguvariian feathers at the zenith of the cavern. Its gigantic size ensured that we remained invisible, regardless of what Ranguvariian secrets Rhydin had managed to discover over the eleven years since Luke's death.

The pang in my heart caused me to hesitate briefly before continuing to walk toward the northern wall of the Dome. Yet, the pang was so old by now that even Sam didn't ask me if I was alright. It was my fault Luke had died. I had long ago accepted that. If I hadn't run off in stupid frustration, he wouldn't have gone after me and gotten captured with me. Oh, how I wished I could go back in time and stop myself from ever leaving the camp. But I couldn't, so the only thing I could do was make Rhydin die for it, just as soon as we could get him alone and perform the *Alytniinaeran* spell – the death spell for short. The special spell that required three Allyens and would destroy Rhydin once and for all.

We were readying for it all the time. With every Rounan or distant Royal we brought back to the Dome, we brought back a mage who desired to join the fight against Rhydin. We had been massing an army for over ten years, whether here in the Dome or in a hidden pocket somewhere in Nerahdis, and our numbers were now in the thousands.

It was time to add the last piece of the puzzle, I told myself for what seemed like the hundredth time. Also, for probably the thousandth time, I told myself that I would not allow Rachel to turn me down again.

Sam and I pushed through the last stretch of sardined passageway, far too narrow and tumbledown to be regarded as a road, and the northern wall of the Dome stretched before us. The northern wall had been the thickest, and so it had been excavated into numerous cavities, almost like an apartment inn. Each cavity had a small opening out into the Dome for air flow, and these windows dotted the northern wall in organized rows, obviously artificial.

Those of us who had been here the longest lived in these one-room dwellings away from the constricted, haphazard city. Mostly the Royals and others in positions of power. While I still balked at the idea that social constructs existed even in the Dome of all places, I had reluctantly accepted that if we wanted people's help in creating an army, we had to cater to them to some extent.

Sam and I had been offered one of these apartments once upon a time. We had refused.

There was a guard posted at the carved, earthen doorway. That was new, I thought as I fought the urge to roll my eyes. We strode right past her and up the man-made stairs. Absolutely everyone in the Dome knew who Sam and I were, Rounan and Gornish alike. The days where no one knew us were definitely over.

We hiked up to the third level and then turned down a tight passageway with lanterns strung along the ceiling, which cast a dim, rather yellow – and not an attractive shade of yellow at that – light upon the hall. We passed several doorways, each strung with some sort of curtain or blanket, until we reached the very last one, and I rapped my knuckles against the rocky wall as if it was a door. At the sound of Rachel's mellow answer, I brushed the scarlet blanket with big, angular designs on it to the side.

Rachel was here very rarely, usually spending most of her time between Caark with our children and the Ranguvariian Camp as she trained to become Clariion, leader of the Ranguvariians, after her grandfather, Arii. This apartment was actually Jaspen's and Bartholomiiu's, who both stayed in the Dome year-round, and it showed.

There wasn't much of a homey feel to it. Nonetheless, one half of the room was relatively neat and tidy while the other half was mostly just random piles of assorted weapons of different shapes and sizes. Warrior culture as they were, it was funny to see the differences between the organized Jaspen and the scatterbrained Bartholomiiu displayed so clearly. Although, this was hardly Bartholomiiu's fault.

Herb-tinged smoke entered my nostrils as we came through the curtain, and it was Bartholomiiu's thin, beaming face that I saw first. He had regained quite a bit of function in the years since his too-close encounter with Rhydin that left him with brain damage, but whenever his eyes shifted colors, as Ranguvariian eyes do, the color was never quite as dark as it should be.

Bartholomiiu gleamed at us. "Hello, Lina and Sam! What can do for you?"

"They're hopefully going to tell me what information they nearly got themselves killed for," Rachel's voice called from the back corner of the room, sounding unimpressed.

I turned to face my part-human, part-Ranguvariian friend. She was huddled behind a quaint, writing desk that was black as coal, which seemed rather comical due to her unnatural, Ranguvariian height. She was wearing her usual orange and yellow Ranguvariian robe. She had yet to look up at us, busy scrawling away at something, but all I could think at that moment was that she had just seen our children last week and would be returning to them soon.

I steeled myself, surer than ever of my resolve.

"Alright," Rachel finally announced, putting down her quill and fixing us in her icy blue gaze, "what did this Auklian noblewoman have to say? And what in Nerahdis happened that you ran into so many of Rhydin's artificial lackeys?"

I crossed my arms tightly over my chest and grumbled, "She wasn't completely truthful with us. She didn't tell us that she had a large family of Rounans hiding in her cellar needing extraction, or that Rhydin's forces were actively tracking her for the information she found. If we'd known the full situation, obviously we would have brought more people."

It was like Rachel didn't even hear my defense. "I really don't see why you have to run all these missions, Lina. They're too dangerous. If we lost you, our whole rebellion would fall apart."

It was a decade-old argument at this point. Rachel wanted me to sit around in the Dome for eternity while I knew that I needed to be out in the world actively helping people and the rebellion. I decided not even to engage her this time. "This one mission didn't go well-…"

Rachel snorted.

I continued, trying to ignore her, "…and I was only able to receive part of the information before she was killed. It's odd…it almost sounds like a riddle."

My red-haired friend's ears almost perceptibly picked up. "A riddle? What is it?"

"She was writing it down for me when the Einanhis attacked. She was too afraid to say it out loud," I mumbled thoughtfully as I fished the scrap of parchment out of my pocket. The whole experience seemed weirder the more I thought about it.

I handed it out to her, and she stood to come study it together.

The throne of sand
must meet its end
to break the curse
that shrouds the First,

Rachel instantly began to puzzle over it. "Throne of sand? That surely doesn't mean Auklia. Obviously, the Great Desert has no throne. Why would it have to end? And what curse? First what?" she questioned over and over, and then threw down the parchment. "You know, Lina, I'd be tempted to think this Auklian noblewoman was just trying to draw you into a trap for something ridiculous."

Sam finally piped up, "Rhydin wouldn't have sent his forces to kill her if the information was meaningless."

"He could have sent his forces simply because she was harboring Rounans," Rachel argued back as she returned to her writing desk. "Either way, as it is now, this information isn't very helpful to us. We can't use it if we don't understand it."

"What if we found the other half?" I asked as I picked up the riddle and held it close. "I feel like this is important. She wasn't done writing when we were interrupted, and there's a comma at the end. She was so scared, Rachel, she *knew* that this was-…!"

"And where do we find the rest of it?" Rachel chastised, throwing her quill back down. After a few moments of silence made her point, she took it back up again. "Just hold onto it for now. Our hands are tied until its meaning is made clear or we discover the rest of it. There's nothing else we can do."

My shoulders wilted. I didn't want that Auklian noblewoman to have died for nothing. Rachel hadn't seen her as I had. Her trembling as she wrote, her anxious eyes that darted back and forth at every corner, her professed belief that *everyone* needed to hear this message. It couldn't really have

23

been all a sham, could it? If it was, this noblewoman was the greatest actress of all time. It couldn't be.

As the room filled with nothing but the sound of Rachel's quill on parchment, Sam turned to leave. However, I wasn't done yet. I took a deep breath, trying to ready myself one last time.

"Rachel?" My voice wavered. "There's something else."

My friend's quill never stopped, but she looked up at me briefly between words, multi-tasking. The act raised my ire a bit.

I began, measuring her expression carefully, "We nearly died today. Nearly died without seeing our children in over a decade…"

Rachel's knuckles turned white as her quill suddenly scrawled to a stop. Sam turned back toward the room, stepping nearer to me like reinforcement.

"I know you wanted to wait until the Dome was safe, but how much safer can it truly get? We've all been here for so long without incident." Heat flooded my neck and shoulders watching Rachel's reaction.

"Lina, they are far safer in Caark then they ever could be here," Rachel chided the same old words. "The Dome is semi-safe, yes, but we're also over-capacity, if you'd take the time to notice. Why do you think I barely have time to answer all these memos from scouts trying to find a new base? We've already had to start creating safe houses across Nerahdis where our people can remain together in pockets of rebellion, but that's not a long-term solution. If we can't continue to hold our people together, our rebellion will lose its momentum-…"

"Rachel," I interrupted firmly, my hands forming fists as tight as my words, "I'm not backing down this time. You've shut me down every time in the past, and that's not going to happen today. It's time to bring our children to the Dome. Now."

Rachel opened her mouth to object.

"*Nothing* you say is going to change my mind this time," I declared, resolute. Sam wearily tried to hide his grin next to me. "For Nerahdis's sake, our children are *teenagers* now. We could be beginning their training, honing their magic. Rayna hasn't had any Allyen training whatsoever-…"

"Her magic has not awakened yet, Lina," Rachel announced harshly as she attempted to return to her writing.

"But in a world like this, it could be forced to awaken any day," I answered quietly. It was a gigantic fear of mine. That something would threaten our children in Caark, and we wouldn't know until it was too late. "I know you are busy and juggling a lot. But you at least get to see your son every so often. Imagine not seeing him for over a decade. You've never even let us visit for fear that someone recognizes us. It's time, Rachel. I've let you rule this portion of my life for too long."

Rachel froze, looking as if I had struck her. I was done talking. I spun on my heel and made for the curtained doorway. Sam hesitated, torn between waiting for a response from Rachel and following his wife. He had just chosen to come after me when I vaguely heard the words "I'll think about it" over my shoulder.

I stormed down the cave-like hall and bounded down the stairs. We walked in silence, Sam trailing after me, as the aquamarine glow above our heads began to dim. The sun was going down outside, and the gigantic, crystalline structure was adapting accordingly. It never went out completely, but the Ranguvariians had some way of adjusting it to help people sleep and go about their days and nights. We entered the maze of narrow passageways and ramshackle tents and buildings, following a path that I could walk with my eyes closed.

It wasn't long before we reached a mid-sized tent made of canvas and patchwork. It sat on the corner of two smaller arteries of traffic, generally only used by the people that camped in the area. Our tent used to sit by itself in the first days, but as our rebellion grew, other dwellings quickly sprung up around it until it was hard to tell where one stopped and the next began. While the Dome could hardly be called a city – a city of temporary houses, perhaps – this was the closest to city life that I had ever experienced. As a farmer, it made me chafe to have so many people living so close. I generally preferred my neighbors no closer than a mile away.

The sooner we defeated Rhydin, the sooner Sam and I could return to Lunaka and restart our family farm with our children.

Sam didn't enter our tent with me. He decided to go find the Ranguvariian healer again before turning in since his ribs were still bothering him. I waved briefly to June, one of the members of my team who happened to live across the road from us. She grimaced at the sight of me, covered in sand with dried blood in my hair from my head. She had become a good friend over the years.

Once inside our tent, I took my sweet time in unarming myself. Of course, my trusted sword remained magically hidden within the old sash bound around my waist. That never came off anymore, even during sleep. But it took some time digging out the various daggers I had secreted away. One in each boot, one strapped to each thigh, and a particularly thin one over my shoulder and between my shoulder blades. I'd been in enough sticky situations in the last year alone to make each and every one of them worth its weight in gold. Once there was no longer anything pointy on my person, I kicked my boots off into a pile near the entrance of the tent, the soles so thin there would soon be holes where the balls of my feet rubbed.

Our tent seemed larger on the inside than it did on the outside. There was one bigger compartment in the middle with two little wings off each side. For not really being material people, or quite frankly not being home all that often, our tent seemed like a catch-all for the most random of junk. We had a shelf of books that held every topic from the useful, such as Nerahdian history, to the oddly specific, such as a book on gardening. I had kept every book I'd ever laid hands on in any raid in the hope that maybe someday I'd actually get to read them all.

The shelf was in the center of the tent, along with a table and chairs that Sam built shortly after we moved into the Dome. Upon the table was oodles of Kidek/Rounan paperwork that I only somewhat tried to keep up with Sam on. It seemed like his work never ended. A quaint cabinet housed our weapons, which seemed grotesquely tiny after seeing Jaspen and Bartholomiiu's apartment, but it was all we needed. We had a couple Lunakan moon plants in the corner that we were experimenting with growing under the Ranguvariian crystals of the Dome rather than the sun. They grew slower and had turned an odd color of blue, but the flowers were still pretty and smelled like home. We might be warriors now, but there was no ignoring our green thumbs.

In one of the wings, I threw myself down on the rickety bed that Sam had also built when from a Mineraltin tree that smelled like syrup. I tried to keep my eyes wandering toward the other wing across the way, but I couldn't help it. It wasn't empty, although sometimes I wished it was. Short shelves lined each of the walls, filled with more books designed for children as well as other neat things I'd found on raids that had made me think of Ky and Rayna. In the center of the other wing were two stubby little beds that matched ours. Sam had made them at the same time, not cradles but bigger beds for young children, thinking that it would only be a few short years before they were reunited with us.

How did we let it become this long? What kind of parents were we?

Parents that were trying their hardest to do the best they could and keep their children safe, I told myself over and over again as my eyes grew heavier and heavier. My bones slumped with exhaustion, and I barely heard Sam come back several hours later. He entered our bed quietly and remained rolled away from me, which I thought was odd. Usually he would come close no matter how long I'd been asleep without him.

I dredged myself from my sleep enough to roll over and scoot up to him, squeezing into his back until there was no space between us that remained. Sam relaxed slightly at my touch, but not completely. Something was off, I didn't need to see his face in order to tell. I croaked, my voice drenched with sleep, "What's wrong? Are you healed?"

"Yeah, I'm fine now," Sam responded rapidly, his voice oddly smooth. He patted my hands which had come to tuck around his stomach. "I'm healing well, but I might need a few more sessions. Anyway, I have good news."

"What?" I asked groggily.

Sam answered joyfully, although with a hint of sleep or sadness I couldn't quite tell, "Rachel's going to bring our kids to the Dome."

CHAPTER THREE

RAYNA

I 'd seen the sea in the morning more times than I could count in my life. But never like this. Not with it stretching out in a million directions for what seemed like a million miles. Not with the water reflecting the pastel colors of the sky so evenly that the horizon melted away altogether, our ship seemingly suspended within it all. I wanted to draw it so badly, but without any colors, I would be doing its beauty a disservice.

When the sun cracked a drowsy eye above the water at our backs, its deep scarlet rays turned everything they touched a brilliant pink. The dark, barnacled stern of our ship suddenly seemed bright and cheery while I tried to ignore the sleepy island in its wake that had long since vanished. A strange sense of yearning had awakened within me overnight, but it was easy to squash with both excitement and anxiety. We were going to Nerahdis! Hopefully we had enough of a head start that even if our caretakers had noticed our absence by now, they wouldn't catch up.

"Rayna," I heard Ky hiss. I turned from the glorious morning to see my big brother barely a step away from the door that led down below. "Get over here!"

I groaned, my reverie over. I strode over to him slowly, so as to not draw attention to myself. "You just have to ruin all the fun, don't you?"

"You know you're not supposed to be up here! We were going to stay in our room until port, that was the deal! If someone figures out who we are on this tiny ship in the middle of the sea, we're goners!" Ky chided me quietly as he not-too-conspicuously dragged me toward the door and down the creaking, moldy steps.

"I was careful! There was only one guy up there, and I couldn't see the dawn through that tiny porthole!" I defended myself as we ducked into our minuscule compartment. "Sheesh, do you think I'm an imbecile or something?"

Ky simply groaned as he dropped onto his hammock. Mathiian was still snoozing in his while Aron lounged with a book he must have brought along. There was barely enough room for the four hammocks, two on top and two on bottom, much less anything else.

Sometimes I wondered if Ky would get his first gray hair by fifteen, not too long from now. If I was the cause, I would consider it a badge of honor.

I settled myself upon my hammock, tortured by the desire to draw the dawn but painfully without the proper tools. I dug my sketchbook out of the big pocket of my cloak anyway and thumbed through its thick, worn pages. The sketches grew better and more complex the farther inward I turned. When I finally hit a blank page, I stared at it mournfully, flipping my charcoal pencil back and forth along my fingers. Black. All I could draw was black. Not the pinks and yellows and oranges and blues of the sky and sea.

To satisfy the urge, I took to sketching and shading Mathiian's slumbering face in the light of one meager oil lamp and the brightening porthole. After all, our ship wasn't due to dock in Canis until noon. His face was much longer than either of my family members'. He was also much taller and lankier, so I figured it was the Ranguvariian in him. Aunt Rachel was partial human, but Jaspen was full-blooded. Maybe that made Mathiian three-fourths? I really didn't know.

The only sounds in our compartment were the *scritch-scratch* of my charcoal and the *woosh* of the waves just outside our puny porthole. Ky had managed to fall back asleep, rocked to sleep by the sea, while Aron continued to read. I never would have thought that Aron and I had something in common until this moment, the two of us enjoying our quiet, individual activities. Although, after a few hours I was beginning to feel sleepy myself, and I was in the act of putting my sketching things away when the ship came to a stop.

It was subtle really. The swaying of the ship became more pronounced now that we weren't moving forward. The waves quieted some since our bow was no longer breaking through them. Had we really arrived an hour early? Had to have been one heck of a tailwind.

I slipped down from my hammock, excited to go investigate and see my parents' homeland for the first time, when the sight of Aron sitting rigid stopped me in my tracks. His hands were gripping his book so hard that his knuckles were white, and his teal-colored eyes stared off in the distance.

"Aron?" I asked quietly, not wanting to wake the other two. "What's wrong?"

My cousin swallowed with difficulty like there was something stuck in his throat. "I...I don't know. My senses... T-There's something *really* dark here, Rayna," he stammered, "So old. So dark."

It unnerved me seeing the calm and cool Aron like this. Sometimes I forgot the kid had emotions. Only seconds passed before Ky and Mathiian both bolted upright, the latter nearly falling onto Aron's head. I watched in confusion as each of their faces paled, their eyes growing into saucers.

Even though I probably should have been panicking at their reactions, instead I found myself pondering what it must be like to sense something. With magic. Like a compass in my head. While the three boys grew more and more agitated, my head remained clear, un-muddled.

Well, I suppose that meant I wasn't going to die today.

I threw on my cloak, all my things tucked safely in the pockets. "Alright, boys. Let's go see what's going on up there instead of hiding down here like scared kids."

"We are scared kids," Aron replied monotonously. "No, it's too dangerous. Mathiian, just transport us the rest of the way to Canis. We can't be more than a couple miles away."

"Uh...about that," Mathiian stuttered, a blush creeping over his leathery cheeks. "I haven't exactly gotten the hang of transportation yet... Last time I tried to go to Calitia, I ended up in the ocean."

"You *can't* transport?!" Ky seethed, his hands balling up into fists, "Our Ranguvariian protector can't protect us?"

"Hey, I can fly no problem! And sure, I can transport if you don't mind possibly getting flattened into a building or drowned!" Mathiian shouted back, his eyes flashing to an unsettling blood red.

Meanwhile, a ruckus had begun on deck. While Mathiian and Ky argued, I first peeked out the tiny door to the hallway, seeing the backs of several other passengers as they all exited their compartments and headed toward the stairs. Then, I crossed between the boys and leaned toward the porthole, trying to hear what was being said above us. Most of it was strange, repetitive swears of fealty to Emperor Rhydin that I could barely make out over the thunder of all the footsteps above and the waves below.

After a few comments like "is this everyone?" and "remove your hood," I realized with a jolt that Rhydin's soldiers, the dark presence that everyone else could sense, were checking all the passengers of the ship. For what or whom, I had no clue, but if they uncovered the very Ranguvariian-looking Mathiian or realized who we all were, we weren't going to make it to Canis.

"Well, Mathiian," I sighed after a deep breath to steady myself, "the only way you're going to get better at transporting is if you practice, and unless you transport us out of here, you're never going to get the chance."

"What do you mean?" Aron asked timidly, having sat back from the argument this whole time.

"Rhydin's soldiers are up there. They must check every ship that comes and goes from Nerahdis for Rounans or anyone else they don't like. They're not going to leave until they search the whole ship if they do their job right," I explained as I anxiously checked myself once more. I'd never transported before.

"What if we just find a place to hide? Maybe they won't find us, and we can just continue on!" Ky offered, his fingers becoming jittery. "We still have our feathers!"

"The feathers don't hide presences this close anymore, remember? If there's a real mage up there, they already know we're here. I'll take my chances with the ocean over being captured by Rhydin. We're trying to help our parents, not show them we're still kids and can't handle ourselves," I responded stubbornly. My mind was made up. "Besides, I trust Mathiian. Shoot for a spot with lots of space, and if that happens to be over a body of water, just hang on tight, and he'll fly the rest of the way."

Mathiian peered at me quietly, a nervous expression on his face. His eyes morphed from the gold of a sunset to the gray of shining metal as he braced himself. When footsteps suddenly stomped off toward the stairs above us, Mathiian reached for my arm. "There is no time left. I can only take one at a time."

"No, I'll go first," Ky announced quickly. He moved closer to Mathiian and pretty much mounted him like he was getting a piggy-back ride. My big brother's face was pale, but I knew he couldn't bear the thought of me going first into the unknown.

Mathiian nodded, taking two deep breaths before he whistled a few familiar notes and his gorgeous wings of glass shards crowded our compartment. He and Ky vanished into a burst of light.

Aron and I stared at where their boots had once been for a few moments. Did it work? Were they safe in Canis? Or were they dangling over the ocean or worse, impaled by a building or ship? I wanted so badly to draw what I had just seen, yet I vanquished that thought until I knew my brother's fate.

Both of us jolted upright when Rhydin's soldiers reached our level and began hammering on the doors down the hall. I was just wondering what we would do if Mathiian didn't come back when, with another flash, Mathiian materialized out of nothing. He was heaving great breaths of air, and his chocolate hair was plastered to his forehead and dripping.

"What happ-...?" I tried to ask, but I was interrupted.

"No time," Mathiian gasped. He reached for me. "You next, Allyen."

I shoved Aron into his grasping hands. "He's the youngest. Go!"

Mathiian disappeared with my cousin, not willing to waste time arguing. Once I was alone in the compartment, I made sure my things were in my pockets and began to prepare myself as Rhydin's soldiers grew ever closer.

This was it. My life would be in danger from other people, and I was trapped in here. My magic would *have* to awaken this time.

I suddenly found myself wishing for some sort of weapon for the first time in my life.

The door next to ours suddenly banged open, and my heart clenched with fear. I turned my arms to stone so they would not shake. This was the moment I'd been waiting for my whole thirteen years.

Our door exploded off its hinges, and in its wake were three hooded figures in black, their eyes white with no pupil. Those eyes narrowed at the sight of me waiting for them with nothing more than my fists. I had never seen them before, but with their eyes and their strange, thin physicality, I knew exactly what they were.

Einanhis. Rhydin's soulless, man-made creations.

"The Allyen," one of them murmured quietly in a grainy voice. Again, "the Allyen," like those were the only words it could say.

Another stepped forward. "I wondered what it was we were sensing down here. Someone shrouded by a feather. Now I can sense it is an Allyen with no magic."

The blood drained from my face as my fingers continued to feel nothing magical whatsoever. The feathers didn't work this close.

The third announced, "We take her to Master. He will be pleased."

Never thought I'd be disappointed an enemy wasn't going to kill me before. My life, at this very moment, was not in danger, but instinct kicked in anyway. I jumped into the air with a little help from a swinging hammock and pretty much crashed into the lead Einanhi, knocking over the other two behind it. Without thinking, I bolted down the thin hallway and up the stairs, bursting upon the upper deck. For a moment, the sun blinded me, but it wasn't long before I realized I was surrounded.

On one side of the ship were all the passengers who had embarked from Caark with us, most of them with bored expressions. On the other side were two more Einanhis, skinny with limbs like spiders. People jolted at my ruckus, and the passengers stared at me in confusion while the Einanhis began to creep forward.

"Allyen!" one of the Einanhis called.

"Allyen!" they all repeated, including the three on my heels.

The Einanhis droned on and on like an alarm. I backed away from them, officially panicking. I looked to the passengers helplessly, but they were now bubbling with the word as well. Some of them latched onto me with their eyes like they wanted to help me but didn't know how. Others looked at me like I was some sort of abomination. Still others turned away altogether, like my fate was sealed.

It sure as heck wasn't!

I threw myself into a run across the deck, through the no-man's-land between the passengers and Emperor Rhydin's unnatural soldiers. I swore I could feel their lifeless breaths on the back of my neck before I leapt from the ship's bow. I braced myself for the shock of the frigid saltwater – or the awakening of my magic, whichever came first – but an entirely different sensation rocked my body. Strong hands looped under my armpits and yanked me upward so hard that it felt like my arms popped out of their sockets.

"You made yourself last on purpose, did you not, small fry?" Mathiian chided as he soared along the ocean, my toes dangling inches above the frothy waves.

"Maybe just a *little* higher, Mathiian?" I wheedled, more terrified than I cared to admit.

Mathiian took mercy on me and cruised upward with several mighty flaps of his glassy wings, banking west. The deck of the ship we had just escaped was quickly becoming a smudge, but there was no mistaking the gaping mouths of the passengers and the alarm of the Einanhis. I was just beginning to relax, thinking we were scot-free, when Canis came into view. All the muscles in my face went slack.

Granted, I had never seen the Canis port before. But even I knew that this wasn't normal, and something very bad was about to happen. Hundreds, if not thousands, of warships were docked in and around the port, too many to be contained. Millions of midnight-colored sails rippled and snapped in the wind, angrily glaring toward the east, riddled with the emperor's insignia, a golden flame with a red orb in the center. Just the sight of all the masts and sails and ropes and soldiers lining each deck like ants made me feel dizzy.

As Mathiian flew further north to avoid flying directly above the humongous navy, my teeth chattered as I asked, "Mathiian? What is that?"

"I am not sure. But that size can only mean one thing," Mathiian responded, his breathing labored as he tugged me higher and higher. "Invasion."

"But there's no-..." I started to say before my throat swelled and cut me off. Emperor Rhydin already controlled all of the mainland of Nerahdis, but I had forgotten. All the ships' bows pointed east. Toward my island. Caark, which had lain undisturbed by any war or Royal dispute for as long as anyone could remember. Where so many had found their solace and kids like me had grown up in peace.

Caark was going to be attacked.

"We have to go back!" I screamed, wrestling Mathiian's arms to get another look at the invasion force. "We have to warn them! We have to save them!"

I continued to fight until Mathiian finally reached the great cliff that stood several hundred feet over Canis and sea level. He dropped me as soon as he could, which I probably deserved. I bounced up and was clawing at his tunic in only seconds. "Mathiian! You have to take us back, so we can warn Caark!"

Mathiian simply crossed his arms stoically, and suddenly my brother's voice piped up from behind me, "C'mon, Rayna. You and I both know we wouldn't make it in time. They're leaving right now."

I let Mathiian go and hurried to the edge of the cliff, straining my eyes to see. He was right. Sails were unfurling all along the coast beneath us, blooming like ink blots on parchment, catching the wind, and propelling the dark ships toward my island. I pleaded, my eyes glued to the ocean we had just crossed, "But we have to help them!"

"You cannot go back to Caark," a woman's voice responded.

I froze. I knew that voice, and I *especially* knew it in that reprimanding tone. I turned slowly to see my Aunt Rachel, wrapped in her usual orange and yellow robe with her cropped, red hair threaded with golden rings. Ky and Aron stood next to her, the first absolutely soaked and the second looking as if he'd dived through a haybale.

"A-Aunt Rachel," I stuttered as my face flushed with heat.

"Mother, I-I can explain!" Mathiian rushed toward his mother, desperation written all over his face.

"Don't bother," Aunt Rachel huffed, her pale, freckled arms crossed tightly over her chest. "In this very, *very* unique set of circumstances, I am glad you all are here and not in Caark."

Looks of relief spread across our faces before she added, "But you all will get a thorough talking-to later."

Mathiian, Ky, and Aron all grimaced. My attention was sucked back toward the ocean like a magnet. I watched for a few moments as ship after ship after ship left Canis's harbor and sailed toward the horizon where my island lay. I was quiet when I asked, "But what about Caark? What about Chelsea and Sonya?"

"They will be here momentarily. I found them on my journey here searching for you all. You owe them both apologies," Aunt Rachel answered monotonously before turning her blue gaze to the horizon as well. "As for Caark…I'm afraid there is nothing we can do beyond what we are already doing in the rebellion. We can help them by helping our cause here."

My heart grew heavy. Each of my schoolmates' faces flashed in my mind, the ones who always bullied me. They had no idea what was coming. As more and more ships left Canis, I mused out loud accidentally, "It's just so big."

As Aunt Rachel helped Ky remove some of his wet clothing and Aron pull sprigs of hay out of his hair, she turned back to me with a curious look on her face. "Of course, it is.

What did you think your parents were off fighting for more than ten years? Just one dictator on a throne?"

I blushed, embarrassed. I remained quiet for some time as we began walking to where we would be meeting Chelsea and Sonya. Between Mathiian and Aron, the boys scrounged together enough extra layers to get Ky into some dry clothes. Aron clutched his book to his chest as he walked, more silent than usual. Mathiian trotted dutifully behind his mother, as if upon eggshells.

When the ocean disappeared from sight, I felt twitchy. When the humidity I'd known all my life vanished, I found the air thin and dizzying. When the grassy plain we crossed began to morph into huge trees with scaly bark and small, pointed leaves that were turning red of all colors, I felt like we were on another planet. The mainland of Nerahdis was nothing like I imagined it to be. Nothing like my island. Yet, we were moving ever closer to our parents, at long last. What if they were nothing like I imagined either? The threat they were facing was obviously nothing I had ever remotely conjured up.

What had I gotten us into?

CHAPTER FOUR

LINA

"They're really coming? Really truly coming?" I repeated for the hundredth time to Sam over our breakfast. Eggs, as usual, fixed one of the millions of ways we had invented during our decade in the Dome with some very overworked chickens. This morning it was victory eggs over easy.

"Yes, dear," Sam answered tiredly as he forked more egg into his mouth, bags under his brown eyes. I might have kept him up for several hours last night in my excitement.

I scraped my tin plate clean and tossed it into the bucket by the door for washing later, too energized to sit still. "I'm just so shocked that Rachel is going to bring them! After so many years and years of begging for her to concede just like that!"

"I know, Lina," Sam chuckled quietly. "I've told you everything I know. She left this morning." His eyes fell slowly to the floor.

"What's wrong?" I asked, suddenly feeling dampened.

"Oh, nothing," Sam responded loudly, not quite meeting my eyes. A beat went by before he added, "Just remember it's going to take a few days for them to get here. We can't spare any Ranguvariians right now if we don't have to, and there are too many to transport for Rachel to handle safely alone."

"Oh yeah." I drooped, but only for a second. "But, still! We have to get ready for them! They're going to be too big for these beds!" My heart was close to weeping from joy.

"I'll work on it soon. I promise." Sam couldn't help but smile as he finished his eggs. "After the meeting, hopefully."

I froze in my tracks as I took his plate to add to the washing bucket. "What meeting? There's not a meeting today, is there?"

"Afraid there is." Sam's eyes gleamed like toffee.

I groaned as he stood from the table and affixed his bandana, the golden-starred, navy and purple swatch that signified him as Kidek, leader of the Rounans, around his head, sprigs of brown and red peeping out from underneath. Some little silver spots peeked out at his temples, which had been growing in recent years. We certainly weren't young newlyweds anymore.

I stuck my hand against my forehead as if I was becoming feverish and sighed, "Back to the real world I guess."

"Not the real world," Sam said as he threw an arm around my shoulders and walked us toward the flap of our glorified tent. "Just a wartime world. One that we work ceaselessly to free until it ends…or we die. Whichever comes first."

"Well, that's depressing," I snorted, moving his hand to mine. "Don't talk like that. Who knows? Maybe this meeting will be a good one."

I couldn't have been more wrong. Then again, I had been far too positive. Every meeting of the Council I could remember from the very beginning of the Dome's establishment had gone poorly. It wasn't necessarily that we all couldn't get along. It was simply that the issues and problems thrust upon the Council were ones that often divided even the best of friends.

The Council was made up of nine people: King Frederick and his sister, Princess Cornflower of Lunaka, King Xavier and Queen Mira of Mineraltir, Queen Sabine of Auklia, James – who acted as his grandfather's correspondent for the Ranguvariians, Sam, my brother Evan, and me. As soon as Frederick, Xavier, and Sabine were crowned, shortly after our forces found the Dome, we started these Council meetings as frequently as possible. The public was always invited, but the number of people who actually bothered to show up varied, especially as the Dome's population grew and room for an audience dwindled. The Council decided everything here. Rules, food management, where we would raid, how to best implement the information we received on Rhydin's activities. In some ways, we were very productive. In others, it seemed like we got stuck in the same rut over and over.

The usual rut, in particular, was miles deep and one that I wasn't sure how to feel about.

"I don't see why we keep talking about this when none of us have budged in years!" Xavier, our red-haired hothead declared abruptly. "You all know where I stand. It's time to appoint an Archimage already, this democracy doesn't work!"

"Xavier, let's move on from this," Frederick responded, my oldest friend on this Council and my original magic tutor. "We can't constantly debate having an Archimage."

"Yes, but we're at a stalemate on this Aatarilec discussion and an Archimage could break it. The Archimage was an imperative job that Nerahdis hasn't gone without for centuries," Sabine rattled off. "My father may not have been perfect, but his job was important! If the Kings of Old had just done what they were told, perhaps none of this would have ever happened!"

I groaned and rubbed my temples, wishing Rachel was here. Whenever she happened to be available, she would sit in on our meetings with her brother, James. She usually had a great argument for why the Archimage was unnecessary now that the Council included more than just the three sovereigns. The Archimage used to be a mage who presided over the Three Kings only, helping them make decisions and dispute their issues so that wars could be avoided. The last Archimage, Dathian, had been killed by Rhydin at the end of the war.

Sam was growing more frustrated by the minute next to me. Anger was rolling off of him in waves, which wasn't quite like him. His temper typically took more time to reach such a crescendo.

It was private knowledge within the Council that Rhydin had once been the First Archimage as a teenager before Emperor Caden's death, but I had told only Sam and Frederick about my strange experiences in the Archimage Palace. The mysterious presence that often came to me when I was alone. It was a helpful presence – it had warned me of Rhydin's armies while we were on the run before heading to Caark – but its existence was puzzling and uncanny. Something wasn't right in the Archimage Palace. Dathian had known it too before his death. I just couldn't help but wonder whether it would be better for us all to bury that palace once and for all.

Before Sam could explode, I butted in, "Even if we decided today that we should elect another Archimage, who would even be a candidate?"

"Anyone with magic, of course. Just like it's always been," Xavier snapped. Mira, his wife and Frederick's sister, placed a pale hand on his shoulder. She had also always been pro-Archimage, but with less vehemence.

"For the past three hundred years, the Three Kingdoms have taken turns appointing an Archimage from the pool of Royal children not destined for the throne," Sabine quipped. She would know better than anyone, after all, being Dathian's daughter. "Auklia supplied the last Archimage. It is Lunaka's turn."

Cornflower blanched, all color leaving her in stark contrast to her red gown. Her two siblings, Frederick and Mira, were both reigning sovereigns of Lunaka and Mineraltir respectively. Mira's children didn't count as Lunakans, but Frederick had two children now, one by birth and one adopted.

Dominick, fourteen, was the heir as his biological son, while Nathia, the same child I saved from the Rounan compound near Stellan, wasn't of age, only sixteen. Frederick had adopted her when she'd shown up at the Dome as an orphan a few years after I met her.

Ultimately, Cornflower was the only option Lunaka had left.

"We've discussed this before," Frederick interceded for his sister, still trying to be the mediator. "My sister has no desire to be Archimage."

"And you think my father did?" Sabine argued, leaning forward onto our glass, octagonal table with both hands.

I stood from the table now, tired of the shouting. "The last thing we should do is elect an Archimage against their will! Cornflower doesn't want the job, and I don't blame her. If we push another person into this job, we'll just end up with another dictator or another Archimage to whom nobody listens."

Sabine's lips curled upward. "So, you agree with me. We need another Archimage. One willing to do the job, of course," she conceded.

"No, that's not what I'm saying…" I tried to explain.

"Everybody, stop!" someone yelled. To my surprise, it was my brother, Evan, and not my temperamental husband.

Evan hadn't changed much over the years. He was as short as he'd ever been before, and while there were lines of silver through his hair, his golden-speckled Allyen eyes were no less vibrant. When the room had fallen silent, including the few commoners that had decided to watch us fight today, he continued in a firm tone, "Do not twist my sister's words. We shall always retain our neutral status on this topic, just as we have for years. Without any willing candidates, or even qualified ones for that matter, there's no point in wasting any more time on this topic."

He was right. There were no other Royal adults to speak of. Sabine was the very last Auklian Royal after Daniel, the previous king, died during the battle at the Archimage Palace where Dathian was killed. Xavier was the last Mineraltin Royal. His father died in Duunzer's Darkness, his mother died bearing him, and his step-mother and step-sister were both executed by Rhydin during the Crushing of the Thrones. Everyone else were the current rulers or not of age, therefore ineligible.

The Crushing of the Thrones. Just the sound of the words in my head sent a ripple through me. It was the day Rhydin put to death all the Royals he possibly could, even the ones who worked for him, so that no one could ever challenge him for the throne. It was on that day that King Adam of Lunaka breathed his last, my first foe as a fledgling Allyen. Jasmine and Ren, too, Xavier's step-family who had been so cruel to him. These were victories in a way because that event had also been the beginning of Nerahdis's turn away from Rhydin and his malice. Regardless of the meager good that came of it, Crushing of the Thrones remained a day that none of us would ever forget because of what it stood for. That Rhydin would do *anything* to keep his throne. Any and all morals were off the table. We actively worked to avoid any sort of repeat.

Frederick, Mira, and Cornflower also lost their mother, Queen Gloria, that day because we were too late to save her, even though we succeeded in rescuing them. That act made Frederick and Cornflower the last Lunakan Royals since Mira had married into another kingdom. Cornflower was technically the *only* traditional candidate in any of the Three Kingdoms, but my gut still told me that forcing this position just wasn't a good idea. I hadn't studied and re-studied that old history book that detailed Rhydin's time as Archimage for nothing.

"Perhaps, the traditional rules are broken. Null and void," Xavier sneered, glaring at his good fist sitting on the table. His bad arm, crushed long ago in the avalanche that caught Xavier and Sam during their army days, remained hidden under his emerald cloak. "New rules, more candidates. Make the age limit sixteen instead of eighteen."

"*Moving on*, please," Frederick said loudly, squeezing his eyes shut. "Our actual discussion topic is a lot more important at the moment."

James, Rachel's brother, finally spoke up, quiet thus far. He looked a lot better than the last time I'd seen him post-battle. "As much as it pains me to admit, it's become clear over the last few years that we need to formally enlist the Aatarilecs to our cause. We need more warriors and resources. Our people have been fighting for years without a lot of gain. They are tired."

"Those water creatures have never bothered to return any of our messages," Xavier replied drearily, his chin resting on his good fist. "I do not see why we continue to talk about that either."

"Because," I declared stubbornly. Some groans piped up from our meager audience. I continued, "we already have two Aatarilecs helping us in Caark, and we made promises to them!"

"Promises that you don't know whether you can keep," Mira chimed in sadly. Her midnight hair gleamed silver around her ears in the aquamarine light of the Dome.

"They're plenty do-able! You all are kings and queens, aren't you?" I began to chide. "If you all can't fix the overfishing of the seas, then who can?"

Xavier, Frederick, and Sabine all squirmed in various levels of discomfort. The last thing they wanted to do was start placing new rules upon peoples they had just begun to lead.

"You also promised Chelsea and Sonya that you would get their banishment rescinded. That's not exactly your decision either," Frederick said slowly, looking at me from across the glass table with an uncertain expression. We very rarely were on opposite sides of an issue.

"*Ahem!*"

Each of us stopped what we were doing and turned toward James. He looked at us with a bored expression, and a small part of me expected his eyes to change color just like his brother Luke's would. But James hadn't inherited that Ranguvariian trait, being part human just like Rachel, and my heart ached yet again over Luke's absence. I wondered if I would ever be able to forgive myself. It was my fault he was dead and that Rhydin cracked all the Ranguvariians' secrets just before we came to the Dome over a decade ago.

"If you all are ready to stop fighting for the day, I can say what I was trying to say," James added grumpily, crossing his lanky arms.

We all continued to stare at him silently. Sam finally looked cooled off, but Xavier and Sabine appeared to be simmering beneath the surface.

"My grandfather, Clariion Arii, was able to make contact with the Aatarilecs. The chieftess will arrive at the Ranguvariian Camp in a few days. He wants Lina to come for the meeting."

"And not us? Why can't the chieftess just come here?" Sabine demanded.

James shrugged. "Who knows, who cares. Can you all just be happy for once?"

I slapped a hand over my mouth to hide my smile, but there was no hiding the crinkles around my eyes. It was about time somebody said it!

"Well, that takes care of that," Frederick chuckled as he scratched the back of his neck. "Anything else we need to talk about?"

"No," Xavier announced abruptly, scooting back in his seat so rapidly that the legs let out a squeal. He clutched his emerald cloak around his arm and stormed off with Mira in his wake. I really couldn't blame him. These meetings were always awful.

Frederick sighed. "Meeting adjourned."

Relief instantly flooded me. Another meeting was done and over with. As the Royals dispersed, Evan turned to me, his voice nearly giddy. "Is the rumor true? Rachel is bringing our children from Caark?"

A smile split my face. "Yes!" I exclaimed, still so happy I could cry.

"I cannot wait to see Aron. Cayce will be so thrilled," Evan said excitedly, the most animated I'd ever seen him. His expression suddenly fell, and he asked, "Will you be here when they get here? If you have to go to the Ranguvariian Camp for this meeting?"

My heart fell into my stomach. "I-... I don't know." I whimpered, "Sam?"

Sam grimaced. "Rachel said it would be a few days before they get here. We might make it back in time, but they might beat us to the Dome, too."

"We?" I asked confusedly, still devastated at the thought that I might not be here when my children finally stepped foot across our secret threshold.

"I'm going with you, of course," Sam answered matter-of-factly.

"But shouldn't you be here for Ky and Rayna if I can't be?" I asked sadly as Sam took my hand and squeezed it.

"Uh, Arii has something for me to do there, too. James told me right before the meeting started." Sam smiled slightly.

"Oh," I responded slowly, unsure of what to think.

"Don't worry," Evan said as he touched my shoulder. "I'm sure you'll be back in time. We all know how important this is to you. If not, Cayce and I will be there to meet them."

I was just thanking my twin brother when James and Jaspen appeared over Sam's tall shoulder. I asked again, "We're not leaving now, are we? I thought the meeting wasn't for a few days, the tent isn't ready for the kids."

"Arii thought it would be best if we got there as soon as possible," Sam replied shortly. At the sight of my downfallen face, he threw an arm around me and added, "Don't worry,

Lina. It'll all work out in the end. They're coming. That's what matters."

I moaned only partially to myself, trying to keep it together to bid goodbye to my brother. We walked in silence out of the Council chamber, which looked like a small circus tent from the outside regardless of the countless important matters that passed underneath its canvas ceiling. This tent had been dug in deep long before any of its neighbors had sprouted up. The one room with its glass table was nestled into the cold earth, and my toes were having trouble getting their warmth back as Sam and I followed James and Jaspen through the clogged arteries of the Dome, away from its heart.

People had created similar lives to what their old ones had been down here. Teachers had created makeshift schools for the surviving children of our rebels, merchants sold and bartered whatever wares they were able to get their hands on during secret sojourns outside, carpenters worked their wood, and smiths hammered away on their swords or pots as if we were all still living in our original towns, free of Rhydin. Several of these people followed Sam and I on our missions, yet several more simply lived down here in safety until the big one. The day we would make our stand and take the fight to Rhydin's entire army.

That would be the day.

The Dome grew infinitesimally less congested as we approached the edge of the city. The people around these parts were new arrivals, still figuring out their footing in their new lives underground, in more ways than one. As a father worked on constructing a hodge-podge dwelling, a little girl played nearby with healing wounds on her arms that I recognized were from magic. I wondered if this was why this particular family abandoned their old lives for the safety and cause of the Dome. There was always something that served as a "last straw," it seemed.

We approached the same "back door" through which we had entered last night, and as Jaspen gently rolled away the enchanted stone that hid the entrance, I abruptly saw stars. Rays of sunlight shone through the doorway and beamed through the darkness of the Dome, offsetting the aquamarine light of the Ranguvariian feather chandelier above. My eyes were dazzled by the sight, and the Dome suddenly seemed so much darker than usual. I couldn't remember the last time I saw the sun like this, fully overhead and not about to dip above or below the horizon.

I walked faster, desperate to drink it in. I left Sam and the two Ranguvariians in the dust and burst outside into the sun. It was so *warm*. I felt its heat from the top of my head down to my chilly toes. The same trees and bushes and grass I'd seen a hundred times before at this entrance had so much more color. Vibrant greens and browns that were stripped away by the night. I breathed in deeply, and even the scent of the forest seemed stronger.

Before I knew it, my hands were stretched out in front of me trying to feel the sun's warmth. I stared at the paleness of my skin, and my mind couldn't fathom it. As a farmer and a child who grew up on a farm, my skin had always been burned and tanned hundreds of times over to create a semi-permanent leathery color and texture. I had never been so pale in my life. I yearned for my old life so hard in that moment. The feel of freshly plowed earth under my feet and grains of wheat in my fingers. It was all I had ever wanted. Not to live underground away from the sun and the wind and the rain that made the crops grow.

Sam had appeared next to me during my daydreaming. He, too, looked white as a sheet, but still strong from years of battle and swordplay. He cracked a smile and chuckled, "I think you might get the worst sunburn of your life on this trip."

"I'm doomed," I laughed, and it felt good.

"Ready to go?" Jaspen asked, having just reinstated the magic stone in front of the doorway.

We both nodded, and Jaspen and James hummed their flying spell, their wings springing forth. There were gaps among their shard feathers because they had given so many away to keep us all safe. Jaspen took Sam's arm, and his wings wrapped around them both before they rapidly vanished in a burst of white light.

As James approached me to do the same, my eyes were drawn to the horizon by a twinkling. The Dome was located in the foothills of the mountains, the great divide of Nerahdis, on the southwestern edge of Lunaka. Even though we were a few miles away, I could see Rhydin's imperial palace higher up in the mountains, the sun playing along its windows as if it wasn't the dark dungeon it was. The Dome was just under his nose, and he had no idea. Nowhere safer than in your enemy's backyard.

"Lina?" James asked, bringing me back to my thoughts.

I turned to look at him. He was all grown up. Rachel's youngest brother had still been a shaggy-haired teen when I first became an Allyen. Now here he was nearly thirty. I had passed that big number a few years ago myself. Where had the time gone? As I stared at James, I found myself wondering if Luke would have looked similar at this age.

"You okay?" James mumbled in his deep voice, truly reminding me that he was no longer the child I remembered.

"Yeah," I answered, clearing my throat. "I'm ready, let's go."

James took my hand, somehow knowing my thoughts, and I welcomed it. Then, I took a deep breath and braced myself. James wrapped his wings around us, and my last thought before transporting was that I was about to see the Ranguvariians' ancestral home – *Luke's* home – for the very first time.

CHAPTER FIVE

RAYNA

"How much farther?" I groaned, each step throwing needles into my feet. We had walked all afternoon and evening yesterday before meeting up with Chelsea and Sonya and making camp, and now we had spent another entire day on the road. I had never once considered myself out of shape, but my perception of walking a mile to and from school every day being enough was quickly fading.

"Just a couple more miles for today, Rayna," Aunt Rachel called over her shoulder. "We're almost to the closest pocket."

"Pocket?" Aron asked quizzically. "Pockets are for trousers."

Aunt Rachel laughed tiredly. "You're not wrong, Aron. You all haven't listened to a single word of my lessons today, have you?"

Ky, Aron, and I eyed each other as we continued to walk. We were still within a forest, which at least kept us shaded. I had spent much of our walk staring at the scenery, wishing I could draw and walk at the same time. This place was just so different. The amount of vegetation was the same, but it seemed *drier* on the whole. The crisp air had absolutely zero humidity, and the temperature was much cooler than I was accustomed to. At some point, I'd overheard Aunt Rachel mention the word "autumn," which was something I'd only read about in books at school. It had something to do with the leaves turning red and falling to the ground or something like that. Caark didn't have "seasons." It was muggy all year round.

"I'll take that as a no," Aunt Rachel sighed, rubbing her freckled temples. Then, she instructed her son, "Mathiian, repeat the highlights to your friends, please."

"The mainland of Nerahdis consists of the Three Kingdoms of Mineraltir, Auklia, and Lunaka, as well as some unincorporated areas like the Great Desert and Caden's Plain," Mathiian recited like he was a textbook. "The Kingdoms' boundaries still exist, but they are no longer considered kingdoms. Instead, Rhydin has placed Einanhi decoys of himself at each of the old castles, which are all now his strongholds packed with military and basic supplies. He often switches between them so no one is really sure where the real one is at any time in order to maintain his dictatorship. The rebels have been trying to discover the difference between Rhydin and his Einanhi decoys for years in order to attempt conquering one of the castles."

Multiple Emperor Rhydins. I had never seen him before, but I shuddered at the thought.

"All of Nerahdis is considered a war zone. People are no longer allowed to gather and are only allowed to leave their property for work or essential goods, which are rationed. There are many other rules too. Rhydin seems to be trying to create a 'perfect' society where nothing 'bad' ever happens, but allows no individualism or steps out of line. The punishment for anything is usually to be sent to a slave site in the Great Desert which produces all the weapons and supplies for Rhydin's reign and armies," Mathiian continued on.

Just as the Ranguvariian boy finished speaking, something black appeared over the next bend of our path. Aunt Rachel never said anything, so we kept walking. Thirty seconds later, we were close enough to see that it was a burned-up wagon, a big one the likes of which I'd never seen in Caark with tall arches down the length of it that must have once kept a tarp in place. Blackened pots and books and other odd items were littered around it. Aunt Rachel acted like she never saw it, like it was commonplace, and that scared me more than the wagon.

The whole place really was a war zone.

Chelsea and Sonya brought up the rear of our walking party. They, too, appeared unnerved at the sight of the wagon. They never left Caark like Aunt Rachel did; they had always stayed with us as we grew up. The dark-haired Sonya never spoke much, but Chelsea's blond brow furrowed over her mint-green eyes as she said, "I cannot believe how bad it has gotten. How has Rhydin not been overthrown by now? Surely nobody supports him anymore like they used to after the War of the Three Kingdoms?"

"The only way he'll be overthrown at this point is if literally *everyone* stands together. Trust me, we've tried every other way. We just don't have the numbers," Aunt Rachel responded tartly. Her blue eyes dipped to her shoes. "And you'd be surprised. Some people still support him. Mostly the rich who get special treatment."

"What about the Rounans?" Ky suddenly chirped. My head snapped in his direction, surprised to hear his voice. "I know Rhydin hunts us. Because he hates us."

Aunt Rachel stopped for a moment. She weighed my brother in her gaze, all fourteen years of him. The future Kidek, leader of the Rounans. I could see the gears turning in her mind, wondering if my brother could handle the truth, if he had broad enough shoulders to bear it. We all could. She abruptly turned and continued walking with the simple answer of, "I'm sure you know it isn't good. Your father can better enlighten you when you see him."

Both Ky and Aron slowed in their walk as Aunt Rachel summoned Mathiian closer to her. She was still trying to give him pointers on how to transport since they were the only two

Ranguvariians here, the only two who could, in case something should happen.

Chelsea quickened her pace until she was between the boys and placed a hand on each of their shoulders. "Come now, boys. Everything is going to be okay."

We were all silent for the next twenty minutes or so except for the two Ranguvariians. I caught snippets of their conversation on how to transport as I tried to ignore my aching feet. At some point, they lapsed into Ranguvariian, and I lost all bearing on what they were saying.

The sun was beginning to stretch toward the western horizon, and the trees were clearing enough that I could see the mountains in the distance waiting to catch it as it fell. I had been surprised to see a forest in Lunaka. People always said Mineraltir was the forest kingdom. But I guess that matched the story of when my mother was a child and was nearly abducted by Rhydin. Aunt Rachel had told me that story hundreds of times, and it always took place in a forest in southern Lunaka. Aunt Rachel's father had died there, she told me once.

When the trees cleared out altogether, prairie opened up in front of us in all directions. Thick, tall grasses stretched up to my waist almost like a pale green sea. *This* was what people had always said Lunaka was like. *This* was my parents' homeland. The sight, even in the fading daylight, took my breath away, and I wondered what it would be like to draw it. Would I be able to portray what it actually looked like, or would it look like just a bunch of vertical black lines of charcoal?

A small bungalow sat just a bit down our path. It looked quaint with firelight in its windows and smoke coming from the chimney. There were faint scorch marks here and there along its walls, but nothing else looked amiss. Aunt Rachel marched us all up to the door and knocked four times in a particular rhythm. After a few moments, a little old dark-skinned man with a thick mustache answered the door. I waited for Aunt Rachel to say something, perhaps as to why there were three adults and four teenagers on this man's doorstep, but instead the man said in a gravelly voice, "Hope shines bright."

"By the tallest shadow," Aunt Rachel replied cryptically, but a smile graced her lips.

The old man smiled too. "Around back, dear. Conriin will be pleased to see you."

Aunt Rachel thanked him, and the world was growing very dark now as the sun crept below the horizon. She herded us off the porch and around the side of the shack to where there were cellar doors. Surely, we weren't going to spend the night in somebody's tiny old root cellar? Where were the other rebels?

Aunt Rachel knocked the same knock on the rusty metal doors, and they resounded like loud, cymbal crashes. The doors swung open on their own, revealing a long flight of stairs whose end I couldn't see. Ky and I eyed each other. This was growing weirder by the minute.

Chelsea and Sonya ushered the four of us kids down the stairs while Rachel waited to close up the doors behind us all. I assumed they had some sort of spell on them since they opened by themselves, but being magic-less, I had no real idea. The stairs were completely dark aside from a small, glowing light at the bottom that I could see now with the outer doors shut, and the dampness of the air almost reminded me of Caark despite its coolness. Indistinct music floated upward towards us, beckoning us deeper.

As we descended, Aron piped up, ever the curious one, as he brushed a cobweb out of his lavender hair. "What were those strange words you said? And who's Conriin?"

"The words are a code that members of our rebellion say to identify each other. Conriin is part of this pocket. He looks after it in a way, but he's not its leader," Aunt Rachel answered simply. It was too dark to see her face. "He's my cousin actually."

"Tell them the rest," I heard Chelsea chide. "Warn them, so they do not stare."

Aunt Rachel gave the quietest of groans, which sounded annoyed but I wasn't sure why. "Conriin is part-human and part-Ranguvariian just like James and I. He is also part-Aatarilec."

"But!" Aron chirped, the expert on every subject. "You've all always said that Ranguvariians and Aatarilecs have hated each other for nearly a thousand years!"

"Exactly," Aunt Rachel and Chelsea responded in unison. I could only imagine that they were probably glaring at each other now, even in the dark.

"Conriin is a little different, but he is a good person and very smart. He cannot talk, so let us do the talking," Chelsea continued. "He is my cousin too, as you humans call it."

"Wait." I stopped mid-step. "Aunt Rachel and Chelsea are cousins with the same person. Are you two related?!"

"*No!*" both women shouted, which caused the lilting, happy sounds below to cease.

Aunt Rachel groaned loudly and suddenly started herding us all down faster. It was an effort not to trip over my own feet as we hurdled down the dark stairs, and relief flooded me when we finally reached the landing and the light.

There were people *everywhere*. Old people and young people. Tall people and short people. People of every skin tone and every kingdom. Gornish and Rounans alike. It was mind-boggling. It was like we had interrupted Friday game night or something. Everyone was huddled together in different groups with food or cards in front of them. I imagined only moments before they were all talking and laughing, but now they all stared at us with weary, cautious eyes.

Aunt Rachel smiled and held up her hands. "My apologies for frightening you all! We are just a few more weary rebels on our way to the Dome."

"The tallest shadow," a few people murmured to each other, over and over until it had crossed the entire room.

I needed to ask Aunt Rachel what this referenced later.

A small, shriveled woman seated a few feet away from me with a mug of juice squinted at me. Only seconds later, she gasped loudly and announced like a rooster, "It's the Allyen! The new Allyen!"

Abruptly, nearly everyone in the room was on their feet, craning from side to side to try and see me. My spine felt cold as whispering filled the room and people gaped at me like I was on display, but that feeling melted away when a man called out, "You're going to save us all!"

"You Allyens will rip Rhydin from power!" a young woman with long emerald braids cheered. "What a glorious day that will be!"

I smiled, suddenly feeling pretty good about myself. Their energy was contagious. "Yes! Yes, we will!"

The room filled with cacophonous cheering. Aunt Rachel eyed me, and I could tell she hadn't wanted to bring such attention to ourselves.

"Madam Allyen!" a scrawny boy called to me as he squeezed between two adults to be able to see. "Do a magic trick for us! Please, oh please?"

A stone settled in my stomach. Pretty sure this didn't count as a life or death situation.

"I-..." I stuttered, my fingers twiddling. How could I tell them that their precious new Allyen still didn't have any magic?

Aunt Rachel instantly cut me off, "My apologies again, dear rebels. We've traveled far and still have a long journey in front of us. Allyen Rayna needs her strength. No magic tricks today."

The entire crowd groaned as if the circus had just gotten canceled, but that was the end of the conversation. Everyone turned back to their original activities. People began to re-deal playing cards, and I noticed a pyromage or two give a quick re-heat to their meals. Ky and Aron were scanning the room left and right, probably searching for anybody using invisible Rounan powers, as Aunt Rachel, Chelsea, and Sonya guided us toward an empty corner. I didn't notice anyone levitating their food or passing their cards without touching them, but I wasn't looking very hard either.

The adults settled us at an empty table, and Chelsea sent Sonya to find us all a bit of whatever everybody else was eating. I never really understood why Sonya, who was so much bigger and stronger than Chelsea, always did what she said. Aunt Rachel gasped all of a sudden, and I noticed a hooded figure had quietly come up behind her. I was about to jump up and help her when she broke out into a huge grin and enveloped the hooded figure in a massive bear hug. "Conriin! It's so good to see you!"

In return, the hooded figure made several quick gestures with his hands, which were very pale with a bit of a lilac tinge to them. I had never seen Chelsea and Sonya in their true, Aatarilec forms, but they had told me once that their real skin was purple. Aunt Rachel continued to talk niceties to him, and he responded with his hands each time. After a few moments, she turned and motioned towards us. "Conriin, these are the children I've been guarding for the last decade in Caark. Ky, Rayna, and Aron. And you remember my son, Mathiian?"

Us kids were all in the midst of greeting Conriin ourselves when the short figure removed his hood. Despite the preparation, we still stared. His face was strikingly human albeit the long Ranguvariian nose and impish Aatarilec cheeks. Aatarilec fangs poked out of his lips on either side, but his hands were claw-less. After a few moments of staring, Conriin's eyes shifted from a light pink toward a daffodil yellow, which was a Ranguvariian trait I knew from Mathiian. However, the pupil was not a slit, but round like a human eye. What must it be like to be a blend of three different species? It was no wonder he kept his hood up.

"Kids," Aunt Rachel warned quietly through her teeth.

All of us immediately averted our gazes somewhere else as Aunt Rachel, Conriin, and now Chelsea continued to talk. Sonya hadn't returned with food yet. My stomach felt like it was eating itself. The scones Aunt Rachel had packed hadn't lasted long for either breakfast or lunch. Aron resorted to digging out the book he had brought while Ky continued to study the room, probably still searching for the use of Rounan magic. My eyelids fluttered closed, heavy from the long day, until Ky abruptly sent his elbow into my ribs.

My eyes flew open, and I was close to tackling him to the ground before he threw his head towards his other shoulder. I looked beyond him to see what he had seen. A boy with dark blond hair was staring straight at us. Ky and I glanced at each other, but when we looked back, the boy was still staring. I was about to get up and demand what he wanted when the boy stood and took a few steps toward our table. He spoke clearly, yet timidly, "I'm sorry for staring. I just can't believe you all are actually here."

Ky answered, his brow furrowed in confusion, "Why?"

"Oh, uh…" the boy's hazel eyes darted downward briefly, "I got separated from my parents because of Rhydin before Rudy brought me here a week ago." He pointed at the elderly man who was sitting at the table he had just left, a shiny, black ring on the boy's finger. "Seeing you all makes me hope I'll get to see them again soon." The boy smiled sadly, and then peered at me sort of funny. "You are Allyen Rayna, aren't you?"

"Uh, yeah," I answered uncertainly, making a quick glance at Aunt Rachel and Chelsea, who were still speaking to Conriin. "And you are?"

"Oh, sorry. I'm Erikin," the boy replied confidently.

"Are you a Rounan?" Ky asked suddenly.

"No," Erikin responded with what I couldn't decide was confusion or disgust. "Does that matter?"

"Don't worry about it," I said soothingly, eyeing my brother who turned away from us glumly. "Do you want to eat with us?"

"Sure!" Erikin cheered as he retrieved his plate and hopped down next to me. He put a big bite of beans in his mouth and asked, "How old are you?"

"Thirteen," I said as I held myself back from stealing some of his food. "Ky, my brother, is fourteen. Aron over there, my cousin, is twelve. How old are you?"

"I'm fourteen like your brother, I guess. Not too far from you though." Erikin smiled mischievously. "Tell me everything, Allyen Rayna. What's having magic like?"

The stone in my stomach grew heavier, suddenly quenching any hunger pangs. "Uh...I don't want to talk about that. Please just call me Rayna," I said quietly.

A plate of food suddenly dropped in front of me, ladled full of stew, beans, and a piece of hard cornbread. It could have been a feast for all I cared, and my hunger came roaring back. Sonya placed similar plates in front of Ky, Aron, and Mathiian, then gave the others she carried up and down her arms to Chelsea and Aunt Rachel.

Aunt Rachel turned to sit at the table with Conriin at her side, but stopped short at the sight of Erikin sitting next to me. "What's this? I haven't gained another teenager to wrangle, have I?"

Erikin grinned sheepishly. "Actually, I'd love to tag along with you all to the base if that's alright?"

"The Dome?" Aunt Rachel corrected, looking at him skeptically.

"Yes, yes that's what I meant," Erikin replied, blushing.

Aunt Rachel's eyes narrowed in that way that said she was studying every inch of this kid. She muttered a terrifying "maybe," before turning back to her food and Conriin.

Erikin became quiet for a few moments, glancing up at Aunt Rachel several times between bites of cornbread. Then, he struck up an innocent conversation with me about what I liked to do. Meanwhile, Ky sulked at his plate, and Aron propped his book against his tin cup so that he could read and eat at the same time. Mathiian huddled next to his mother, staring at Erikin every so often, his eyes continually shifting between a nervous brown and an annoyed orange. Chelsea sat on Conriin's other side, talking to him briefly but not as much as Aunt Rachel, while Sonya wordlessly ate her food. She was never a talker, that one.

The evening crept into the late hours as Erikin attempted to teach us how to play one of the card games everyone was playing, Mineraltin Blitz. It involved constantly flipping through your hand in the hopes of being able to slap cards down on other players' piles. The game moved faster than I could comprehend, and Aron utterly destroyed us in all three rounds. Toward the end of the third round, the adults in the underground room began to move all the tables and stack them against the earthen walls. There was obviously a system to this place as everyone perfectly spread out their sleeping paraphernalia on the cleared floor. As families huddled together, I found myself wondering how many of these people stayed in this pocket and how many were simply passing through.

Aunt Rachel, Chelsea, and Sonya corralled us into the same empty corner where we had eaten and tossed us our blankets from the night before. The three adults spread their blankets around ours, effectively creating a barrier between us and the rest of the rebels in this pocket. I didn't really understand why at the time. We were supposed to be in a safe space.

Erikin dragged his sleeping roll as close to us as he could get without a glare from Sonya. He didn't seem to care about remaining close to Rudy, his elderly companion, any longer, which I thought was a little weird. But I supposed that living in this cellar with the same person for even just a week would wear on anybody.

I flopped backward onto the hard ground with a groan. My feet were still aching, and my toes throbbed from where they had rubbed against my boots for the past two days of walking. Aron was still reading his book as the adults across the room started dimming the blackened, rusty chandelier in the middle of the ceiling, snuffing candles one by one. He gave up when it became too dark and rolled over toward where Mathiian was already snoring away.

Ky had lain down too, but I could tell his mind was still awake, poring over the general lack of Rounans in this pocket and what that could possibly mean. I reached over and placed my hand on his arm, whispering only loud enough for him to hear, "The Dome will be different. There'll be way more Rounans there, I know it."

My big brother grumbled in response, but he tapped my hand a couple times before his breathing grew deeper and more relaxed.

I was almost too excited to sleep. It would only be a day or two more before we would see our parents! But my exhaustion banished any restlessness, and I quickly slipped away to sleep. It was a good thing, too, because we were only going to get a few hours' worth before the night came crashing down around us.

CHAPTER SIX

LINA

M y jaw dropped to my toes when the white light of transportation dimmed. The Ranguvariian Camp was nothing like I had *ever* imagined. I certainly wouldn't have ever defined it as a camp.

Hundreds of Ranguvariians walked about doing their daily business, each of them dressed in a rainbow of colors, some of which I didn't know the names of. Monstrous trees dominated the settlement, each of them several feet in diameter with decorations made of fabric strips wrapped around their trunks and strung through their branches. Wooden houses with perfectly shingled roofs hung suspended in the treetops, all of them painted with different designs and colors.

Ranguvariians left and right simply flew up to their doorsteps with their beautiful wings. Wind chimes made of their shard feathers, like the one Rachel had brought Sam and I as newlyweds, were absolutely everywhere, and their tinkling chimes echoed throughout the village. The air was cool, clear, and crisp, just as I would expect in northeastern Lunaka, huddled up against the mountains before they dipped into the ocean.

We had landed on sort of a big, padded area the size of a large building back in my hometown of Soläna, the capital of Lunaka. It was like a gigantic drum with a homemade tarp tied tight, and a brief wondering of whether or not young Ranguvariians learned to fly here crossed my mind. James had to pull me forward off the landing pad to make room for other Ranguvariians that were coming in and out. Jaspen and Sam stood at the edge, and my husband looked just as dumbfounded as I felt.

"This is…" Sam breathed as he continued to stare, "amazing!"

"What? You didn't think there were just a dozen of us living in some tents, did you?" James scoffed.

Sam and I rapidly shook our heads. No, no, of course not.

"Let's go then! We'll head to Grandfather Arii's house, the Clariion's Lodge," James declared.

As James led us toward the heart of the village, Jaspen bid us goodbye and joined the traffic heading back toward the tarp, getting ready to transport back to the Dome. I just couldn't see enough of this place. My eyes traced the intricate designs on the houses and the goods being sold along the pathway. Leather concoctions I could only imagine their uses and strange-shaped fruit, which made the air smell sweet. The mountains were barely visible over the gigantic treetop canopy that blanketed the entire village, which was turning beautiful crimsons and golds as the world turned toward autumn.

"If you think it's silly that we thought you lived in tents, why have you all called your home the 'Ranguvariian Camp' all this time?" I asked as I watched a little Ranguvariian girl sprint up to her mother with some sort of childish treasure in her hands.

"Did it make you humans think we were small with no resources and not remotely a threat?" James answered facetiously.

I harrumphed. "I see your point."

James chuckled, and the path ahead cleared enough to see where we were going: the largest tree of them all. This one made the rest look like twigs. Its trunk was wide enough for twenty or thirty people to circle around, and its decorations were the grandest. Entire banners of the same fabrics I had seen throughout the "camp" waved along its branches, and each one was decorated in an art style that I didn't recognize though they seemed to be scenes. Up in this tree was the most majestic domicile we had seen so far. It was a large, multi-room dwelling that was totally encased within the leaves of this tree, almost like a simplified manor house in comparison to the other small houses around us.

In front of this enormous center tree, hundreds more Ranguvariians were kneeling, facing the trunk of the Clariion's Lodge. Around the trunk was a large, wooden dais, and upon it were three figures. When we grew closer, I was able to make out Clariion Arii in the middle, wearing his typical orange robe, but the two on either side were Ranguvariians I didn't know. They were dressed in their full warrior regalia as if they were about to head off to battle, the man in blue and the woman in red. Abruptly, the couple knelt before Arii, and he placed the back of the man's hand against the woman's cheek. All the Ranguvariians around us launched into a choral song with multiple harmonies, and a glow appeared between his hand and her cheek. When Arii removed the Ranguvariian man's hand, the pattern that had been there was now imprinted on the woman's cheek.

I suddenly realized that we had just witnessed a Ranguvariian wedding. Rachel had told me years ago just before we left for war about her *matrii*, the lime-green mark on her cheek that signified her marriage to Jaspen and allowed her to speak to him anywhere. Ranguvariian males were born with them, and it was copied to their wives' cheeks on their wedding day. I remembered being jealous of it since Sam had just been forcibly drafted into the war, and we didn't know where he was when she told me about it. I would have given anything to be able to speak to him then. Today, I was pretty thankful I didn't need a mark on my face to speak to my husband.

Now that the *matrii* had been transferred, Clariion Arii led the gathering in another song that was much more upbeat and rhythmic before the wedding disbanded. Arii saw us almost immediately from his place up on the dais, and while I expected him to wait for us to approach him, he hurried his tall, three-hundred-and-forty-year-old frame over to us. He wasn't even out of breath when he reached us and said happily in a soft voice, "Welcome to the Ranguvariian Camp! I am so thrilled to have you both here."

I smiled and was about to respond when Arii turned to Sam a mite urgently. "The companions I sent word to you about are standing over there" – Arii gestured to the left of his tree in the opposite direction that the wedding guests were heading – "and they should start as soon as possible."

"Okay," Sam answered a little breathlessly before giving me a long look. My confusion had to be obvious upon my face. He added, "It's just a small project for the Dome. I'll catch up with you later, okay?"

"Alright," I replied uncertainly. Something didn't feel right.

Sam gave me a quick hug, whispering the words "everything's gonna be fine," and then trotted awkwardly over to where two Ranguvariians stood waiting for him, both dressed in a light green.

Well, now something *definitely* didn't feel right.

James appeared confused as well, and Arii's expression was serious for a few seconds before he turned back to me and said, "Come with me, Allyen Linaria. I have something to teach you before our meeting in a couple days."

My eyes lingered on Sam's back until he disappeared, and when I turned back to Arii, he presented his arm to me. I took it, and I walked double-time to keep up with his long strides toward his house. When we reached the dais where he had just performed a wedding, he hummed the flying spell and gracefully flew me up to his doorstep a hundred feet off the ground.

A neat, wooden threshold met us, and it was odd to enter a door in the air. Gauzy curtains fluttered from the doorway, buffeting our entrance. Inside was a large entryway filled with what I imagined were Ranguvariian mainstays as befitting the receiving area of their leader: suits of Ranguvariian leather and armor, displays of about every weapon imaginable, and also décor made to look like Ranguvariian feathers but weren't. The room as a whole was very neat and symmetrical, not an item out of place, in way that almost made you want to start pulling out your hair.

Arii seemed to be watching me absorb the details of his living space, and he chuckled, "This is just the official entrance. You will not discover much about me as a person from this room."

He walked us forward several steps to the center of this perfect entryway where I realized that was a hole in the high ceiling, a neat circle adorned with beads. Again, Arii flew us upward through this hole to the upper floor. I guess stairs were pretty useless to creatures who could fly.

This room was much more what I considered to be like Arii. The room was taller than it was wide with a ceiling of glass panels to let in green- and red-tinted sunlight due to the changing leaves outside. Swaths of colored fabric were hung every which way across the ceiling and down the smooth, wooden walls to create a cozy feel. There was a place for a fire on the far wall in a higher area, and while most of the room itself was vacant, every wall was lined with shelves. All sorts of knick-knacks were on these shelves, and there was a general lack of books, which surprised me.

"You seem intrigued. Why?" Arii asked curiously. He was sitting against an immaculately carved desk with his long arms crossed.

I shrugged. "I'm just surprised all these shelves aren't filled with books. You seem like a book person."

"Ah," Arii replied in his soft, old voice, "that is because Ranguvariians do not have books, or a written language for that matter. Everything we pass on is oral and in song. The few books you see are all written by humans. I collect them. I would have more if it was possible for me to enter a book shop without terrifying the poor keeper."

I suddenly felt sad, as well as an overwhelming urge to bring Arii some books next time. On one last look around, I noticed a portrait of a red-haired woman hanging behind his desk. She was human, and she was beautiful. "Is that your wife?" I asked. "The Mineraltin princess?"

Arii's voice became more subdued. "Yes, it is. Her name was Emily."

"How did you meet her?" I asked again, my curiosity winding me up. "How does a Mineraltin princess end up married to the leader of creatures nobody thinks are anything more than a scary bedtime story?"

Arii chuckled. "She was the youngest sister of a Mineraltin king many decades ago. She was not treated very kindly there, and she ran away. I found her in the woods close to death, but our healers were able to help her. The rest is history." The old Ranguvariian smiled. "The portraits beneath hers are our children, Laveniia and Siimeon. They were the only children of ours to live to adulthood. Laveniia was Rachel, Luke, and James's mother. Siimeon was Conriin's father."

My brow furrowed. I had never heard anything about Rachel's mother. Only that her father, Viincen, died protecting me from Rhydin as a child. Conriin, whom I'd met only a handful of times, also lost his father in that battle. Laveniia looked so much like Rachel in the photo, totally human except she had the high-boned, long-nosed face of a Ranguvariian. "What happened to them? Emily and Laveniia?"

"Emily died birthing one of our other children that died as an infant. I raised Laveniia and Siimeon by myself," Arii answered quietly. "Laveniia died twenty years ago when her hunting party was ambushed."

"By Rhydin?" I asked.

"By Aatarilecs." Arii met my gaze with eyes that flickered between an angry red and a calm green.

I thought about Rachel's hatred toward Aatarilecs, and it abruptly made a lot more sense than just a centuries' old rivalry. No wonder she and Chelsea continued to have a tenuous relationship. "How are you able to consider this alliance with the Aatarilecs? They'll be here in two days, and they killed your daughter." My voice became firm, and my words became more of a demand than I intended.

"Because Rhydin is the greater enemy," Arii responded simply, "and I have had many, *many* years to hope that peace with the Aatarilecs can someday be possible. That, perhaps, I can leave my people with no enemies when my time as Clariion is over. I promised myself that I wouldn't stop my aging until Rhydin was truly gone. How nice would it be if Rhydin was destroyed and an Aatarilec alliance was created in the same stroke?"

"Really nice," I muttered. To myself, I wondered if Arii was setting himself up for disappointment.

"Anyhow," Arii abruptly became much louder, "let us get on to our magic lesson."

"Magic lesson?" I laughed. "I've been an Allyen for nearly fifteen years. Don't I know everything about magic by now?"

"Close, but not everything," Arii chuckled. "Have a seat."

I pulled up one of the soft, leather chairs to Arii's desk as he sat down behind it. The difference in our heights was still unmistakable. An autumn chill raised goosebumps on my arms as Arii withdrew three glasses, a couple of beads, a pitcher of water fashioned to look like Ranguvariian feathers, and a sponge. I was beginning to wonder if this was really a magic lesson or a children's science experiment.

"How many types of magic are there, Allyen Linaria?" Arii asked.

I couldn't help but wonder if this was a trick question. School had *never* been my strong suit. I could barely read anything too difficult without Frederick's help. I stammered, "Uh…well, there's fire magic, water magic, light magic like mine-…"

"No, er… Perhaps, *origins* of magic would be a better term for it. My apologies," Arii interrupted me nicely.

"Oh," I breathed, and then thought for a moment. "Three? Maybe? Gornish, Rounan, and yours?"

"You are on the right track." Arii smiled. "There are four."

Arii lifted the first empty glass and set it in front of me before taking the pitcher and filling it with water. "This represents all Gornish magic, or the magic of the Royals due to their ancestry from the continent of Gornan, as well as all Rounan magic, the magic of the people descended from the continent of Rounia."

I was instantly reminded of the history lesson that every child knew by heart. Gornan was the first continent, ruled by humans with iron fists. The rulers there had the same elemental powers our Royals did, and they ruled over their people using fear. However, when Gornan hit a famine and the land was dying underneath them, all of the original Gornish people left and invaded the second continent, Rounia.

In Rounia, every single human had an invisible force magic, just like the Rounans of today. The Gornish made the Rounans their slaves, and soon the same malpractices caused Rounia to die as well. The Gornish emperor had nine sons, and the youngest, Caden, set out to find a new continent and change the ways of his dark father. They found Nerahdis a little over three hundred years ago.

Of course, our old history books claimed that the land was empty, but the history book I found in the Archimage Palace said otherwise. Nerahdis was inhabited by the Ranguvariians and the Aatarilecs, and we humans tricked them into ceding their land to us. The Gornish quickly took over, creating new kingdoms, and they continued to mistreat the Rounans and tried to wipe out the magical creatures. It was an awful story, but it was the truth and therefore needed to be told.

"How can Gornish magic and Rounan magic be in the same category? They've hated each other for centuries, if not millennia!" I raised my voice unintentionally, but it was only because I had seen the stigma first hand as the Gornish wife of the Kidek, leader of the Rounans, back when we lived in the Compound.

"Magic has nearly nothing to do with love or hate. It is a neutral force, only used or abused by its wielder," Arii answered solemnly. "The Gornish and Rounan magics are the same type of magic because people with these powers are automatically born with them. Their magics do not require any sort of awakening or gifting, just as this cup is already full of water."

I thought for a beat before asking, "Isn't my magic Gornish? Allyen magic has to be awakened."

"To some extent, but Allyen magic belongs to a different category. We'll get to that and why later," Arii answered nicely.

Instead of turning to one of the other glasses as I expected, Arii extended a long finger and drew a glowing square on his desk with magic. Then, he took the pitcher once again and filled the square with just enough water to cover the surface of his desk. "This represents an Einanhi. They are a man-made being created completely of magic with no permanent form, and only the magic of their creator gives them life and keeps them in line."

I groaned, "Those are hard to create. I've only managed to do it correctly once or twice. They usually end up flat as a pancake on the ground or totally haywire."

"They are difficult. I find Einanhis to be an unnecessary type of magic, but we must count them nonetheless," Arii sighed before moving the sponge to the forefront of his desk and pouring water over it. "This represents magical creatures. Ranguvariians, more specifically, but Aatarilecs count here too. We are saturated with magic. Our very existence is magical, but we are not created as Einanhis are."

"Okay, so Gornish and Rounans, Einanhis, magical creatures...what's left?" I asked. My mind was beginning to fill up.

Arii cleared the desk and placed the last two glasses in front of me. Into each, he dropped one of his pretty colored beads, but he never touched the pitcher. "These are the Allyen and Rhydin."

"Whoa, whoa, whoa," I said loudly, holding myself back from standing up, "Rhydin and I *can't* be the same type of magic. My magic is good and light, and his magic is dark and evil!"

"Remember, we are talking *origins*, not what magic looks or feels like," Arii chided. He knew this was bristling me. "Both the First Allyen, Nora Soreta, and Rhydin Caldwell, as he was once known, were Gornish people born with a very small inclination toward magic. It was buried deep in their genes from a relative."

"Like Rayna?" I asked. After all, my daughter had originally been born to Frederick and his late wife, Cassandra. We had to hunt for a new Allyen child when it was foreseen that neither Evan or me would have one naturally. Rayna had an inclination for magic through her father, but it had not been defined yet.

"You are correct. I will return to that momentarily." Arii suddenly became a little nervous. "These beads represent the Gornish seed of magic within Nora and Rhydin." – Arii poured a little bit of water into only one of the glasses – "I helped Nora discover and refine her seed into something new. I watered her seed." The bead in the glass dissolved and turned the water a beautiful sky-blue, and the liquid filled to the brim perfectly without any more water from the pitcher, just like the other glass representing Gornish/Rounan magic. "Rayna is the same way. We watered and refined her Gornish seed into Allyen magic. The rest of the Allyens are not quite like this because you gained your powers by birth, even though they still follow the same rules of awakening and such. This is what makes Rayna different, and this could become important soon."

My head was spinning. I would have to process this over several days. "What about Rhydin?"

Arii suddenly pulled out three other pitchers of water from under his desk, each dyed red, blue, and yellow. He used the original pitcher of clear water to begin the cup just as he had done with Nora's, and the water began to turn blue again. But then, he used each of the other three pitchers to continue filling the glass. The waters blended and became murky before turning an ugly black, and the liquids burst beyond the boundaries of the cup.

My eyes widened. "What are you doing?"

"This is what happened to Rhydin Caldwell. We know from the history book you found that he was made Archimage at eighteen years of age. Rather than cultivating his aptitude for magic as I did with Nora, Emperor Caden pumped him full of all three Gornish magics together. He was overwhelmed with powers unnatural to him, and as the cup loses its bearing on its water, so does Rhydin."

"Which is why he's so powerful," I continued with a slight moan.

"And also why many of his words and actions do not quite make sense. His 'perfect society' which is actually rather awful, for example," Arii clarified. "I believe it is why he is the way he is. He has lost a few marbles, rather than water."

I sat back in amazement. It all made sense. Why Rhydin was so crazy and illogical. It made me angry at the people who forced him to be Archimage, who forced all their powers into him. If they had just never done that, what would our lives be like now three hundred years later?

Arii gestured to his desk, and my eyes wandered back toward it. The black, swirling liquid from Rhydin's cup had crossed the desktop to where the other items of this lesson were sitting. The saturated sponge, which represented Ranguvariians, was beginning to dissolve where the dark water touched it. It took me a few ticks to realize what it represented.

"Rhydin's magic hurts Ranguvariians. The inhumane combination eats you away like poison," I said breathlessly. "How does that work with the Aatarilecs' ability to stop that from happening by being near?"

"I have not quite worked that one out yet," Arii chortled. "I've had over three hundred years to work out this lesson. We have only known about the Aatarilecs' ability for a tiny fraction of that time. Hence the surprise."

I nodded and thought about everything I had been told for a few moments. Arii began cleaning up his desk and putting things away when I asked, "So why now? You could have given me this lesson when I became an Allyen at nineteen, but you didn't. And what does this have to do with Rayna?"

"I believe this information is becoming more and more pertinent with every day that goes by. It did not seem as important when you were a fledgling Allyen. However, I have overwhelmed you with too much information today already, and I am not one-hundred-percent positive on my new theory yet. I will share it when I am. For now, let us go and join the festivities down below," Arii replied as he came around his desk.

Sure enough, the light had begun to fade behind the glass ceiling and millions of tree leaves. Arii flew me back through the Clariion's Lodge, and to my surprise, hundreds of Ranguvariians cheered when he brought me down from the tree top. There was no sight of Sam anywhere in the crowd, or any other humans for that matter, although Arii assured me that he was fine and his assignment had been detained. I was given a feast of sweet venison and goat, as well as roasted purple roots and a rye roll. I watched as a group of Ranguvariians stepped upon the dais, and they sang and acted out a retelling of my vanquishing of Duunzer in their language, which was extremely embarrassing.

We were all up far too late, laughing through thin, mountain air. I had nearly forgotten all of my stressors until Arii escorted me to the chamber I would use in the Clariion's Lodge and informed me that Sam would be staying the night elsewhere as his mission continued to take longer than anticipated. Arii wouldn't answer any of my questions about what he was even assigned to do up here, so I flung myself onto the bed in the very simple, unadorned room. I tossed and turned until I fell into a fitful sleep, dreaming of cups and beads and far too much water.

Chapter Seven

---*ᦔ᷎᷾*---

Rayna

M y island had never looked so beautiful. I was standing
in a tiny rowboat, and Caark beckoned to me in the
distance. Its palms fluttered in the ocean breeze, waving hello,
and the sandy beaches glittered in the sun. Humidity wrapped
me close like a warm hug. I felt safe, ever so briefly.

But suddenly, all I could hear was screaming. "Help,
help!" the palm trees cried. "Help, help!" the waves and the
sand and the jungle foliage cried. The sun was struck from the
sky, and darkness descended, ripping through everything that
made Caark my island.

I was thrown from my little rowboat by the roiling waves,
but instead of landing in the icy ocean, I landed on hard, dry
earth. I jolted from my nightmare to true screams of help as
Aunt Rachel shoved us all back into the corner of the room.

Embers were raining down over our heads, and the cellar
was filled with black, inky smoke. The rusty chandelier
screeched over and over as it rocked side to side. Chelsea and
Sonya drew their swords as Aunt Rachel muttered furiously
to the glowing symbol on her cheek that let her magically talk
to her husband.

"What's going on?" I whimpered, my head throbbing from the smoke and so little sleep.

Aunt Rachel ignored me as she drew her own blade, shouting for Conriin at the top of her lungs. We could hardly see anything there was so much smoke. I began to hear the clangs of swords meet and the booms of magic fired, but it was agony to not be able to see or sense *anything*. This cellar was no longer a safe refuge, but a trap with no way out.

Abruptly, Erikin was next to me, and I wondered groggily where he had come from. "You were followed from Canis! Rhydin's forces have come for us!"

"How can that be?" I wondered out loud sleepily. We had been so careful.

"*Conriin!*" Aunt Rachel yelled again before the smoke cleared momentarily. The room that had been a warm respite the night before was unrecognizable. It was the house above us that was burning, as fire licked the wooden beams above us. Was the nice old man okay? Was anyone that we had spent time with last night okay?

"That's it, I'm taking you *now*," Aunt Rachel shouted as she turned toward me and latched onto my wrist. I was in the middle of refusing to go without my family, but just as Aunt Rachel began to hum her flying spell, blades appeared at both our throats.

"Drop your weapons!" an Einanhi soldier demanded, its features bland and mass-produced by Rhydin.

Aunt Rachel begrudgingly dropped her sword, and so did Chelsea and Sonya. I didn't dare breathe until the cool dagger at my throat relaxed a mite. All of our wrists were rapidly bound tight. Now would be a *great* time for my magic to awaken, but Rhydin wanted me alive. Never once thought that would be a problem.

Ky and I glanced at each other, and fear filled my brother's eyes. More of Rhydin's artificial soldiers surrounded us, several of them pointing weapons at Aunt Rachel and Mathiian in particular, and they began to herd us through the embers and smoke back towards the stairs that would take us to the surface. We could barely hear some of the conversation echoing down the stairway to us. The only part that I could make out was that evidently someone had tipped Rhydin's forces off that the new Allyen had been seen here. Who in Nerahdis would do such a thing?

The world was still dark when we emerged. The one moon I was accustomed to and the second Lunaka-only moon were both only slivers. The house that had once sat on the border between woods and prairie was a smoking pile. I was just getting a good look at the swarm of real, human soldiers and Einanhis dressed in black – Ky barely stepping onto solid ground behind me – when things abruptly moved very fast.

Quick as a flash, a shape burst out of the forest. I only barely recognized it as Conriin before he summoned a pair of wings, which were much smaller than the average Ranguvariian's, and plumb tackled Ky, the closest one to the tree line. They were gone instantaneously, and that threw the rest of the world into chaos.

The Einanhis surged toward where Conriin and Ky had just disappeared. Erikin screamed like a baby, clutching the black-studded ring on his finger. My heart thundered, not knowing what to do. Mathiian tripped forward out of the cellar stairs and pretty much fell on top of Aron, his wings springing forth as he grabbed him with his tied hands. The two of them vanished. Two more to safety, although with Mathiian's transportation skills, there was no telling where they had just landed.

Aunt Rachel snapped her ropes with a sharp bracelet and threw herself into a spin, the tough leather guards on her arms knocking away all of the blades pointed in her direction. Her arm was bleeding when she dove for me, and my world filled with too bright light.

Our ragged breaths were deafening during the split second we spent in the white void, transporting away. The scenery wasn't all that different when the world reappeared: dark, trees, prairie grass. It was painstakingly quiet.

"Stay here!" Aunt Rachel commanded before she vanished yet again.

I suddenly felt very small. Silence roared in my ears. I was alone, my wrists still bound in front of me, and my worries over my family and friends threatened to overtake me. Where did Aron land with Mathiian? What about Chelsea, Sonya, and Erikin, who could not transport? What would Rhydin do to them?

"Rayna?" a quivering voice called out from a nearby bush. I'd know that voice anywhere.

"Ky!" I gasped in relief. I trotted over to him and took shelter with him behind his bush. Odd how such a small plant could make you feel just a little bit safer. "Where did Conriin go?"

"He transported back to save someone else," Ky whispered quietly. His hands were shaking as he cut my binds with a small blade Conriin must have given him, and then he pulled me into a big, brotherly hug. "I'm so glad you're okay."

I was about to thank him when Conriin flashed out of nowhere, his tiny wings fading from view, with a little purple person in his arms. My eyes bugged out at the sight of this fanged, long-clawed creature. I knew it had to be Chelsea or Sonya in their Aatarilec form, a form I knew about but had never ever seen. They were so much tinier than I had ever imagined!

"Conriin, *put me down!*" the little creature shrieked, its voice much higher than usual. Glistening tears were in its eyes. "Sonya's still back there, and there's no water!"

Why did that matter? I wondered, just as Aunt Rachel flared back to us. To my great surprise, it was Erikin in her arms and not Sonya. They were both spattered in crimson blood, and I couldn't help but stare. I had never seen the liquid of life before.

The Aatarilec hopped down from Conriin's arms, snapped her wrists free with a flick of one deadly claw, and raced over to Aunt Rachel, screeching, "How *dare* you save that useless boy instead of Sonya!"

"Chelsea-..." Aunt Rachel tried to say as she dropped Erikin on the ground unceremoniously.

Chelsea continued to rage, her lavender skin blushing a royal purple, "You just couldn't let go of your hatred of Aatarilecs to save her, could you?!"

Aunt Rachel grew angry. "I may despise your people for what they've done in the past, but-...!"

"She was *my best friend!* She's taken care of me since we were *children!*" Chelsea continued to scream, her mint, spikey hair becoming wild.

"*She was already dead!*" Aunt Rachel bellowed.

The woods suddenly fell silent. Chelsea blinked her big, golden orbs at Aunt Rachel, gleaming tears steadily falling down her rounded cheeks. She mumbled, "What?"

"You and Sonya were the reason I returned," Aunt Rachel answered firmly. "You were already gone, so I tried to get Sonya. The Einanhis already had her, and they executed her before I could reach her. This sorry brat just happened to be sniveling at my toes, so I brought him."

Chelsea began to cry loudly. Her anger was gone, so she began to grow and morph back into the Chelsea I knew. Aunt Rachel looked a bit sorry as she withdrew a hankie and started wiping the blood off of her, before briefly disappearing again.

I looked at Conriin for an idea of what I should do right now, but then I remembered he couldn't speak. Erikin was jittery where he sat on the ground, twiddling the ring on his finger, and he was looking all around us like he would see some sort of landmark in the dark night. Ky stepped forward and released his wrists too.

Aunt Rachel reappeared with Mathiian and Aron, twigs embedded in the latter's lavender hair. I would have to ask Aron later to where Mathiian had accidentally transported him. Fleetingly, I felt relief that we had escaped Rhydin's forces again. Yet, while our number was the same, we weren't all here. My relief vanished, and sadness replaced it. While I hadn't been necessarily close to Sonya, she had still watched over me for as long as I could remember. It felt strange to know I would never see her face again.

I had never known someone who had died before.

"Let's go," Aunt Rachel said after a few moments of silence. "We won't be truly safe until we are inside the Dome."

We all summoned the last of our strength and put our weary bones into motion. Every step put me closer to my parents, I told myself. It wasn't long before the trees cleared enough for us to realize that we were very close to the mountains, their peaks in sharp contrast to the treetops as they blocked out all the stars. One mountain, in particular, was nearly double the height of the rest. I figured my sleepy eyes had to be playing tricks on me in the dark, so I leaned over and asked Aron, the smartest one, "Is that a really tall mountain or something else?"

"That's Caden's Peak," my bookish cousin answered. "It's the tallest thing in all of Nerahdis."

My mind suddenly clicked. "The Dome is right next to Caden's Peak. It's inside the tallest shadow."

Aron nodded like it was obvious, but I was proud of myself for figuring out the riddle on my own.

It wasn't long before we were up close and personal with one of the larger foothills of Caden's Peak. I imagined that during the daylight hours, this area was shadowed for a good chunk of the day. Aunt Rachel approached a rather large, round stone and placed her pale hand on it. As she concentrated, the edges of the rock glowed, magically unsealing. Conriin trotted forward and helped her roll the stone away from a doorway, the entrance to the Dome. My arms prickled with goosebumps.

"Before we go inside, children, I want you to look over there," Aunt Rachel announced as she pointed to the north.

We all turned and immediately saw where she was pointing. Even though it was a few miles away, there was no denying the hundreds of lit windows in the night.

"Emperor Rhydin's imperial palace," Erikin breathed, his eyes widening into windows.

"Oftentimes, the safest place you can be is right beside your enemy. That is, as long as he doesn't know you are there," Aunt Rachel said firmly. "The location of the Dome is our most important secret. You all are now carriers of that secret and therefore members of our rebellion, but our cause is more important than any single life. Remember that."

I gulped. What an introduction to Dome life.

When we entered the tunnel, the smells of dirt and fire assaulted my nose. Aunt Rachel and Conriin restored the stone and re-sealed it magically. My heart began to pound as we walked for a few moments in total darkness. I was about to see the place my parents had been my whole life.

We arrived in the main cavern, and my breath left my lungs. It was *gigantic*. And aptly named. This foothill was totally hollowed out like a bowl turned upside down, and an entire city lay underneath it. The edges were still empty dirt, and the outer boundary was made up of tents and other temporary lodgings. Toward the center, I could barely see what looked to be more like cabins and buildings, people who had been here far longer. At the very top of the Dome was a huge, blue-green crystal – like a big, glowing stalactite – and its light filled the entire area.

"What is that?" Aron asked as he pointed at the crystal. He always had to know everything.

"The world's largest cluster of Ranguvariian feathers," Aunt Rachel answered, a prideful smile spreading across her face. "With that number, Rhydin can't sense us right under his nose."

Aron's jaw dropped. Erikin looked like he couldn't believe it all and was going to be sick. Mathiian gazed up at it in wonder. Chelsea just rolled her eyes.

I was losing my patience. I couldn't wait any longer! I asked excitedly, "Where are our parents? Are they sleeping, or can we see them right now?"

Aunt Rachel's smile faded. She reached up and scratched the back of her neck. "Um…you know, Rayna, it's really late. It's only a couple hours after midnight. I think it would be better if we all just got some sleep for now. We'll talk about it in the morning."

I deflated, and so did Ky and Aron. It was impossible to mask our disappointment. I could tell Aunt Rachel felt bad, as she guided us away from the central city and toward one of the walls of the Dome that looked like it had windows in it. Ranguvariian guards were posted at a stairway, and Aunt Rachel led us past apartment after apartment in a dim, lantern-lit hallway until we reached one on the end with a red curtain.

This apartment had to belong to Ranguvariians. Probably two of them considering the tidiness of one half of the room and the utter disaster of the other. Candles were lit along the ceiling, and they were definitely burning something judging by the herbal scent that gave my nose a break from the dirty, fire smell. All the furniture had been pushed to the edges of the room, and a bunch of sleeping mats had been rolled out along the floor. At least one person must have known we were coming.

"*Cy-liire!*" Mathiian exclaimed suddenly, making me jump. I'd no sooner turned to face him, wondering what he had said, when he threw himself across the room and into someone's arms that had just come through a doorway from another room. It was a very tall Ranguvariian man dressed in a yellow robe with a thick, strong frame and brown hair that was long on top and cropped short at the bottom. I remained confused until I noticed that his hand was imprinted with the same symbol that was on Aunt Rachel's cheek.

My heart sank, but I tried to smile. It was Jaspen, Mathiian's father. This was the kind of reunion for which I had waited for so long, and it hurt to see someone else receive it when it seemed mine was no closer. The two bantered back and forth to each other in Ranguvariian, and I finally had to turn away. As we all put down our packs and readied for sleep for the second time tonight, I tried to soothe myself with the idea that I would get my reunion in the morning.

No such luck.

Aunt Rachel let us all sleep in for a couple of hours past what she had ever allowed back on Caark, but that didn't make her first news of the day any better to bear as the underground city bustled below. Her hands were folded neatly in front of her, and her voice was tight when she said, "I'm afraid that Lina and Sam are not in the Dome at the moment. They are away on very important business, and they will be back very soon. Our journey was sped up, otherwise they would have been here."

Ky's shoulders slumped. My stomach clenched. How could we be so close, and yet so far?

"You all will have to stay with me until your parents come to claim you. We can't have you kids just running about the Dome. This is a place of work, and it must be kept secret." Aunt Rachel kept talking. I had pretty much tuned her out at this point. She turned to Aron. "Your parents will be here shortly."

The biggest smile I had ever seen spread across Aron's round face, his teal eyes sparkling. I couldn't help but hate him a little bit in that moment.

"What about me?" Erikin piped up. "My parents aren't here."

Aunt Rachel put a hand on her hip. "I thought you said in the cellar that you got separated from your parents and were hoping to find them here?"

"I, uh…I said I got separated from them a while ago, and I wanted to come to the Dome," Erikin replied, becoming a bit defensive as he touched his black ring. "I don't know if they are here or not."

"What are their names?" Aunt Rachel asked matter-of-factly, like it was that simple.

"Uh…" Erikin hesitated. We were all staring at him by this point. "Mikael and Rosetta North."

Aunt Rachel's eyes flew open. Jaspen spit out his coffee. Conriin and Chelsea both looked at each other, confused.

What was the big deal? Who were Mikael and Rosetta North?

"Did she used to be Rosetta Harvey?" Aunt Rachel demanded as she rushed toward him. When Erikin shrugged his shoulders, she added, "Was she from Soläna, Lunaka?"

"I-I think so?" Erikin answered. "That's where I last saw them."

"Stars above," Aunt Rachel breathed. She glanced at Jaspen, and he lifted his hands in defeat. His eyes became brown with nerves.

"Uh…why is that such a big deal?" Erikin asked innocently. Ky, Aron, Mathiian, Chelsea, Conriin, and I were all asking the same question with our eyes.

Aunt Rachel took a deep breath, obviously deciding whether she wanted to tell us or not. "Your mother is Allyen Linaria's younger sister. She's been lost to us for years. Her husband – your father – is one of Rhydin's Followers."

All of a sudden, I didn't know how to look at Erikin. His mother was *my* mother's sister? His father was a bad guy? *We were related?*

"What have I done?" Aunt Rachel gasped. She clutched the collar of her tunic like she was about to have a panic attack.

"No, no, you've got it wrong!" Erikin exclaimed fearfully. "My parents don't work for Rhydin anymore! They left a long time ago. M-My mother is a teacher, and my father works at the city library in Soläna!"

Aunt Rachel paused, studying Erikin. She and Jaspen shared a long look.

Erikin kept speed-talking, "W-We got separated when Rhydin moved his decoy into Lunaka Castle and tightened his grip on Soläna...I didn't know where to go until Rudy found me and took me-..."

"To the pocket," I finished for him. His story made complete sense to me.

Aunt Rachel sighed, "Mikael and Rosetta were so bookish as kids. They *would* have those jobs."

Erikin began to relax a little.

"*However*," Aunt Rachel continued loudly, "you will never leave my sight, young man, until we can verify your story."

Erikin deflated. I tried to smile at him to make him feel better.

Aunt Rachel downed the rest of her coffee and strapped her sword to her hip. After a few moments, she announced that she wanted us all to meet the Royal children and join them in their magic lessons to start building our powers. Hundreds of shivers shot down my spine. I gave a small wave goodbye to Mathiian and tried not to think about anything whatsoever as Aunt Rachel trooped us all up a few more floors to the very top. Instead of hallways and singular apartments, the stairs let out into one gigantic room hollowed out of the wall of the Dome. She was just saying the words, "you all will be spending a lot of time together," when the magical *booms* stopped and the figures across the room turned to face us.

I gulped, suddenly wishing I had bothered to do more with my appearance this morning than simply run a brush through my reddish-brown hair.

There were six of them. Four boys and two girls. Two boys looked nearly identical to each other and were much older. They had hair the color of a red sunset and unnaturally green eyes, so I assumed they were Auklian. Closer to Ky and I's age were a girl with wavy, chocolate brown hair with a blond patch on top, a skinny blond boy with freckles, and a boy and girl with bright copper-colored hair who looked like siblings. My mouth went dry.

"Your Highnesses," Aunt Rachel announced loudly, which brought them meandering in our direction, "might I introduce to you Ky and Rayna Greene, Aron Harvey, and Erikin North. They will be doing their magic lessons with you from now on."

"Um…" Erikin stuttered. "I don't have magic."

The wavy-haired girl's nose turned up. The twin boys gained mischievous smiles. The copper-haired girl gave us a nice smile while her brother stared blankly into space.

"Then you can watch, because you are not allowed to leave this building," Aunt Rachel responded crisply. She eyed the Royal children's reactions and continued, "Let me clarify. This is the *Allyen* and the future Kidek with their cousins. I trust that you all will be amiable."

All six Royals' mouths gaped. When Aunt Rachel's icy-blue gaze didn't relent, they all began bobbing their heads like sitting ducks on water. She chuckled, "I'll leave you all to it then," and walked back toward the stairs.

After a couple moments of awkward silence, the skinny, blond-headed boy piped up, "Um, I guess we should introduce ourselves, too. My name is Dominick Tané. King Frederick of Lunaka is my father. And this is my sister, Nathia."

The girl was maybe sixteen, and I eyed the strange mixture of chocolate-brown waves and golden bangs. I couldn't help but wonder if it was natural or not. She grimaced. "*Adopted* sister."

Nathia thrust out a hand which lifted a gigantic rock in the center of the room and flung it toward the far wall. We all stared at her, Ky happily, before she began to walk away and pointed a finger at us. "I'm watching you. If you know what's good for you, you'll remember that *I'm* in charge of all the Rounan children around here."

Ky's grin vanished.

"Uh...she's joking. Mostly, I think," Dominick laughed uncomfortably, then gestured to the staring boy and smiling girl. "These are my cousins, Taisyn and Lyla Rollins. Their parents are King Xavier and Queen Mira of Mineraltir," – he then pointed to the older twin boys, whose hair reminded me of squaw birds back home – "and these two are Chretien and Willian Cedal. They are Queen Sabine of Auklia's wards."

So many important words. So many important people! I could hardly grasp that in less than a week we had exchanged our simple school friends on Caark for the children of Nerahdian Royals. It remained to be seen whether they would be friends or not.

"Ky and Aron, you might do better training with Nathia. She's the most powerful Rounan I know," Dominick said cheerily, and then he turned to me, "Allyen Rayna, I know my wind magic is nothing like your light magic, but would you like to train with me?"

Adrenaline knocked all the air out of my lungs, and I responded with the very first thing that came to my mouth, "Oh, um, you know what? My magic is, uh, sort of weird, I can't really use all of it yet, uh – there's just so much of it, y'know – but, uh, it'll come any day now, and I'll definitely train with you then! Could even be tomorrow!" I gritted my teeth together to get myself to stop talking.

Dominick appeared confused, but not offended at least. Until the quiet, copper-haired boy in the back called out, still not looking at me, "Your magic hasn't awakened yet. Has it?"

It felt like the entire room was now staring at me. Ky and Aron were the only ones who already knew, and they looked at me with pity instead of shock.

"Taisyn," his little sister chided, much younger than the rest of us.

"Some Allyen you are," Taisyn, the prince of Mineraltir, grumbled. He placed his pale hand on his sister's shoulder, and she began to walk away with him following, still holding her shoulder. Hatred began to bloom in my heart.

"Hey, you're not allowed to use your magic either, Blind Boy!" one of the Auklian twins cackled at his back. "Might burn yourself, Daddy says."

A fierce drove of fire licked into existence and narrowly shaved the Auklian prince's rose-red hair. The boy started patting his hair frantically, some of the ends singed. The rest of us stepped backward automatically. Taisyn hadn't cast it and hadn't reacted to it either, remaining there stoically. His pint-size sister, on the other hand, stood ready to summon another. "Shut up, Willian!"

With that, Lyla and Taisyn walked together to a different corner of the room than Ky, Aron, and Nathia were now using. Dominick mumbled something polite about looking forward to training together before being stuck with Chretien and Willian in the third corner of the room. I could tell the twins apart now that Willian had some blackened hair. That just left me and my newfound cousin, who had not stopped staring at me since the news that I couldn't use my magic like it was his world that had been shaken.

Erikin asked quietly, kindly, "Do you want to go sit somewhere? They're all jerks anyway."

I nodded slowly, trying to swallow the lump that had formed in my throat. "Not all of them," I muttered as I glanced at Dominick and Lyla. I hoped I was right, but as Erikin and I walked to the last available corner, I found myself wishing I'd never left Caark.

CHAPTER EIGHT

LINA

T he light of dawn trickled through the mountains, refracting off the ocean waters on the other side. The Ranguvariian Camp was cradled against the mountains by spiny trees only found in the very northern reaches of Lunaka, and the camp was quiet ever so briefly this early in the morning. Even at night, the chimes of thousands of Ranguvariian feathers fell silent when the wind settled down to sleep. The first noise of the morning was the blacksmith firing up her forge and banging on the hundreds of Ranguvariian blades that came through her shop every day. It wasn't quite like a human blacksmith shop, but I didn't know what else to call it.

I found myself thinking about the first sounds of Soläna in the morning. The churn of the mines as they beat to life and the bells of the castle tower. It had been so long since I'd seen my hometown and heard its sounds. Not since I had vanquished Duunzer. I could not give up the hope that I would see it again someday.

That hope charged me with energy as I threw myself through the movements of the spell that we now knew would destroy Rhydin. The Ranguvariians had taken to calling it

Alytniinaeran, which meant "death by three lights" in their language because it had to be performed by three Allyens. However, that word had five syllables, so for brevity and ease, Evan and I had started simply referring to it as the death spell.

Nora, the First Allyen, had invented the death spell with Arii's help to destroy Rhydin. She was way more powerful as the first, she made Rhydin disappear for three hundred years, but it wasn't enough to destroy him totally. Grandma Saarah and my father, Robert, split the locket in two and tried the spell as two Allyens to destroy Rhydin the night of Evan and I's birth, but that wasn't enough either. It had to be three Allyens, and thanks to my father, we now had three pieces of the locket.

Robert was murdered by Kino before we had a chance to complete the death spell a decade ago, right after he'd freed me from Rhydin's dungeon. I still saw red every time I thought of that snake-like woman. Evan and I practiced the spell every chance we got, and it made me think of Robert and how much I missed him every time. Evan and I still retained our thirds of the locket, and the last one was buried in the Dome, waiting for Rayna. All this time, we had been waiting for Rayna to grow and learn her magic to have another chance. She had just turned thirteen in the summer. So old and yet so young.

My anxiety flared. Now that she was coming to the Dome, where would danger come from to awaken her power? And when?

I was finishing the arcing motions of the spell, thrusting my large orb into an imaginary middle where Evan and Rayna would meet me, when I suddenly heard clapping. I dropped my hands immediately, my magic vaporizing. This was the second morning I had hidden myself behind the Clariion's Lodge to practice. Who had found me?

"Your grandmother would be proud of you. And your father," Arii added quietly. "All the Allyens before you would be." He was standing upon one of the wooden balconies a couple hundred feet over my head.

I blushed in spite of myself. "They'll only be proud if it works."

"I have no doubt that it will," Arii said reassuringly. Wings sprouted from his back, and he floated downward to the little haven I had found behind his home.

My voice grew quiet. "You see the future sometimes, right?"

"Sometimes," Arii responded vaguely, his brow furrowing.

"Have you seen anything about when Rayna will acquire her magic? When we can start training her for the death spell?" I asked anxiously. Desperately.

Arii pressed his lips together. "I have not seen when. Soon, I think. But I have seen where, and that is what concerns me."

I tilted my head, confused. "Why? Where does her magic awaken?"

Arii hesitated, obviously weighing in his mind whether he wanted to tell me or not. "The Archimage Palace."

My heart free-fell into my stomach. "Wh-Why in Nerahdis would she ever be there?"

Arii simply shrugged. Even I knew future-seeing had its limits. Both times I'd experienced it, it was terrifying. I still got shivers down my spine whenever I thought about foreseeing Duunzer and Sam's being grievously injured back in the war.

I thought for a moment and licked my lips. "Does this having anything to do with your saying Rhydin's and Rayna's magics are similar? My father told me that before he died."

"He did?" Arii asked almost immediately, his eyes flashing a brilliant orange. "What exactly did he tell you?"

I racked my brain, trying to remember that conversation so many years ago. We had been running from Rhydin's imperial palace. He had just helped me escape, and we were on our way to the clearing to help our friends. Where he would be murdered by Kino as he, Evan, and I tried to perform

Alytniinaeran to destroy Rhydin once and for all. I spoke slowly, "He said that our magics are similar...that they are linked somehow, because they are both man-made. Like what you taught me yesterday. He thought that might be important but didn't say how."

"I see," Arii exhaled, studying the ground and his toes. He looked back to me abruptly. "I believe he may be right. But I am not quite sure how yet either. As is normally the case with seeing bits of the future, only time will tell."

I looked away from the tall, old Ranguvariian. It was starting to make me feel physically sick to imagine my daughter being linked to my worst enemy, the darkest man in Nerahdian history. *She was only thirteen*, I thought over and over.

Arii cleared his throat. "Allyen Linaria, our meeting with the Aatarilec Chieftess is about to begin."

I brushed my hands together and straightened my clothing. I hated feeling like my job as Allyen had become somewhat political, but I couldn't ignore that aspect forever. I walked to Arii's side, ready to let him guide me to wherever this meeting was taking place, but not before I said firmly, "As soon as the meeting is over, I would like to return to the Dome. It is very possible that my children are already there."

"I understand," Arii replied quietly. "I imagine Sam will be done with his task by that time."

Sam. I hadn't seen him since we'd arrived here two days ago. I trusted Arii, but it was about to drive me insane that no one would give me a real answer as to what he was up to.

Arii walked me around to the front of the Clariion's Lodge and down a major pathway different from the one that led to the transportation area. Today felt different in the camp. There weren't Ranguvariians walking to and fro happily going about their business. The doors and shutters to their homes were all closed up. There were no children playing outside with wooden swords today.

We approached another large clearing within the village that encircled a beautiful, pristine pond surrounded by more fabric streamers, Ranguvariian feathers, and small bells. The water reflected the sky above perfectly; its depths could not be seen. All the Ranguvariians in town were on the outskirts of this clearing, just waiting in the trees. I couldn't help but notice that they were all heavily armed. A table that looked like it'd had half its height sawn off sat in front of the pond, and it was toward this table that Arii walked me. There was only one chair at this table, facing away from the pond. To my surprise, he gestured for me to sit in the grass at this table, and he did so as well.

The camp was so quiet now. The wind blowing through the various chimes was all we heard. The table was bare except for some tiny cups of water. I kept looking around, wondering which direction the Aatarilecs were coming from. I glanced at Arii once, but he appeared to be meditating with his eyes closed. For how many people were gathered waiting here, the silence was surreal.

The water in the formerly still pond began to bubble and glow with an eerie, green light. My hand couldn't help but inch toward my sash, which magically contained my trusty sword. Dozens of Ranguvariians around the edges of the clearing did the same. The bubbles burst upward into a spray like a fountain, and suddenly three Aatarilecs were standing in the center of the pond. The tiny bells around the perimeter were ringing now as the water sprayed them, far louder than I ever would have guessed, and I realized that they were a warning system.

The two Aatarilecs on either side, a male and a female, appeared to be guards or escorts. Their spiky hair was slicked back, and while they had no weapons beyond simple spears, their claws were the deadliest I'd ever seen on an Aatarilec – even though I had only ever seen two, Chelsea and Sonya. The creature in the center was dressed elaborately, a lacy dress with pearl accents over her lavender, frog skin. She had mint-colored hair that reminded me of Chelsea, and she wielded a large, impressive staff decorated with large, clear orbs in her old, wrinkled hands. She was obviously the chieftess.

I leaned over toward Arii ever so slightly and whispered out of the corner of my mouth, "How did they get in your pond? Underwater tunnels?"

Arii finally opened his eyes, and they were the color of lush, prairie grass. "Transportation magic. Theirs works through any body of water."

That information washed over me in big waves as the three Aatarilecs walked steadily across the surface of the pond, their feet sending the tiniest of ripples in every direction. The bells were no longer ringing. I felt like I finally understood the Ranguvariians' fear of these creatures. They could transport right into the middle of their camp and unleash havoc at any time because of this pond, an irreplaceable source of water and life. How awful.

"Jaana," Arii said from his seated position at our short and stubby table, "how nice to finally meet you somewhere other than a battlefield."

"Arii," the chieftess rasped, "I would much prefer the battlefield."

The Clariion gave a tight smile and gestured for her to sit in the lonely chair. She evaluated it for a few moments as if it might leap up and bite her before taking it hesitantly. It was then that I discovered why we were sitting on the ground and the chieftess sat in a chair. This way, Arii and Chieftess Jaana were seeing eye to eye.

I could only hope they really would. Our entire cause rested on this one meeting.

"Let us get this over with, Ranguvariian," Chieftess Jaana halfway snarled as she threw a look over her shoulder. "It's just plain wrong to be here in the daylight. What do you want?"

I could have sworn a tinge of red entered Arii's eyes, but I admired his ability to remain as cool as a cucumber.

Arii said slowly, succinctly, "As I said when I invited you here, we need your help. The rebellion against Rhydin needs your help."

The chieftess's arrogant façade faltered for a split second. "While it chills me to even consider that those words came out of your mouth, what in the mighty oceans do you think we could do for you?"

"You have numbers and resources," Arii replied, folding his hands neatly on the table as if he'd rehearsed this. He probably had. "You have powers of transportation that humans do not."

"Those are all things you giants can also supply," Jaana answered, flipping her hair annoyedly.

Arii winced at the derogatory term but kept on as if nothing happened. "You provide an element of surprise that Rhydin would never expect. And your numbers more than double ours."

Chieftess Jaana leaned forward menacingly on the table, her fangs discolored. In a sickeningly sweet voice, she said, "Tell me what you really mean, Arii. Tell me what I already know."

I squirmed in my seat. I had no idea how Arii was keeping it together.

Clariion Arii took a deep breath and stretched out his hands, like the answers were on his palms. "My people are not enough. We have tried, and we are failing. We cannot stand up to Rhydin's magic, but with Aatarilec help, we can."

Jaana grinned widely, showing all of her pointy teeth. "Say it. You *need* us. The Ranguvariians are lost without the Aatarilecs."

Arii all but groaned. "It is true. We need you, but you also need us."

"What could possibly make you think that?" Jaana quipped as she leaned back in her chair, crossing her purple arms.

Arii cleared his throat and nodded at me. I tried to still my nerves before I responded, "We know about the overfishing problem. Your people are hungry and going without. I am close to the Royals and can stop this if you help us. Not to mention the fact that it's only a matter of time before Rhydin begins hunting you the same as the Ranguvariians."

Jaana glared at me and hissed, "Who told you that?"

"Two exiled Aatarilecs I met in Caark who are now pledged to our cause," I said confidently, sitting straighter.

Jaana cackled like that was the funniest thing she'd heard all day, "Onna and Rami? I exiled those two traitors years ago. They are dead to me."

My brow furrowed. "I don't-…"

"Ah, they've totally abandoned their true names now that they parade around as humans, hm? I believe last I heard, they went by 'Chel-sea' and 'Son-ya'?" the chieftess said mockingly.

I deflated; my confidence gone. I struggled to speak. "Who cares? You still have a major problem that we can fix if you choose to help us against Rhydin."

"Actually, there is another solution," the chieftess raised herself from the table, now towering over our sitting positions, "Rhydin will eventually destroy anyone who stands against him, and Nerahdis will have a much lower population which cannot possibly overfish our waters. Problem solved."

"He will come after any power that is not his own, you know that!" I stood as well, unable to keep my voice down any longer. Arii remained sitting silently.

"But are you humans worthy of being saved? That is my question," Jaana answered cruelly. "I'd like to see Rhydin hold his breath long enough to get remotely close to our grotto. He cannot transport there if he does not know where it lies. From what I have seen, humans are absolutely incapable warriors. Until you humans prove that you are worthy of my help, I have no inclination to enter a battle that is not mine."

My face flushed with heat. She was walking away. Our only chance at getting enough numbers and resources to take Rhydin on, to give us even a chance at performing the death spell, was walking away. "Please!" I called after her and took a few steps in her direction. "You're our only hope. We'll give you anything you want. I beg of you!"

Arii put his hand on mine.

"Begging and sniveling will never win me. You must earn it," Chieftess Jaana snipped. "Tell my daughter and her treacherous handmaid that they'll never see our grotto again." She tossed a bubbly laugh in Arii's direction before turning on her heel and stepping back out onto the water with her two guards. They swept the surface gracefully, their feet not even wet, until they reached the center where they swiftly slipped underneath in the blink of an eye. The green flash told us that they were gone.

My fingers felt numb. That wasn't it, was it? I suddenly started to feel lightheaded. We had failed.

My mouth was dry as I turned to Arii and said, "That couldn't have gone any worse."

"Oh," Arii replied quietly, "it could have."

I looked around us at all the Ranguvariian warriors waiting in the shadows ready for a war. They were all breathing sighs of relief now that their mortal enemies were gone, having no idea that our meeting had gone so badly.

"So now what?" I asked as Arii finally rose from the table and brushed off his orange robe. "And who's her daughter?"

"Onna, or Chelsea as you know her. I apologize, I thought she had told you," Arii answered quietly. "As for what to do now…I do not know. We can only take one step at a time until our path becomes clear."

I groaned long and loud. I didn't even have it in me to feel shock or anger that Chelsea never told me she was Chieftess Jaana's daughter and Sonya her loyal handmaid. "Arii," I warbled, "I want to go home."

"I understand. I will tell James to come as soon as possible," Arii responded in a soothing voice. "Please feel free to go anywhere you like in the village until he can return you and Sam to the Dome."

I nodded half-heartedly as Arii walked away to a gaggle of older male and female Ranguvariians vying for his attention. From what little time I had spent in the Ranguvariian Camp, I could guess that these people were part of Arii's council of elders. Each one wore a different color primarily, which I had learned represented each Ranguvariian's station or job. Arii wore orange all the time because it was the color of the Clariion. James frequently wore some orange because he was part of his house. Rachel wore both orange and yellow because Jaspen's father was the head of the Ranguvariian warriors, who wore yellow. Green was healing. I hadn't figured out what the other colors meant yet. One elder from each area was part of Arii's council, and he was just calming a grumpy elder in red called Altatiino when I walked out of earshot.

I spent hours by myself. I was too depressed to explore the village as Arii suggested, so I wound up planted right by the big tarp, tight like a drumhead, where all the transporting in and out of the village was happening. It was fascinating to watch, and I lost track of time completely. None of these Ranguvariians had passengers, obviously. No humans allowed here. They just approached an empty area of the tarp, hummed their wings to existence which wrapped around them like a cocoon, and they vanished into a blink of white light. A couple times, a group transported in together at high speed, appearing mid-flight and crashing hard into the springy tarp. A few of them were injured, and Ranguvariians in green rushed up to them to help. I assumed the ones injured by magic had been found by Rhydin or his forces while the ones with bloody gashes had run into Aatarilecs.

When the sun sank beyond the horizon – which was grassy hills and trees this far east, instead of mountains – torches were lit around the landing area. The amount of traffic never fluctuated. Nearly all of the arrivals stared at me briefly on their way into the village, their eyes flashing colors in confusion and realization of whom I was. My bones were weary from sitting in one place for so long when someone finally tapped my shoulder.

"Sam!" I exclaimed before throwing myself into his embrace. Then, I looked him up and down, making sure he was okay after not seeing him for two days. "Where have you been?

"Oh, uh, I was running an experiment for Clariion Arii," he replied. He looked pretty okay, but he moved like he had just run a mile. "Nothing super important."

"Are you okay? You look tired," I said softly, touching his cheek.

Sam shrugged. "Ah...I haven't been sleeping well. It's nothing to worry about. Just some of the Rounans back in the Dome are beginning to give me stress, that's all."

"Why?" I asked, confused.

"Uh, it's a long story," Sam replied as he looked over his shoulder. I followed his gaze to see that James was finally coming. "Several of the Rounans are starting to ask what life will be like after we destroy Rhydin. Whether Rounan persecution will end or not. I don't really know what to tell them because the Royals haven't said anything about it."

"Well, we'll have to bring it up at the next Council meeting," I said nonchalantly. "Nothing to lose sleep over."

"If you say so." Sam gave a small, sad smile. "I hope you're right."

"Are you two ready to head back to the Dome?" James asked happily, as if I had not spent all day waiting for him. I was thrilled to see Bartholomiiu next to him, my old *Alyen nou Clarii*, or soldier of the Allyens. He had saved my life back in the war, and he was recovering from his brain injury all the time.

Bartholomiiu smiled, his eyes turning a pale green, not the normal vibrance as other Ranguvariians but far better than the unchanging white they used to be. "Hello, Allyen Linaria. You, to see, is good again."

"Good to see you, too, Bartholomiiu." I grinned, then continued, "This place is amazing, boys, but if I spend one more minute waiting to see my children whom I haven't seen in eleven years, I'm going to box both your pointed little ears."

"Ma'am, yes, ma'am," James laughed. The sound almost made me forget how disastrous of a morning I'd had.

James and Bartholomiiu walked Sam and I out into an empty spot of the landing area, and I turned around to give the Ranguvariian Camp one last look. For all I knew, I would never see it again since I was a human. It felt like no time at all before we were transported hundreds of miles from the very northeastern corner of Lunaka to the very southwestern, right over my hometown of Soläna in between. Bartholomiiu transported back almost immediately upon landing, but James took us into the Dome through the tunnel I had seen thousands of times.

I found myself anxiously searching for their presences before I remembered that my son was a Rounan, unable to be sensed unless I was already looking at him, and my daughter had no magic to be sensed yet. It was like feeling blind, and my body automatically began moving toward the apartments in the stone wall like there was a magnet there drawing me in. Sam and James followed in my wake, and I was about to burst into a run at the sight of the stairs when my eyes found Rachel sitting on them, waiting for me.

My brow furrowed. This was odd. I jogged up to her, leaving Sam and James behind. Motherly panic consumed me. I cried out, "What's wrong? Did something happen? Where are Ky and Rayna?"

"Relax, Lina," Rachel chuckled slightly. "They're fine, and they're upstairs eating dinner."

I gasped, a high-pitched sound escaping my throat, and I tried to move around her desperately.

"But there's some things I need to tell you first," Rachel said as she stood, blocking my entrance.

"You said they were fine!" I squeaked, my worries coming back all over again.

"Ky and Rayna are," Rachel said again firmly, "but we lost Sonya getting here. We stayed in Conriin's pocket of rebels on our way here, and it was ambushed. We were lucky to escape being captured."

"Captured," I repeated, imagining the toddlers I left on Caark in Rhydin's clutches. "But they're okay," I reminded myself as I moved to try and mount the stairs again. "How's Chelsea?"

"Grieving, understandably," Rachel answered as she once again moved in my way and placed her hands on my shoulders. Sam and James had caught up by now. "But there's something else. We brought an extra teenager here. We didn't know who he was before we got here. It's better for you to process this before you have an audience."

"Rachel, will you *please* spit out whatever it is you need to say, so I can go see my kids?" I pleaded with her, a lump rising in my throat.

Rachel gave a big sigh. "There's a fourteen-year-old boy up there named Erikin. He's Rosetta and Mikael's child."

CHAPTER NINE

RAYNA

E rikin and I spent a *long* day doing absolutely nothing. I tried to ignore the Royal children as they flexed their magical muscles, I really did. But it was downright impossible. Erikin blabbered for hours about all the things he liked to do in his hometown of Soläna, not really telling me his life's story, although he sure asked a lot of questions about mine. The answers I gave were always short, and while my attention was elsewhere, I wasn't meaning to be snippy. I'd led a very sheltered existence on Caark where we went to school and went home, period. I didn't have a whole lot to tell.

I was able to put my anger aside just enough to be fascinated by the magics in front of me. Nathia was leading Ky and Aron to do bigger exercises than I'd ever seen them do before, tossing absolutely gigantic rocks. Dominick was the only aeromage in the room, and he spent most of his time making little twisters to suck up dirt on the floor. He didn't seem to be much of a fighter, I thought to myself, but this made me see him as even more of a potential friend.

Chretien and Willian, on the other hand, seemed to be showing off. They were doing *big* moves, swirling two silvery snakes of water all around their corner of the room, having them dive together and apart like some sort of show. Willian, in particular, kept glancing over his shoulder to see if I was watching. Each time he did, I just glared back at him. I felt like looking away would only make me seem weak.

At some point in the morning, Aron's parents arrived. His father was a short, Lunakan man with brown hair while his Auklian mother was an older, female version of Aron with long, lavender curls. When they found Aron, they ran toward him, calling his name. My cousin ran to them as well, and then they were all hugging. It was hard not to hate the whole show. Ky bid hello to Uncle Evan and Aunt Cayce, and he pointed in my direction shortly after. After talking for some time, Aron left with them, off to spend some quality time, while Ky continued to do magic with Nathia.

As the day went on, I found myself most intrigued with the Mineraltin siblings' training. Taisyn looked like he was my age while Lyla looked a few years younger. Maybe ten or eleven? But she was the one casting all the fire. She and Taisyn would face each other and begin moving through their forms, which were big and powerful. Taisyn may have been blind, but he certainly knew these moves so well that it almost looked like he was mirroring his sister. Fire came out of Lyla's palms with every move she made, but nothing for Taisyn. He kept his hands closed while hers were open. I couldn't help but feel like there was something behind this.

While a Ranguvariian had brought a sandwich lunch to all of us up here, when it came time for dinner, all the Royal children were putting any training stuff they had used away. Dominick waved Erikin and I over as they all approached the stairs, and for a brief moment, I could pretend that we were a part of the group, too. But after an ugly look from Nathia, I was reminded of my place.

Magic-less. Useless.

We went down a floor to a large room filled with tables and chairs. I didn't even notice what was for dinner. I twiddled my fork over my tin plate. The Royal children were all bubbling with conversation, and Ky was a part of it. The only one not joining in was Taisyn. I stared at him briefly over my bite of potato as Erikin jabbered to me about how his parents had given him his ring before they'd gotten separated when suddenly the door to the mess hall opened with a bang.

Everyone stopped what they were doing and turned toward the door. Standing there were a petite woman with brown hair and a tall man with a scar on the side of his face. There was a locket around the woman's neck and a bandana tied around the man's fading brown hair. My eyes snagged on them. I nearly choked on the fire peas in my mouth.

It was like my drawing had come to life. Except they had faces.

The man – my father – had a long, but narrow nose. His face was very angular, and he had soft brown eyes. My mother's eyes were brown with golden embers within them, like mine. Allyen eyes, I had been told. All of her features seemed small compared to her big eyes. There was at least a foot in height difference between the two of them, if not more. My mother's eyes latched onto Erikin ever so briefly, and something in her expression seemed pained before she found Ky and I.

I put my fork down and stood, Ky close on my heels, and the two of us rushed toward them. Before I knew it, we were being smothered in their embrace. I tried so hard to stop the tears, but I couldn't. I pulled away and stared at their faces, only inches from mine.

This was real. This was completely and utterly real.

"Oh, Ky. Oh, Rayna," my mother said to each of us in turn as she touched our faces, tears streaming down her face, "I am so sorry. We never meant to be away from you this long."

I clung to her. Smelled the deep scent of the forest on both her and my father's clothes. I opened my mouth to say something only to realize that I didn't know what to call them. I had pined for them for so long, yet now that the moment was actually here, I didn't know what to say.

"I missed you," I mumbled against her shoulder. She wasn't that much taller than me. Ky was taller than she was, and she exclaimed as such.

When our parents finally released us, I looked around at them and Ky. This was how it was always supposed to be, I thought sadly. But this will be the way it will be from now on, I reminded myself.

"Papa," Ky said, his nerves evident in his eyes, "how many Rounans are safe here in the Dome?"

Our father smiled at the sound of the name, but it quickly vanished. His voice was light. "Too many to count, but I always wish there could have been more."

Ky seemed to relax at that, although I was sure he would want more details later. I suddenly noticed that the mess hall around us had gone back to its former clamor. I stood there, awkwardly. Now what?

"Can we join you?" my mother asked anxiously, her hands fidgeting in front of her.

Ky and I had thankfully been sitting toward the end of the table, so we beckoned them over to eat with us. The rest of the children grew very quiet again and wide-eyed, glancing up to stare at our parents every few seconds, except for Taisyn of course. Even the arrogant Auklian twins suddenly seemed to have forgotten how to blabber. Nathia, on the other hand, became an entirely different person. A terrifyingly bubbly person compared to her usual scathing looks, and her attention to my father rubbed me every wrong way there ever was.

What was she playing?

Dinner was filled with uncomfortable small talk in front of our audience, so the moment we were done, our mother leapt at the opportunity to bust us out of the apartment building. Erikin waved a sad goodbye to me, which made my mother stare at him even more, while Ky was the new Mr. Popular with all the Royal kids as he nodded goodbye to them. I'd have to trip him up later to remind him I still existed.

Ky chattered more than I'd ever heard him before as we walked down the stairs and out into the main area of the Dome. He talked about everything he could ever talk about. What we were learning in school when we left Caark (the mechanics of sailing). What he liked to do in his spare time (see friends, dig around in the dirt trying to grow random plants because he knew our parents used to be farmers). Even as specific as what meal Chelsea and Sonya had made him when he turned fourteen (Aatarilec fish rolls). Me, on the other hand? I had to keep reminding myself that Ky wasn't telling his whole world to total strangers. Because they weren't. But they were?

Our parents guided us down busy pathways that transformed from wide dirt roads with a few shanties on either side into ever narrower alleyways with cobblestones here and there, squeezed between buildings that grew taller and more permanent as we went. When we reached the corner of two thoroughfares, my father abruptly turned right into a decent-sized tent that had been set up with a more solid frame like a house. This definitely wasn't what I had ever imagined, but I was beginning to understand why they hadn't come for us. In Caark, we had a safe, sturdy home, a reliable source of supplies and food in the city of Calitia, and a normal routine of going to school. My resentment began to lighten up a bit.

"Well," my father said, a hint of embarrassment in his voice, "this is home. At least for now. I'm sorry it's not more."

There were three "rooms," if you could call them such. A large main area with a table covered in papers, a bookshelf, and some plants that looked like they desperately needed watered. Two smaller rooms jutted off from the main area, and while one of them contained a big bed and some more shelves of more random knickknacks, the other was curtained off.

"Um, I know it's been a long day. You two have been through a lot on your way here, and your father and I haven't been home for several days. So why don't we call it night, and we start fresh in the morning? Sound good?" my mother asked, glancing back and forth between Ky and I anxiously.

"Sure, Mama," Ky answered happily, like it was the most natural thing in the world.

Before I knew it, my father was settling my mother and I into their bed and setting up places for him and Ky to sleep on the floor in the living area. I didn't know what my mother had been off doing, but she was asleep almost as fast as her head hit the pillow. The tent grew dark, especially as the giant crystal on the ceiling of the Dome seemed to become dimmer as well, and her face relaxed as she slumbered. I stared at her, her nose only a foot away from mine, and I hoped that when I woke, this would seem less foreign than it did right now.

But when morning dawned, she wasn't even there.

I bolted upright, briefly forgetting where I was. "M-Mother?"

Had I dreamt the whole thing?

"Rayna," my father called from the living area. When I didn't respond, the patchwork curtain to the room inched to the side. "She's off practicing the spell like she does every morning. She'll be back. Come on out, and eat breakfast with us."

Hmph. She could have warned me. I slipped out of the bed, only wearing my long tunic, and pulled my trousers on, tucking my shirt in. My cloak was lying on a chair in the corner of the room, my sketchbook still nestled inside its big pocket. I decided to leave it there for now.

I emerged into the living area to see my father and Ky sitting at the table eating a style of eggs I didn't recognize. Father had moved all the papers on the table enough for him to eat in peace, but Ky pored over them like his life depended on it. He exclaimed, "These are *all* the Rounans in the whole world?"

"The ones I know about anyway," our father chuckled slightly. "It's not as accurate as I would prefer. The only hard and fast numbers are the ones that live here in the Dome."

"That's so *amazing*, Papa!" Ky shouted, unable to contain himself as he forked more and more egg into his mouth.

As the boys bantered back and forth, I poked my head out of the flap of the tent. Tons of people were already bustling up and down the street, and every little sound of the settlement echoed off the domed walls above us. The energy briefly reminded me of Calitia, although this city was much more haphazard. I said from the flap, "Where did she go?"

My father looked up at me, sensing my unease. "She's out back today. Perhaps, it would be better if you eat breakfast instead. She'll be in soon."

I ignored him and stalked right through the middle of the room to the back of the tent where there was another flap that was tied shut, almost not even visible. I untied it piece by piece and walked through to a very tiny yard of sorts. A ramshackle fence where every single post was a different item marked out the boundaries of the dirt area. When a flash of light caught my eyes, I ducked down behind a stack of firewood to watch.

My mother was waltzing around the small yard in circles like she was dancing. Her arms arced over her head in coordination with each foot, each time dragging an ever-larger orb of golden magic along with her. It took me a minute to realize that Uncle Evan was out there with her. He was several steps away from her, doing the same movements she was doing at the same time. They were two points in a circle with a larger gap on one side.

At the end of the dance-like spell, she and Uncle Evan met together in the middle of the circle, still with a gap between them on one side, and made their orbs of magic merge into a much larger one. It was so big and so powerful, so much more than I ever imagined. Then, abruptly, the magic disappeared and so did its warmth on my face. I had never seen Allyen magic before. I had never seen what my magic would look like before. It was golden and glowing and warm, and I wanted it so much more than I ever had before.

As my mother and Uncle Evan began their weird spell again, I jumped as my father placed his hand on my shoulder and sat behind the firewood with me, grunting with the effort. "Can't contain your curiosity, can you?" he said cheerily. "You're just like your mother."

"What are they doing?" I asked, never taking my eyes from them.

My father's lips turned into a thin line. "They're performing *Alytniinaeran*, which means 'death by three lights.' It's the spell that will destroy Rhydin for good. We call it 'the death spell' for short."

"Three lights?" I asked again, finally tearing my eyes from the gigantic display of magic. My kind of magic. "What does that mean? There's only two of them."

"I really shouldn't be the one to tell you this, but uh…" – my father scratched the back of his head underneath his bandana – "it has to be performed by three Allyens to have enough power to truly destroy Rhydin for all time."

My heart suddenly sank to my boots. "B-But," I stuttered, "I don't have any magic yet."

"I know," my father answered warmly, like it was the most normal thing in the world. "Don't worry about that. It'll come with time. I have complete faith in you."

The ice sliding down my spine warmed. This was the first time I had told someone about my absent magic, and I wasn't judged or attacked or belittled. "Thank you," I replied softly, and added as my heart thawed a little, "Papa."

Papa beamed. He wrapped a lanky arm around me and scooted me closer to him. He was so big and tall. I couldn't help but feel like nothing could hurt me here in his embrace. I leaned my head on his shoulder.

This. This right here was what I had waited my whole life for.

Uncle Evan and my mother ran through the spell with the big, five-syllable name that I couldn't pronounce one more time before calling it quits. If they'd practiced this every morning for the last eleven years, they'd done this 4,015 times. And they'd run through it three times this morning. They ought to be able to do this in their sleep. Would I be able to perform it remotely as well as they could when my magic awakened?

My mother stopped short on her return to the tent when she saw Papa and I sitting behind the stack of firewood. Her eyes looked fearful. "H-Have you two been here long?"

"It's okay, Lina," Papa said softly as he pulled himself to his feet, "she deserves to know."

I was liking him more and more all the time. I was sick of secrets.

My mother took a deep breath before answering, "You're right." Then, she turned to me slowly, almost like she was afraid of me. "Do you have any questions? About the spell, or...being an Allyen?"

"I don't think so." I shrugged. "Not right now anyway."

"Don't be afraid to ask if you ever think of one," my mother said with a smile.

"We're going to be late," Uncle Evan huffed from behind her. "The Council meeting is going to start in just a few minutes."

My mother groaned. Papa laughed at her. I didn't get it.

"Can I come?" I asked curiously, folding my hands behind my back.

My parents' eyes met. "Might as well. You're going to figure out everything going on down here sooner rather than later anyway," my mother replied as she walked toward the tent to get ready. "I hope you like watching people argue."

I'd laughed when she said that. But that was before I'd realized just how dead serious she was. Within minutes, the whole family was trotting toward the center of the Dome. What my parents referred to as the Council chamber looked like an elaborate tent dug deeper than the buildings around it directly underneath the gigantic, aquamarine stalactite of Ranguvariian feathers hanging at the top of the Dome. They gave us a quick overview of what the Council was and whom it consisted of as well, but nothing could have prepared me for the sheer level of arguing that went on in only an hour.

I spent the first ten minutes or so gawking. A week ago at this time, I was sitting in my little one-room schoolhouse hundreds of miles away on a tiny island, and now I was surrounded by the nine most important people in Nerahdis. Having spent so much time with their kids the day before, it was immediately apparent whose parents were whose. Dominick was the spitting image of his father, King Frederick, and they acted the same way. Queen Sabine was bold and ruthless in her arguments, which reminded me of Chretien and Willian, her wards. Queen Mira didn't speak much, but her quiet presence resembled Lyla's. King Xavier seemed like he was angry at the world, and Taisyn wasn't too far from that. The only one I couldn't pick out was Nathia. She didn't act like either King Frederick or Princess Cornflower. She was a puzzle, that one.

At first, the Council argued briefly about something called an Archimage, but that got shut down quickly. Seemed to be a frequent argument. Next, my mother gave a summary of her recent trip to the Ranguvariian Camp, and I hung on every word. Mathiian, too, who was here with his mother and his Uncle James, looked enraptured. I hoped I could go if there was ever a next time, and I was starting to feel like my mother was a pretty cool person.

"So, the Aatarilecs said no? Why am I not surprised?" Queen Sabine muttered annoyedly, running her tan hand through her emerald tresses.

"They didn't necessarily say no," my mother clarified. "Chieftess Jaana just said that humans are unworthy of their help, and we have to prove we deserve it."

"Which is basically a no," King Xavier chimed in ferociously. "How would we even prove that to a bunch of magical imps? We don't even know where they live."

My mother crossed her arms defensively. "I don't know, but I'm not willing to give up on that yet!"

King Frederick rushed to speak before King Xavier could continue the argument, "Lina, how about you work on that and get back to us when you have an idea. We need all the help we can get."

"Yeah, especially since we have no idea whether your daughter will be able to pull off the death spell! How we're going to get her magic awakened is the real topic we should be discussing!" Queen Sabine shouted over the murmuring in the audience. "If she can't do it, everything we've worked for – and all our lives – are lost!"

I was seated in the stands directly behind my parents. With the strange overhead lighting in the Council chamber, Queen Sabine likely couldn't see that I was here. That didn't stop both my parents from defensively taking a step backward. Ky took my hand. Aron was on my other side sitting with his mother, and he leaned closer to me as well.

A roar came up from my mother's petite body, "Allyen Rayna is present at our meeting today, and I have absolutely *no* doubt in my mind that she will do what needs to be done! I personally witnessed my magic enter her body at her birth, and with the dangerous world we live in, it's only a matter of time before her magic awakens. We need to be ready at any moment."

Queen Sabine suddenly looked guilty. King Xavier appeared intrigued, while his wife, Queen Mira, wore an expression of shock. King Frederick looked like he was holding back tears, and Princess Cornflower, his sister, placed a hand on his shoulder. The audience had gone silent. I abruptly realized that Willian was sitting in the stands on the opposite side as me, and he gave a smirk and a wave.

Aunt Rachel's brother, James, suddenly cleared his throat, having been silent all this time. "I just have one announcement before we adjourn. The Ranguvariians have been studying Rhydin and his Einanhi look-alikes at all the castles for the last year, and we are getting close to being able to determine when Rhydin himself is in a particular castle or it is one of his decoys. My grandfather is curious whether the Council has decided upon a primary target for when we can know for sure it is a decoy at that location and not the real deal."

The sovereigns of Mineraltir, Auklia, and Lunaka all looked at each other for a few moments. It seemed to me that they had spoken about this before. King Frederick answered, his voice weary, "Lunaka Castle. It is the closest, and if we can shut down Rhydin's access to Soläna's coal mines, we can hinder his armies."

Both my parents took a breath. They'd grown up in Soläna, I remembered. So did Erikin. I couldn't help but wonder what it used to be like.

James accepted that answer. Abruptly, the meeting was over, and the Royals began to disappear. My mother's face was sorrowful when she turned around and met my eyes. I tried to shake it off in front of her, but I knew I needed to get away before I couldn't hide the mounting pressure I was beginning to feel. I gave a quick response that I wanted to go see my friends now – if only they knew that was really just Erikin at this point, maybe Dominick tops – and bounded out of the Council chamber before they could object.

I walked briskly in the direction of the stone apartments. Thankfully, they were so tall within the Dome wall that they were easy to see even over the hubbub of a city I didn't know yet. The gears of my mind kept cycling Queen Sabine's words over and over. *"If she can't do it, everything will be lost."*

No pressure.

"Rayna?"

I skidded to a halt and looked around. Who knew my name in the Dome already? It took me a minute to glance behind me and see Dominick's father, King Frederick of Lunaka. My face flushed with heat. I must have walked right past him. I didn't bump into him, did I?

"Uh," I stammered, grasping at what I should say. Something random I remembered from a school book popped into my head. "Your Majesty, what is it?"

King Frederick gave a weary smile. His pale face was full of worry lines, and his crown looked like wheat. He hesitated before saying, "Are you heading to the apartments? I am headed there to see my children. Would you like to walk with me?"

"Sure," I answered through gritted teeth, even though every bone in my body was threatening to melt from anxiety.

The king caught up with me, and we commenced walking together. He asked me a few questions about Caark and how I was settling into the Dome. I replied with the polite, not-completely-true answers. My nerves were about to strangle me by talking with a Royal. My mind was dwelling on this when I realized that King Frederick was asking me another question about the meeting we had just left. "Do you have any questions about anything we discussed today?"

I thought about it for a moment. "Yes, actually. You all were fighting about something called an Archimage at the very beginning. What's that?"

"Before Rhydin became emperor, there used to always be someone called the Archimage who helped the Three Kings get along. He, or she, was like a mediator," King Frederick answered, his blond brow knit tight. "The Archimage was never an emperor. They didn't rule over anything. They just served as a sort of supervisor. The Three Kingdoms took turns supplying an Archimage from the pool of Royals that weren't slated to inherit."

"Oh," I exhaled as I walked, "that sounds like a great system."

"It worked when the Royals listened to the Archimage." King Frederick briefly made a face. "And when the Archimage was a good person and wasn't power hungry."

"Hm. Fair enough," I replied shrugging. "I can hardly imagine what the old Nerahdis must have been like."

"It wasn't perfect," King Frederick said, meeting my gaze with his warm, blue ones, "but it was better than this by far."

We walked in silence for a few moments. People in the roads, doorways, and windows all around us would suddenly bow when they saw King Frederick walk by. It was amazing and embarrassing all at the same time. My parents may have held important positions, but I couldn't imagine being the child of a king, even if King Frederick seemed like a really nice man. I found myself wondering what had happened to his wife. His little sister, Princess Cornflower, was the one consoling him during the meeting today, my parents had said.

We were just reaching the edge of the city, only a few more minutes from the apartment stairs in the Dome wall when I asked out of nowhere, "What happened to Dominick's mother?"

King Frederick slowed to a standstill. He didn't look like he was fighting tears this time, but he swallowed hard once or twice. He looked at me oddly and spoke like he couldn't breathe, "She died. In childbirth. Giving birth to...my daughter."

I quirked my eyebrow. "Is she here? I only saw Nathia up there, but she said she's adopted."

King Frederick gave something that was like a laugh or a grunt, or both. "My daughter is gone. I adopted Nathia when she was six and first arrived at the Dome with no parents. I guess maybe I thought it would help."

Well, that got real personal real fast. I backtracked rapidly, "Thank you for walking with me. I'm going to go upstairs and see if my friends are there. I'll tell Dominick and Nathia you're here."

Before he could respond, I bounded past the Ranguvariian guards and all the way up the stairs to the very top floor, the training area. To my great surprise, Taisyn was the only one there. He was huddled in the far corner, working over something.

Part of me wanted to just leave after how rude Taisyn had been to me about not having magic the day I'd met him. But King Frederick was likely still downstairs and I wasn't ready to see him again. So, I started walking toward him, not thinking about what I was doing.

As I got close, Taisyn suddenly shouted in a frightened voice, "Who's there?"

"Oh, uh," I stuttered, "it's Rayna. Sorry, I didn't mean to sneak up on you."

"Hmph," Taisyn grumbled, turning back to his corner, "sure."

I rolled my eyes. This kid definitely wasn't going to be a friend. But I kept walking toward him anyway, being noisy about my footsteps so he couldn't claim I was sneaking up on him. "We could be friends, you know," I called as I walked funny, my feet crisscrossing. "Sounds like we're pretty similar if you can't use your magic either."

"I have magic. You don't. That is not the same," Taisyn argued without turning around. "Plus, it doesn't seem to me that you were blinded as a baby by Rhydin's Followers."

I halted mid-step. That sounded absolutely awful. Guilt ate away my confident attitude. "I'm sorry."

"If you wanna be friends, don't be. I get enough 'sorry' from my parents and my sister and everybody else around here," Taisyn growled, hatred seething from him. "They have me up here for lessons every day so that I'm 'the same,' but they won't let me cast fire because they're afraid I'll 'hurt myself.'"

"Okay." I shrugged. "I won't be sorry for you. You're fully capable of everything I can do, if not more, fire boy."

Taisyn abruptly stopped everything he was doing. He turned a little bit, the light glinting off his unseeing eyes. "Thanks."

"You're welcome," I said as I finally reached him. He shoved whatever he was working on into his pockets. I crossed my arms, feeling rebellious. "Try casting fire."

"What?" Taisyn asked, his freckled face confused.

"Just try it!" I encouraged. "You can't burn yourself if you don't aim at yourself. I want to see it, I'm the only one here."

Taisyn seemed to think about it for a grand total of five seconds. Then, he threw himself into his usual routine that he did with Lyla. This time flames licked at his fingers and fired from his fists. It was beautiful, in an odd way. However, I realized a fraction of a second too late that while Taisyn had the movements of this spell memorized, I did not and was standing a mite too close.

I lifted my hands to block the brightness of the flames, and before I knew it, my palms and fingers felt like they were riddled with thousands of needles.

CHAPTER TEN

―――――⟨∘⟩―――――

LINA

E vening was approaching. Once upon a time, I used to look up from my fields and see the sun lazily sinking toward the horizon, its golden eye hued crimson. Nowadays, I didn't have any of the usual celestial orbs to tell time, and I'd learned long ago to read the time by reading people.

Were the people of the Dome near their ramshackle dwellings? Or, were they congregated in the center of the Dome's beating heart? Were the smells of game meat and potatoes wafting from the open windows or tent flaps? Or, were the scents of working leather and blacksmithing assaulting our noses? If the people were in their homes with the smell of food, it was evening time.

I tried to hurry up. I was huddled on the complete opposite side of the Dome as the apartments, well away from the edge of the city and the glow of the Ranguvariian feather cluster. I dug with a rusty trowel, one that I'd picked up on a raid years ago thinking maybe I'd use it for a garden somewhere, which never happened. My hole was two feet deep before I finally unearthed a swatch of leather. I cradled it in my hands and shoved my trowel in my belt as I stood, content to leave my hole as it was since nobody would ever be over here. As I turned to walk home, I unwrapped the leather blanket to reveal the third piece of the Allyen locket.

This piece was identical to mine with its silver face and swirling lines, although there were no gems of amber. When there were only two halves, I had possessed the entire exterior of the locket while Evan used the interior piece, a small disc decorated with the same design that could slip inside my piece if we needed to combine our powers.

For hundreds of years, the locket had only been one piece before it was split in two by Grandma Saarah, but it was broken into thirds thanks to Robert, my father. My half was halved again by separating the front and back faces of the locket. This piece had lain undisturbed for eleven years in the dirt. I wrapped it back up and shoved it deep and tight into my pocket. I would have it handy now for when Rayna's magic awakened, whenever that may be.

I was lost in my thoughts as I walked, barely seeing those around me as I worried over when my daughter's magic would come. It was true, I had seen the magic transfer to her the day she was born. I *knew* the magic was within her after everything we fought for all those years ago. Clariion Arii had transformed Frederick and Cassandra's newborn daughter into the new Allyen because Archimage Dathian had foreseen there would be no Allyens born to either Evan or I. Arii had even altered her genes to change her appearance to match Sam and I, so no one would ever question that she was our daughter or the strength of the Allyen line. Yet, every time I saw Frederick, I had to live with always wondering if he thought I stole her from him. He hadn't even been there when the choice was made. I tried to force the notion from my mind for the millionth time.

Just as I was turning down the little artery that would take me home, my body halted all of a sudden. In front of me was a dirty-blond-haired boy with hazel eyes that reminded me so much of my sister I felt ill. He froze when he saw me too, and I grasped for something to say.

"Erikin," I said hesitantly. "I'm surprised to see you here. Aren't you supposed to be in the apartments with Rachel?"

"Oh, she gave up on waiting for someone to claim me," Erikin answered sheepishly. "She didn't have time to watch me anymore."

I groaned inwardly. Rachel had wanted to keep him until his parents claimed him. Of course, the last time I saw his mother – my sister – was when I rescued Sam from Rhydin's prison tower in the Great Desert. The last time I'd seen his father? Shortly before he revealed himself to be one of Rhydin's Followers and kidnapped my sister, dropping a limp Einanhi in her place to make me think she was dead.

Erikin's parents weren't here, I knew that for sure. That made me the only family he did have in the Dome. I'd refused initially. His presence had ruined the reunion with my children for me. But could I really be this cruel?

Giving a big sigh, I replied, "If you need somewhere to go, you can come with me."

Erikin looked surprised. Truly touched, even. "Th-Thank you, Madam Allyen."

"Don't call me that," I grunted as I began walking again.

Erikin quickly joined me. "What should I call you then?"

The name "Aunt Lina" popped into my mind, but I shook my head hard. Definitely wasn't ready for that. "I'll think about it," I conceded.

Erikin remained quiet for our walk, taking on and off a peculiar black ring, but it was probably a good thing he was silent. Anger was bubbling in my veins. How could my sister not tell me she had a child? Rachel said he was fourteen, which was Ky's age. That meant she would have had him already the last time I saw her. How could she not tell me?

"So, Erikin," I said as we reached my tent, "where did you grow up?"

"Soläna," my newfound nephew responded like it was the simplest thing in the world. "My parents work there."

"That's where your mother and I grew up," I replied thoughtfully. "What do they do there?"

"They work at the library and the school," Erikin answered easily, seeming to be sincere.

Well, if that didn't sound like the two little bookworms that used to read in my kitchen all the time, I didn't know what did.

We entered the tent to find Rayna and Ky hunched over the washbasin against the far wall. I thought this was odd, so I asked, "What're you two doing?"

"Nothing!" Rayna responded far too quickly, still turned away from me even as Ky spun towards us with fearful eyes.

Every fiber in my being wanted to ask. But for right or wrong, I let it go. We'd been a family for not even twenty-four hours yet, and Rayna was struggling to warm up to me. No need to be an apprehensive mama right now, no matter how badly I wanted to know.

However, in spite of myself, I mentally swept the room for any new magical presences. The only ping that came back was Ky's Rounan powers, and I tried to not feel too disappointed that Rayna still had no magic to sense.

"So, uh," I said awkwardly, trying hard to brush it off, "Erikin, how did you spend your days in the rebel pocket?"

"Oh, I hadn't been there long. Only a few hours before your kids showed up," Erikin replied nonchalantly as he meandered around the living area of the tent. He, too, seemed a mite distracted by whatever Ky and Rayna were doing at the washbasin.

Abruptly, Rayna turned around. I gave a sigh of relief when I saw that she looked unharmed, although her hands were tucked deep into her cloak sleeves. She tilted her head to the side and narrowed her eyes as she asked, "I thought you said back at the pocket that you'd been there with Rudy for a week?"

"Oh, uh, yeah, you're right," Erikin stammered rapidly, his eyes darting between Rayna's and mine, "I-I meant that Rudy and I had gone out for the day and had only returned a few hours before you all arrived. That's all. We'd been *living* in the pocket for a week."

"Oh," Rayna said slowly, her golden, Allyen eyes rolling upward as she thought it out. "Do you think Rudy is okay? I didn't see him during the attack."

Erikin's shoulders slumped. He stared at the floor. "I don't know."

"Hmph," I uttered unintentionally. Erikin's story was becoming muddled, and that wasn't a good sign. The last thing I needed was someone to babysit, but Rachel couldn't handle everything. At least if he was here, he could maybe tell me more about Rosetta.

I walked over to the washbasin to cleanse my hands, discreetly eyeing Rayna's cloak pockets where her hidden hands now resided, and said, "Ky, help me get supper on the fire. Your father should be back soon. Erikin, if you don't mind, I'd love to hear more about my sister."

Sam ended up not returning in time for supper, which was reheated squirrel stew from the night before. Therefore, it was just me at a table of more teenagers than I ever expected. Erikin became more closed off to my questions after the confusion concerning his time at the rebel pocket, but I was able to glean that he had been born in the Great Desert and the family moved to Soläna shortly after Rhydin became emperor. This meant that they had been in my hometown the entire time we were traveling across Lunaka to take our toddlers to Caark. We even passed through Stellan, a mere twenty miles from Soläna, where Sam's sister died of the Epidemic and I saved Nathia as a child, such a powerful little Rounan even back then.

Rayna somehow managed to eat her dinner with only the tips of her fingers showing beyond her cloak sleeves, which looked fine. I halfway expected them to be dyed blue with how she was acting. I had hoped we would get to talk more this evening, but no sooner than her plate was cleared, she vanished into Sam and I's bedroom which we had shared last night. Ky dutifully cleared the table, and then he helped Erikin find some sleeping materials. I waited briefly for Sam to return after the kids had all gone to sleep, but my eyes were too heavy to wait for long. I settled to sleep in my bed, fighting the temptation to look at Rayna's hands in her sleep.

"Lina!" Sam's voice called an unknown number of hours later.

The curtain to the bedroom was whisked away, but there wasn't near enough light for it to be morning yet. I groaned, my mind foggy, "Wh-What?"

"Our crew was called out on another mission while we were gone, and they've gotten themselves into a tight spot," Sam spoke so fast I could hardly make sense of what he was saying. "We need to go right now, or they're all going to die!"

That shook the fog off like a bolt of lightning. I jumped out of bed and worked to put my trousers and boots on over my tunic. "Okay, let's go."

"Papa?" a small voice called sleepily from the other side of the bed. It both excited and killed me that she had finally taken to calling Sam a term of endearment, but she had not done so with me yet. Rayna was soon rolling over and trying to dress as well. "I want to go with you."

"No," Sam said firmly as he handed me my sword and my other various blades that I started shoving in every nook and cranny of my clothes. "It's too dangerous. Maybe another mission sometime. This one has already gone far south."

Sam whirled around and I followed him through the curtain and toward the entrance of the tent. Ky and Erikin were suddenly on our heels in addition to Rayna, and Sam did a double-take at the sight of the blond boy. His voice deepened and darkened into something I very rarely heard as he warned, "You all are staying here. End of story. We'll be back in a few hours."

We escaped into the cool, dim cavern, the rest of the Dome city slumbering in eerie silence. I looked over my shoulder a few times to make sure the children had all stayed, and no one followed. It was only minutes before James and Jaspen met us on the pathway and flew us to the exit tunnel, hastening our journey.

Lunaka was unnervingly still outside the Dome, but the two Ranguvariians were already transporting us to where our crew was evidently stranded. When the white transportation magic faded, we were dumped directly into the fray. I barely had time to raise my blade when I saw a familiar white head of long hair a short distance away.

June, my second and my favorite neighbor, shouted over the clangs of swords and blasts of magic, "I'm sorry, Lina! We thought we had it under control!"

"Save it for later!" I yelled, too busy blocking the blows of at least three Einanhis that were trying to pin me down.

"Lina, be careful!" Sam screamed over the chaos as he parried and thrust his blade into an Einanhi, reducing it to sand. "Their blades are poisoned!"

"What?" I called as I kicked one Einanhi to the ground and shut down another. "How in Nerahdis do you know that?"

"I can smell it!" Sam bellowed before he was too far away to hear.

I tried to sniff whatever it was he claimed he could smell, but there was just too much going on for that. How had this mission gone so badly for this large of a battle to happen?

"June!" I shrieked as I ducked under an Einanhi's arm to get closer to her. "What happened here?"

June grunted, her glistening white hair caught in the breeze as she decapitated yet another Einanhi. They were swarming now. "We got word of information on the Rhydin decoys in the castles and tried to follow it! We just never expected *him* to show up!"

Him? As my sword transformed another Einanhi into meaningless silt, I whirled around, scanning the battle. We were surrounded by sand on the edge of a body of water to the south. Must be the Great Desert, or perhaps a sandier portion of Auklia. Our crew was made up of a half dozen people including Sam and I. There were easily triple as many Einanhis, Rhydin's soulless creations.

I was beginning to wonder when I'd actually seen a human on his side last, but every train of thought came to a standstill when I saw the figure standing halfway up the nearest sand dune. He had thrown his billowing, midnight cloak to the ground, the one that still inhabited my nightmares, as he dueled Calvin, another of our people. It only seemed like seconds before our man was laid out on the ground.

Rhydin's pale lips curled into a cruel grin as he said, "You have finally arrived, I see! Just in time to see your precious rebels destroyed."

He stalked toward another of our people, Brade, and I kicked myself into action to help. I blasted Einanhis away from me left and right with magic, the warmth making my fingertips feel like they were humming, and lifted my sword high above my head as I rushed in between Rhydin and Brade. Brade skedaddled right out of there and started working his way toward Sam while Rhydin's amethyst gaze bored into me.

"You rats seem to think that you can just *steal* any information you like from me!" Rhydin raged. He flipped his blade and broke it lengthwise into two, so now he had one in each hand. "Well, *no longer!*"

He thrust rapidly with his twin, midnight swords, but he wasn't aiming very well. I blocked with one move and shoved his blades into the air to get his arms up, firing a blast of magic toward his chest. He raised one of his hands and whirled my bolt of light to the side.

I goaded him, "What's wrong, Rhydin? Off your game today?"

The dark emperor growled, and our duel continued wordlessly. As we fought, I tried to remember the last time I had seen Rhydin this close. It had been nearly six months since I'd last seen him from afar, but I hadn't dueled him like this in a decade. Not since the day he murdered Luke, my anger reminded me.

Rhydin had always been so cool and calculated in the past, and even when he had grown angry, he never sacrificed his precision. He was still an excellent swordsman and sorcerer. It still took every ounce of physical and mental energy to keep up. But with every slightly off-balance lunge and every unstable violet charge that crackled loudly and exploded larger than ever, I knew more and more that something was different about my nemesis who was supposedly frozen in time.

"What's wrong with your magic, Rhydin? Looks a little unstable," I mocked him again, craving vengeance for Luke. "You *are* what? Three-hundred-ish years old? Feel free to stand down anytime!"

To that, Rhydin did a backflip off the rebound of his last magical charge and landed several feet away from me. There, he threw his swords down and opened his hands at his sides. Gigantic violet orbs appeared in each hand, popping like lightning searching for its next target, a showcase of his massive power. The sly smile vanished from his face.

This was not the Rhydin I battled last eleven years ago. Twisted anger had replaced poised cunning, and the new instability of his magic appeared to have only doubled his power.

We needed to get out of here *now*. This was not a battle we could win.

I yelled at the top of my lungs over my shoulder, "James! Jaspen! Get everybody out now!"

As the two Ranguvariians moved to follow my orders, Rhydin crowed, "You have plagued me for too long, Allyen! I *will* make Nerahdis a better place than Caden ever dreamed it could be! Only then will Amelia see!"

His blades flew into his hands, attracted to his lightning like magnets, and he stalked toward me. I backed away from him for a few paces, trying to get closer to my friends before

I had no choice but to engage him. My chest heaved for air as I tried to keep up with him, blow for blow, shot for shot. Soon, it was taking all my strength to even hold my sword up to block whatever Rhydin threw my way. He seemed to gain in energy as mine faded away.

In the distance, I could see James and Jaspen struggling to fly our team out of here, their magic too eroded from Rhydin's presence to transport. June and Sam were gone. Calvin and now Brade, too, were dead. I couldn't see our sixth person from where I stood, so I could only hope that she had gotten out.

Before I knew it, I was knocked to the ground, my sword flying from my grasp. My leg became wet because I had fallen into the water. I rolled farther into the water just before one of Rhydin's blades gouged the gravelly sand beside me. He splashed forward until he planted a foot on either side of me, and he reared back for another blow. His grin was maniacal at this point. "Your death is only the beginning! Your brother and daughter are next! So ends the Allyens and their doomed rebellion! My reign will be eternal!"

"Never!" I screamed.

Rhydin swung his other blade downward as I clapped my hands together, creating a golden orb the size of a small pumpkin over my chest. His sword hit my defense spell squarely, and with a buzz of crackling magic, his blade rebounded back at him and cut into his shoulder. His black sleeve was immediately stripped from his pale arm, but an empty crack loomed in the place where blood should have been spilling forth. It was just like when Sam wounded Rhydin's cheek in the Archimage Palace when he tried to save Dathian. Where was Rhydin's blood? Why did he crack like stone?

I had no more time to think. Rhydin rapidly grabbed his other sword, ready to end me, at which point I was suddenly dragged underneath the water's surface. Bubbles released from my mouth as I screamed once. I couldn't see in the dark, murky water, but something had caught tight hold of my foot. Panickily, I tried to kick whatever it was with my other foot as my lungs began to burn. My sword was gone. I flung magic in every which direction, trying to see or hit what was dragging me.

After everything I'd been through, I couldn't die like this!

Green light blinded me for a second before my head was abruptly pushed above water. I gulped as deep a breath as I could manage before lapsing into a coughing fit, liquid pouring out of my mouth.

"So dramatic," a high-pitched voice said that I recognized but couldn't quite place. "You're welcome!"

I wiped the water out of my eyes to see Chelsea – or Onna, as I now knew – in her Aatarilec form lounging against the wall of a fountain...*the* fountain that we'd built in the Dome on top of a spring!

I instantly looked straight up to see the familiar, blue-green Ranguvariian feather cluster that gave us light and safety, and I laughed crazily, "I can't believe it! I thought I was going to die, and here I am back in the Dome!"

"Exactly. You're welcome," Chelsea snipped, although there was a smile on her impish face now.

"Thank you, Chelsea. I mean it," I chuckled. The city around us was still quiet. Morning hadn't quite arrived yet. I slowly lifted myself from the floor of the fountain, my hair and clothes sopping wet. I was going to have to explain to the blacksmith how I'd lost my sword yet again, I thought as I reached to make sure my third of the locket was still safe around my neck and Rayna's was still buried in my pocket. I watched Chelsea regain her human disguise, growing a foot taller and her mint-green hair flashing gold again, thinking. I said carefully, "I met your mother."

Chelsea froze, her now blue eyes meeting mine slowly. She sighed, "I'm sorry I never told you. I always meant to when you came back for your kids, but-..."

"I know," I cut her off. "It's okay. I'm just hoping you can help us prove to Chieftess Jaana that we're worthy of her help."

Chelsea scoffed and answered grimly, "She banished her only child and heir for making friends with a human to try to fix the overfishing problem. And killed that human, for that matter, because he wasn't 'worthy.' I don't know what she means by it."

"Hmph," I groaned. I'd been hoping that Chelsea would have the answer. I looked around again, the city still quiet. "Where are the others? Sam and my team?"

"They are in the apartments being healed. Those of them that made it anyway," Chelsea replied quietly as she turned in that direction. "Let's go."

Chelsea and I took off down the empty pathways. Chelsea was already dry due to some sort of Aatarilec magic, but I felt like I weighed five pounds heavier with all my soaked layers. As we got closer, I could see that all the open windows of the apartment wall were a flurry of activity, which was odd at this time of morning.

Please, let Sam be okay, I thought to myself over and over.

There was no Ranguvariian guard at the entrance this time, and I knew that wasn't a good sign. We bounded up the stairway toward the room next to Rachel and Jaspen's, which was larger and where all the healing magic took place. The room was a big hub-bub of activity, most of my team were spread out on stretchers minus the ones I had seen fall in battle, but the movement in the room stalled when Chelsea and I entered.

"*Lina!*" I heard Rachel before I saw her whip out from behind a curtain at the back of the room. "We've been looking *everywhere* for you! We were starting to think Rhydin captured you. Do you know how *bad* that would have been?!"

At Rachel's outburst, Sam stood up from a chair in the corner of the room, and he swept to me instantly. My heart melted in relief that he was okay.

"I know, I know," I said in a high voice, holding up my hands in defense as Sam wrapped his arms around my shoulders. "Chelsea got me out of there. I'm fine, not a scratch."

Rachel eyed Chelsea for a minute before uttering a rare "well done" and rushing back behind her curtain where I could only assume was one of my crew in bad shape.

"Who's back there?" I whispered to Sam as I looked him up and down, searching for any wounds.

"June," Sam responded wearily. He looked like he had been awake all night. "Rachel isn't sure she'll make it. She has several deep wounds from the poisoned blades."

"What? Ranguvariian healing magic can't fix that?" I asked, astounded.

Sam shook his head sadly, his eyes on the floor. His voice was a little hoarse when he added, "They've tried everything."

My heart sank. June had been my second all these years, the one who was my twin on the battlefield just as Calvin was Sam's. Not to mention the hundreds of mornings we had spent together as neighbors.

I was just about to rush back to her side when I noticed a figure hovering in the doorway to the healing bay. He edged a little closer to the light where I realized it was Frederick, and upon seeing him, I remembered I had something very important to tell. I motioned him toward me, "We need to talk."

"About what? What's going on here?" Frederick asked sleepily, bags under his eyes. Chelsea took that moment to disappear.

I abruptly remembered that Frederick's apartment was directly above the healing room, but I couldn't help that now. "Our team was off scouting something when Rhydin and a ton of Einanhis arrived. We tried to go help, but it was no use. This was the first time I've actually spoken to Rhydin in *years*, and I'm telling you, something is off with him."

"What do you mean?" Frederick asked, seeming to wake up a bit more. Sam, too, peered at me curiously.

"He seems...unhinged," I replied slowly, feeling out the right word. "He was angry and off-balanced and said things I don't understand. Talking about someone named Amelia? He always used to be so poised, and even if he got angry, he was always very calculated. And his magic...it's like lightning! Unstable and unpredictable, yet way more ridiculously powerful than I ever remember! Plus, he was wounded, and I saw his lack of blood again."

The king of Lunaka reached up to stroke his beard-less face. Sam was deep in thought, staring at a wall. I had no idea.

Frederick was still gazing at his toes when he responded, "I'm not sure what any of that means. I'll update the Council, but actually Lina, this could be a really good thing."

"*Why?*" I asked, appalled. "His magic is twice, if not triple, the power it used to be!"

"Because we've been trying for months to figure out when it's the real Rhydin at any of the castles and when he just has an Einanhi decoy stationed there," Frederick explained, his excitement growing, "The decoys have always been as cool and cunning as Rhydin used to be. If he's starting to act different and his magic is starting to look different, this could help us pin down when there's only a decoy at Lunaka Castle!"

"And he's slipping," Sam added, my favorite lopsided grin appearing on his face. "We've noticed for a few months that his Einanhis haven't been as human-looking, like they're losing quality. If he's slipping *that* badly, whether mentally or magically, even if he's more powerful an opportunity to dethrone him might be coming up quick."

Hope flooded my system. Could it really be that close? Anxiety immediately squashed it. Rayna didn't have her magic yet. What if the opportunity arose, and we didn't have a third Allyen to make the full might of the death spell possible? I voiced only one question, "What about the fact he cracks like stone and doesn't bleed? It's just *wrong* on so many levels."

"We don't know what he did to gain immortality." Frederick shrugged like it was nothing. "I don't know what the answer to that is."

After a couple beats of silence, Sam gave me a quick peck on the cheek and said, "I'm going home. Kids will be up soon."

I nodded slowly, feeling lost. I expected Frederick to turn and leave too, even just to attempt to get a little more sleep, but instead he said quietly, "I talked to Rayna yesterday. She seems like a really neat kid."

Tears threatened to choke me. "She is, Frederick. I can't take much credit for that though. We've been gone for eleven years."

"I'm sure she understands," Frederick replied, looking out over the room and not at me. "Dominick and Nathia were also sequestered for a while, just like the other Royal children. They know we just wanted to keep them safe."

"I know," I groaned.

"She even looks like she's your daughter," Frederick chuckled sadly. "She favors Sam, but I see a lot of you in her, too."

I couldn't take it anymore. "I'm *sorry*, Frederick. If there was any other way to continue the Allyen lineage all those years ago, I swear, we would have done it!"

Frederick sighed and placed a hand on his forehead wearily. "I know. I may not like it, but I understand."

With that, he turned and disappeared into the hallway. I rubbed my face with my hands, wishing for the billionth time that none of this had ever happened. Then, I shored myself up and walked to the back of the room where June lay on a cot dying of her deep wounds and the deadly poison seeded deep within them. I didn't leave her until she was gone.

Sam walked briskly from the apartments to the inner city where his and Lina's tent resided, but he had to stop a few times to catch his breath. It was getting worse, he thought to himself as he halted a moment to get air into his burning lungs. It had started with just pain and tiredness, but now he was having trouble breathing with too much activity. The Ranguvariians had never been able to give him a timeline. All he knew was that it was inevitable.

He paused again before entering the tent to make sure no one noticed his gasping, but all the teenagers were still asleep when he came inside. Ky slept soundly while Erikin snored on the dirt floor around their simple kitchen table, and the curtains were still dark where Rayna slumbered in the bedroom.

Relief flooded Sam that his children hadn't awoke to an empty tent and become afraid, but he also found himself jittery. He hoped they would wake soon, so he could spend as much time with them as possible.

Sam wandered into the other wing of their tent that had never been used. He drew the curtains closed behind him and pulled his tunic up out of his belt. The nastiest scratch Sam had ever seen stretched across his ribs. It had long since scabbed over and even become a white scar after the insane amount of healing he had received from the Ranguvariians. Yet, purple fingers of poison were reaching forth from the scar like deadly roots into the soil of his flesh.

This was the true reason he and Lina had been allowed to visit the Ranguvariian Camp, where the most powerful Ranguvariian healers resided. Lina hadn't actually been needed at that meeting.

This was the true reason that Rachel had caved and brought the children from Caark. Not because she had a change of heart or because Caark was now occupied by Rhydin's military – although that would have likely brought them anyway.

Sam was dying. And there was nothing anyone could do about it. Just as June lay dying in the infirmary with far more of the poison invading her veins.

That was how Sam had known that the Einanhis' blades were poisoned now. He knew from experience. Every moment of every day, Sam used his Rounan magic to slow the poison as much as he could. He wanted every minute possible with Lina and his two teenagers that he was just getting to know.

Sam sat on one of the two child-sized beds in this wing of the tent. Lina had tried so hard to make this room into something Ky and Rayna would like when they always thought they would return to them as young children. Certainly not teenagers. And certainly not just in time for his fourteen-year-old son to inherit his position as Kidek, leader of the Rounans, at such a young age. Sam had been roughly that age when he became Kidek and hated it. He had vowed that he wouldn't let that happen to Ky, but he couldn't uphold that promise.

Lina was going to be crushed. That's why he hadn't told her. He wanted her to act normal for the time he had left. He wanted the small window of time his children would get to know their father not to be plagued with sadness. Was that wrong?

He sat there for an unknown amount of time. His mind whirling with all the things he wanted to do with his family before he died, the things that needed done to help transition the Kidekship to Ky, and he wondered how he could make sure Lina would be taken care of.

He was thirty-six years old, and the list was too long for how much time he imagined he had left.

When rummaging sounds began in the living area, Sam knew he'd have to lock up these thoughts for a while. It was time to make his kids breakfast, and he would pretend that he would be able to do this every morning for years to come.

CHAPTER ELEVEN

RAYNA

B efore I knew it, it had been a week since we'd arrived in the Dome, and then two weeks. While time had always seemed to drag on Caark, the harsh, island sun limping across the humid sky above my old school, it seemed to fly here. Our days were often full, spending the mornings with the Royal children on the training floor of the apartments and spending the rest of the day with one or both of our parents. Our mother and Papa were busy people as the Allyen and the Kidek, but Ky and I soaked up every minute we got with them in the later parts of the day. I'd spend all day with Papa if I could, but he had to be the Kidek in the mornings so I grudgingly dragged myself to training with Ky every day.

Erikin had stopped coming to training. Now that I had come up with something to do during that time, and someone to talk to for that matter, he had lost all interest. I had used my sketchbook to draw every one of the movements to the death spell that would destroy Rhydin for good. Papa told me that its real name, *Alytniinaeran*, meant "death by three lights," or Allyens, in Ranguvariian. I was the third light, and I had no intention of letting anyone down.

I got to the training area early this morning, and I threw myself into my new routine. With the big room all to myself, I could spread out and not worry about any wandering eyes. I ran myself through the routine five times, trying to imagine the hum of my magic in my veins and the glow of the magical orb I pretended to wield. I flung the perspiration from my brow away, trying to complete the spell faster and faster until I was sure that I was performing it even faster than my mother and uncle.

"You're doing that *far* too fast," my new friend called from the stairway. "If you were actually chucking magic around, you'd have shot yourself by now."

I stumbled, ruining my routine. Angry, I whirled on Taisyn and yelled, "You messed me up!"

Taisyn scoffed as he approached me, "Well, you'll just mess up more when you're actually putting magic to those moves."

I groaned loudly, "With how well-protected the Dome is, my magic will never awaken at this rate."

"It'll come," Taisyn answered confidently, a far cry from what he'd been like when I met him a month ago. The copper-haired prince sat on the ground and began to tinker with something he had pulled from his pocket. "I dare you to do that spell as *slow* as you can. I bet you'll know it a lot better if you do."

"Hmph," I grunted angrily as I plopped down onto the floor next to him. I peered into his hands, trying to see what he was doing.

Taisyn scooted away from me like he could see my attempt, made a few more rapid movements to the tiny thing in his hands with his fingers glowing red with fiery warmth, and then presented the item right in my direction, which surprised me.

Upon his hand was the smallest metal sculpture I'd ever seen. It was a delicate bird as if it had been folded from paper, not heated and welded together by the fingers of a pyromage.

A blind pyromage at that. Its wings even had little indentations to denote its feathers, and he had rubbed ink into its eyes to make them stand out. My jaw dropped open at the sight of it.

"It's for you," Taisyn said sheepishly, turned away from me, "for not telling anyone that I burned you. My father *really* would never start teaching me to be a pyromage if he knew I'd burned the Allyen. Thank you. I know it must have hurt."

I felt the stinging heat along the palms of my hands again just thinking about it. They'd healed well, not much of a scar to be seen. Once the pain subsided, the hardest part was keeping the secret from everyone but Ky, who had found me failing to bandage them on my own at home. Taisyn had felt awful. He had given me some salve he had on him for when he burned himself and walked me home that day. From then on, he suddenly stopped being a jerk to me and became my friend, making the entire experience worth it.

"Thank you," I gushed, transfixed by the miniscule details. "How in Nerahdis did you make this? It's amazing!"

Taisyn chuckled uncomfortably, "This might sound odd, but my magic helps me 'see' in a way. When I use magic, it fills the room with a red glow and helps me see where people are or what objects are near me. Like outlines. I still can't see colors or what people look like, though."

I stared at him wistfully. Everything I loved about the world was visual. The sunrise on the ocean or the waves beating the shores of Caark. The things I tried to replicate in my sketchbook. What would life be like if those things were taken away? Or worse, I couldn't fathom those things because I'd never seen them and never would?

I took a deep breath and let it out slowly. "I'm a few inches over five feet tall. My hair is a light brown color with a few red streaks in it, like my Papa's, and I usually wear it in a braid. I have my mother's golden Allyen eyes. People would probably consider me tan because I grew up on an island, but the longer I'm down here that'll probably change. We're sitting in a giant room bigger than any building on Caark, and the whole south wall is open to the rest of the Dome. It looks like it's been carved out by a giant mole or something. There are torches along the other three walls, which gives it an odd light when it clashes with the blue-green light from outside."

Taisyn turned his head toward me slightly, his eyes remaining still and thoughtful. "Thank you, Rayna. No one has bothered to describe themselves or this room to me before. You are good at it."

"Well," I shrugged, "someday you'll be a king. Then you could make people do it if you wanted to."

The Mineraltin prince grimaced. "I don't want to be king."

"What?" I gasped. "Why ever not? You could do anything you want!"

"Eh...maybe. I really just don't want to. I'm not a people person, if you haven't figured that out," Taisyn replied, pulling his knees up to his chest. "Lyla would do a better job. She'd be a perfect queen. Mineraltir deserves a ruler that isn't broken, whom they don't have to worry will burn somebody or himself."

"You're not broken!" I said firmly, and my hand clamped onto his before I realized what I was doing. "You will know your magic so much better once your father agrees to train you!"

"Well, well," a new voice lilted over from the stairway, "am I interrupting something?"

Both Taisyn and I jumped to our feet. Willian stood at the top of the stairs with his arms crossed arrogantly. I rolled my eyes at the sight of him. Over the last month, Willian had started sticking to me like glue every time he happened to see me, especially outside of magic training. I, on the other hand, had decided that he was an obnoxious showoff, and I was glad that he was the younger twin with no throne to inherit. His attention never seemed to be genuine interest in friendship.

"Just go to your little corner and practice whatever Queen Sabine assigned you today," I grumbled. "We're busy."

"Terribly busy," Willian mused as he looked from Taisyn to me to the little bird sculpture still in my hands. "I think you two will want to see what milady has me working on right now."

It appeared we didn't have much of a choice. Willian closed his frog-green eyes and concentrated. In front of him, down on the floor, a glowing blue orb of magic appeared. Taisyn's face went slack like he could either sense it or see it with his magic, but I felt nothing as usual. The sapphire globe grew to the size of a stool and sprung a couple of off-shoots, one with a diamond-shaped end and the other pointed. The Auklian prince opened his eyes after a few more moments and whispered, "*Anadlu.*"

The blue sphere popped like a bubble, and in its place was a coiled, blood-red snake, which raised its head and hissed. I started to back away, and when Taisyn didn't, I grabbed his arm and pulled him with me. I cried, "What is that?!"

"It's an Einanhi, duh! I just made it," Willian boasted happily. "Now I can give it whatever command I want. Snake, slither up and make a hat on Blind Boy's head!"

Taisyn's expression turned dark with hate. But the snake didn't move from its position. Instead, it began to coil taller and look around, hissing even louder. It peered at each of us before it looked at Willian again, beginning to creep toward him.

"What's happening?" Taisyn whispered to me, his fingers glowing as he stretched his hand toward Willian and the snake.

"What's it doing, Willian?" I asked fearfully, eyeing the back of the red snake's diamond-shaped head.

Willian's confidence had vanished. The seventeen-year-old suddenly looked afraid for the first time. When the snake continued to advance, he turned on his heel and began to sprint around the room, but the snake only followed with unnatural agility.

I shouted at Taisyn, "The snake is chasing him! Why is the snake chasing him?!"

"I can do this," Taisyn declared, and he abruptly took off, chasing after the snake and Willian with the help of his magic.

While I stood there useless, trying to figure out what I should do, Willian was screaming bloody murder. The snake was growing closer and closer to him, and as it did, a stream of blue particles appeared in the air over Willian's head and began siphoning over to the snake.

Fire flared from Taisyn's fists, using them to see in his own, unique way. Willian was rapidly running out of steam around the time a slew of Ranguvariian guards came scampering up the stairs and spilling out onto the floor of the training area, trying to make sense of the screaming and why two princes were dashing around the room as fast as they could.

Finally, Taisyn caught up enough to shoot a ray of fire that stopped the Einanhi snake in its tracks. The whole length of it burst into flames briefly before it dissolved into a narrow pile of sand.

Aunt Rachel had reached the top of the stairs just in time to see this happen, and she yelled darkly, "You three, right here, *now!*"

Yikes. I'd heard plenty of Aunt Rachel's tones over the years, but even the worst one didn't quite match this. We slowly worked our way toward her, Taisyn breathing hard while Willian was totally out of breath and bewildered. Something extra seemed wrong with Willian on top of having run around too much.

Aunt Rachel dismissed several of the Ranguvariian guards until only a handful remained, and then she fixed us in her icy glare. She asked firmly, "Who created the Einanhi?"

Both Taisyn and I unceremoniously pointed at Willian without a single word. As we did, all the other Royal children appeared at the stairs behind Aunt Rachel, chattering like any other day. They all froze at the sight of the scene around them, and Aunt Rachel motioned to them. "Good, you can all hear this lesson. Get over here and listen up because this is one lesson your life may depend on."

Dominick and Ky looked surprised to see me here. Nathia roundly ignored me. Chretien was staring at the state of his twin while Lyla cast a concerned gaze toward her brother. When they had all filed in behind the three of us troublemakers, Aunt Rachel went at it.

"*Most* of you know the rules," Aunt Rachel said as she eyed the older Royal children: Chretien, Willian, and Nathia. "Einanhis are *never* to be created without supervision! They are one of the hardest spells to master, and when they go wrong, they *really* go wrong. All of you are powerful mages. You wouldn't be able to create Einanhis if you weren't. But Einanhis have a direct link to their creator's magic. It's how they function. An Einanhi given too little magic lies practically dead on the ground, but an Einanhi given too much? You may as well kiss your magic and your life goodbye."

"Why?" Dominick asked curiously. "If an Einanhi is made from your own magic, how could it steal from you and kill you? Why can't you just reabsorb it like normal?"

"Because when an Einanhi is given too much magic, it's no longer under your control! Or anyone's control, for that matter," Aunt Rachel answered grimly. "When you give your magic to an Einanhi willingly, during its creation, that magic rejuvenates over time. When your magic is stolen from an Einanhi, after its creation, it's gone forever until it's destroyed. Prince Willian will get his magic back now that the snake is gone. Einanhis are made from your magic, therefore they can steal your magic away. We're learning more about this all the time. If it steals too much-…"

"We die. We get it," Nathia interrupted, her arms crossing over her chest.

"I don't think you do," Aunt Rachel said in a low, dangerous voice. "If I catch *any* of you creating an Einanhi without supervision, there will be severe consequences."

The hairs on the back of my neck prickled. I liked to test the limits, but even I knew not to mess with that voice. Aunt Rachel seemed to be done talking, so the rest of the Royal children dispersed to their usual corners. Willian appeared too shaken to move quite yet.

I was turning to Taisyn to ask him if he wanted to go somewhere else when Aunt Rachel moved to me. "Something unexpected has happened. We are about to convene the Council to discuss it. It might not hurt for you to attend. As an Allyen."

I gulped. A magic-less Allyen.

"I'll come with you," Taisyn said softly. "I've had enough exercise for today."

I had to work pretty hard to keep the smile off my face in front of Aunt Rachel, so I took a fistful of Taisyn's sleeve and dragged him off down the stairs where I could cackle in peace. We jabbered and giggled all the way to the Council chamber about how Aunt Rachel had put Nathia in her place and how Taisyn couldn't wait to tell Lyla about what had actually happened.

As we grew closer to the heart of the cacophonous, underground city, there seemed to be a flurry of activity. People were more agitated and congregated, not partaking in the usual activities that I had gotten used to by now. It was only then that I started to wonder what exactly Aunt Rachel had meant when she said something unexpected had happened.

When we entered the Council chamber and the entire audience section was absolutely packed, I really knew something was up. I whispered a description of the room to Taisyn, although he probably knew by the roar of whispers and rumors that something was up. With nowhere left to sit, I took a deep breath and decided to stand next to my mother. I was wanted here "as an Allyen," after all.

My mother smiled at me and gave a warm look to Taisyn as well. Papa was sitting at the glass table, which was odd. Normally all the leaders stood, not bothering to make use of the chairs behind them since they were all typically arguing anyway.

"Let us begin," James announced loudly, which was also abnormal. Aunt Rachel's human-looking brother *never* started any meetings. She stood behind him with her arms crossed like some sort of bodyguard.

King Xavier and Queen Mira of Mineraltir, King Frederick and Princess Cornflower of Lunaka, and Queen Sabine of Auklia all gave him their undivided attention. They, too, knew that this was strange. The smile fell from my mother's face, my father waited, and Uncle Evan touched his chin, bracing himself. The audience became silent.

"The mist has returned to the Archimage Palace," James declared, meeting each person's eyes around the table.

There was immediately a ruckus around us of murmuring. Several of the Royals glanced at each other, astounded. My mother looked like she might faint. I tapped her shoulder and whispered into her ear, "What's this mist?"

My mother swallowed awkwardly before saying, "The Archimage Palace is enchanted with a mist-looking spell connected to the life of the elected Archimage. It hangs along the ceiling of the great hall. When Dathian, the last Archimage, was alive, he could use this mist to view anything and anyone in the world without having to leave his palace. It fell to the ground like rain when he was murdered by Rhydin and left nothing."

"What can this mean?" King Frederick asked firmly, leaning forward onto the table in James's direction.

"We are still trying to figure this out," James answered calmly. "Nobody has been there in at least five years, and there was no mist the last time we were there. My grandfather,

Clariion Arii, was in need of a book on healing to help someone and traveled there to search Dathian's vast library, only to find that a new mist has appeared."

"You said before that the mist 'returned.' Now, you say a *new* mist has appeared. Which one is it?" Queen Sabine asked crabbily, but there was a glint of desperation in her crimson eyes. "My father's mist was a sky-blue color."

"It is not blue like Archimage Dathian's. My apologies," James replied hesitantly. "This mist is much smaller, and it is starting to take on a purple color. This is what leads us to believe that it is a new mist."

"Which means what?" King Xavier asked impatiently. He never was one to beat around the bush.

James took a deep breath. His confident façade was fading. "My grandfather surmises that it means that an Archimage walks Nerahdis." A collective gasp went around the room before he added, "An Archimage who is not Dathian, that is."

"How can this be?" Queen Sabine asked ferociously. Both Willian and Chretien had appeared behind her by now. The buzzing in the Dome must have finally reached the apartments.

Queen Mira piped up matter-of-factly, "That's impossible. We haven't elected a new Archimage."

"It's just a theory!" James reacted defensively, trying to break up the shouting and conjectures by both the Royals and the audience. "In order to look into this more, my grandfather is still at the Archimage Palace, and he has requested that Allyen Linaria come to aid him."

"Just Lina? He doesn't need me?" Uncle Evan asked confusedly.

"Just Lina," James affirmed. "He thinks her experiences in the Archimage Palace will be helpful."

My mother suddenly froze. I had to stare at her for several seconds to make sure she was even breathing. At long last, she bobbed her head in agreement, but it was rigid. What had happened to my mother in the Archimage Palace?

"Keep us updated as you learn more," King Frederick stated as he glanced at my mother, trying to move things along. Dominick and Nathia had materialized next to him as well. "Meanwhile, you all will be happy to know that we are getting much better results in discerning when Rhydin himself or one of his decoys is at Lunaka Castle. I think we will be ready for an assault very soon, so please start checking in with your respective peoples to get them ready. The supplies there will be an immeasurable help to our cause as we approach another winter."

The meeting churned on without much ado before coming to an abrupt end. After all, it was an emergency session, not the usual meeting. Papa was holding my mother's hand like he seemed to know what was going through her head. I turned to her and said, "I want to go with you to the Archimage Palace."

My mother snapped out of her episode and looked at me fearfully. "Rayna, I-…"

"Please," I interrupted her, "I want to understand. I don't know anything about the Archimage or Nerahdis before Rhydin became emperor. Going with you could really help me understand how they all fit together."

My mother gazed at me for a few moments, seeming to weigh more than one thought in her mind, and Papa squeezed her hand. He said slowly, "Let her go with you. I'll stay here with Ky and Erikin. She's right."

I beamed when my mother hesitantly agreed, although I realized at Papa's words that Erikin wasn't here while Ky was now on the other side of Papa. I wondered where he was, but that thought quickly vanished.

I gushed, feeling like a child, "Can Taisyn come too?"

One of my mother's eyebrows raised. "Only if Xavier and Mira say so."

Taisyn instantly bounded off to the other side of the room, his fingers glowing so that he could squeeze between departing audience members and find his parents. As I watched him go, I realized both Willian and Nathia were looking at me. The former looked sad, perhaps because I had not asked for him to go, while the latter looked absolutely livid.

I grinned at her. Somebody needed to put that bossy girl in her place, and if my going to the Archimage Palace over her did that, then I was thrilled.

Within the hour, we were all gathered around the exit tunnel outside the Dome. It had been a month since I'd last been outside, and I basked in the sunlight. I spread my arms, feeling the heat, and noticed my mother doing something similar. I was thankful we emerged during one of the few times the sun happened to strike the Dome's shadowy location.

When my eyes adjusted, I was flabbergasted to see that all the leaves had changed colors. The canopy of the forest's entrance was a melting pot of scarlets, gingers, and golds unlike anything I had ever seen, and half of the canopy lay browning at the trees' toes. Caark didn't have seasons, and I decided that I had been utterly missing out on this phenomenon called autumn.

James, Chelsea, and Conriin were coming with us, and I was shocked to learn that Aatarilecs could also use transportation magic to and from any body of water. They were off to the side waiting for us to leave, and Conriin was rapidly making several hand gestures to James since he was mute. Chelsea, his cousin on the Aatarilec side, seemed to understand exactly what he was saying, while James, his cousin on the Ranguvariian side, only shouted something about being unable to tell whether Conriin was frustrated or just really wanted a cookie.

I said a quick goodbye to Ky and Erikin. Ky didn't seem to care too much – after all, it didn't appear that we'd be gone for too long – but Erikin was acting oddly. He had become my closest friend a month ago when we had first arrived, and over the weeks, he had spent less and less time with me. Now, as we said goodbye, he looked downright sad.

When Ky walked away to join Papa, I asked him, "What's wrong? We're coming right back."

"N-Nothing," Erikin stuttered, gripping his ring tightly. "I just...I'm sorry."

"Sorry for what?" I questioned again. Now he wasn't making any sense.

Erikin hesitated, his hazel eyes dropping to the ground. "For...For not spending time with you anymore. I'm sorry. I don't know why I did it. You're the only friend I've ever had, and I did this to you."

I smiled in understanding. "Don't *worry*, Erikin! When I come back, there will be plenty of time to fix that."

Erikin didn't respond. He just continued to stare at his toes glumly before he walked back toward the tunnel into the Dome. I shrugged, not thinking much of it, and walked over to stand by my mother, waiting for what felt like another adventure. Aunt Rachel and Mathiian stood at the entrance of the tunnel, and I gave a quick wave to my Ranguvariian friend, whom I also hadn't seen in a while.

"I love you. Come back soon," Papa said wistfully as he pulled my mother in for an embrace. He held her there tightly for a minute before, to my surprise, he did the same to me. It was several moments long, like he was really trying to make it count.

"We'll be back before you know it," my mother answered cheerily, trying to remain positive. "I love you, too. I doubt we'll be away for more than a couple of days. Just meet with Arii and come home."

"I hope so," Papa replied quietly. I hadn't really pegged him as an emotional man, but perhaps I was wrong. He grudgingly backed away with Ky to re-enter the Dome, watching us until he couldn't any longer.

"Your father is acting strangely," my mother muttered to me as we joined the others.

"Yeah, he is," I agreed.

"Wait!" a voice called from the tunnel. I turned to see Taisyn, and relief flooded me. I had been beginning to think King Xavier and Queen Mira wouldn't let him come. He came running up to me, just in time. "Sorry, my mother was fretting."

With that, my mother laid claim to transporting with James while Taisyn and I were assigned to water-bound transportation with Chelsea and Conriin. Apparently, Conriin could transport by both flight and water, but he preferred the Aatarilec way. Thankfully, there was a creek nearby, but I joshed with my mother that she just didn't want to get wet. The bond between us was getting better day by day.

James and my mother disappeared in a flash of white light, and Taisyn and I trekked after Chelsea and Conriin toward the creek to follow perhaps ten minutes after. I tried to still the electricity in my nerves. Taisyn was excited too, he hadn't left the Dome since he had arrived a few years ago. I couldn't help but think that the Archimage Palace might be the ultimate adventure.

I could have never guessed what – or whom – was awaiting us there.

CHAPTER TWELVE

LINA

It had been eleven years since I'd last stepped foot in the Archimage Palace. Not since the night our Rounan Compound had been razed by Rhydin's Followers, and we needed a place to re-group before heading to Caark with our infant children. Rayna had been only a year old then, and now she stood next to me with thirteen years under her belt.

How could time pass so quickly?

James dropped me off just outside the palace, and everyone else appeared in a small, mountain spring with a flash of green minutes later. I watched Rayna's expression as she took in the giant palace that blended in with the mountains around it and then rapidly began describing it for Taisyn in the kind of words an artist used. The palace had been camouflaged to help keep the Archimage position a secret over the centuries.

I remembered the first time I had come here during the war as we walked up the slope of the mountain. Archimage Dathian had summoned me because he'd dreamt of a future where no Allyens would be born to Evan or I, setting off our quest to find a Royal newborn who could take on the magic.

Ironically, both candidates we considered stood before me now. Taisyn was born first, and my father, Robert, while he was still working for Rhydin, blinded him and tainted him with dark magic to keep us from turning him into a new Allyen. Just a few weeks later, Rayna was born. Cassandra had told no one that she was pregnant, not even Frederick, but Jaspen and the other Ranguvariians fought tooth and nail to protect her until we could transfer the magic. Arii magically changed her into my daughter and her midnight hair became the exact shade of Sam's as Cassandra lay dying. Frederick was off in Auklia with no idea any of it was occurring.

Would I ever be free of this overwhelming guilt?

"Why is it disguised as a mountain? Where are we? How many Archimages have there been? Why...?" Rayna rattled off a dozen questions, and I suddenly realized that it was a good thing she had come. Taisyn, too. The new generation was taking on our fight, and they needed to know everything.

That didn't stop me from being on pins and needles. Arii had dreamed that Rayna's magic would awaken here at the Archimage Palace. It seemed impossible at the time, yet here we were. I tried not to jump at every shadow.

As we walked across the already lowered drawbridge into the abandoned palace, I tried to answer as many of Rayna's questions as I could. "We're in the far northern reaches of Lunaka. The northern ocean is just on the other side of the palace. It's camouflaged because the Archimage position was kept a secret from everyone except the Royals. I don't know how many Archimages we've had, but there are portraits of them all in the hallway on the top floor."

Rayna positively gleamed with all the new information, and she asked a flurry of new questions that I did my best to answer. Most of them I couldn't, so I made a mental note to arrange some one-on-one time for her with Arii. She grew quiet as we passed through the busted stone door that used to be two stories high and entered the palace that once put every other Royal castle to shame. The palace had been mostly put together the last time I'd been here only a year after Dathian's death. Thirteen years' abandonment had left its mark.

Anything deemed valuable was long gone. The navy carpets were all ripped up or stained with old, brown blood from the battle where Rhydin took Dathian's life. The great marble columns that stood between the onyx floor and the ivory ceiling were coated with dust, and a few of them had huge chunks missing or scorch marks. The chandelier had crashed to the floor, and most of its gold plating and crystal beads had been torn off. The old servants must have returned, or told others where the palace was, to loot it.

My attention, however, immediately turned to the ceiling where, just as Arii and James had said, there was a new mist. While Dathian's had been plentiful, light blue, and churned in an invisible breeze, this new one was a fraction of the size, a dull lavender, and barely moved, if at all.

Rayna was chattering at the speed of light so that Taisyn could "see" everything that she did. I could listen to her descriptions for hours, and pride swelled up in my chest. I may not have been there for most of her childhood, but my daughter had grown into a good person.

Across the room sitting upon the dais was the Archimage throne, made of twisting black and white marble similar to the rest of the room. The three small stained-glass windows of the First Three Kings of Nerahdis were still intact, but the gigantic round one above them was smashed to bits. The one of Rhydin Caldwell, the First Archimage.

I shuddered at the thought.

"Hello," Arii called from the entrance of the back hallway behind the throne, "I am glad you all are here. Let's get to it, Lina, shall we?"

"Okay," I said, bobbing my head. The sooner we got this over with, the better.

"Can we go explore?" Rayna asked excitedly, stars in her eyes. "Please, please, please?"

I swallowed hard. Was this it? The moment I allowed something dangerous to happen to her? I hadn't forgotten what had happened the last time I was here. The strange, invisible presence that had warned me when Rhydin arrived with his armies to kill us right after we'd fled the Rounan Compound. There was something not right with this place, and the strange mist above our heads was only more evidence of that. The mist's magical presence was unreadable to me. However, my desperation to bond with my daughter got the best of me, and I told myself that once her magic awakened, it would protect her as it had done me. So, I found myself saying, "Only if you stay with one of the adults."

Rayna groaned, but there was no denying her eagerness. Taisyn, on the other hand, looked less enthused, and I began to wonder if my daughter was dragging him around against his will. Rayna cheered, "Thank you, Mama!"

My heart soared, my fear disappearing. It was worth it only to hear that name.

Rayna bounded off with Taisyn in tow toward Chelsea, and I turned to follow Arii past the great staircase and down a hallway I'd never noticed before. The hallway was dark, although very wide, so I imagined it used to be very grand. As Arii walked quietly before me, I asked the burgeoning question on my mind. "Why am I here, Arii? Why is there a mist when there hasn't been one for so long?"

"That is what we are here to discover," Arii answered as he cracked a double door open at the end of the hallway and ducked inside. "I believe that you already know the answer to your first question."

I entered the room with him to discover the largest library I'd ever seen in my life. Books lined every shelf of every wall to the very top of the three-story room. There was some debris by the door, but aside from that, the room was untouched by all the thieves who had filched the rest of the palace's goods. My jaw dropped. I still wasn't the greatest of readers, but my sister would have died upon seeing this place.

"Only the Archimages' magics have ever been linked to the mist in the throne room. There has not been an Archimage since Dathian, which only leads me to speculate that an ancient Archimage has returned," Arii said slowly as he sank into a velvet chair with fringe in the corner of the room.

"B-But that can't be," I stammered, still standing and taking in the room around me. "All of the Archimages are dead, aren't they?"

"Supposedly," Arii replied vaguely as he crossed his long, Ranguvariian legs. "That's what we're here to figure out."

"Well, I saw Dathian die with my own two eyes. Who was Archimage before him? Maybe he's actually still alive," I theorized.

"That would be Archimage Andromeda, formerly a Mineraltin princess and the sister of King Josip and my wife, Emily. She was only Archimage for a handful of years before dying of a stroke at age fifty-one," Arii rattled off like he was a textbook, almost appearing bored.

"Arii," I said, trying to keep my voice in check, "it seems to me that you already know the answer since you keep dismissing my questions. How about you let me in on what it is?"

Arii eyed me, his eyes gleaming emerald. "My apologies. I have but a theory, Lina dear, not the answer. You told me once that you could sense a strange presence within these walls. One that you could interact with to some degree, that could guide you to only history book left in the world that contained Rhydin's former identity, and that it perhaps even saved your life."

I shifted uncomfortably, finally finding myself a chair. "You're not wrong."

"Can you sense it now?" the old, Ranguvariian leader asked.

Hesitantly, I closed my eyes and focused on my warm magic within me, sending out invisible feelers throughout the palace. I couldn't sense any of my companions because we were all either Ranguvariian or wearing Ranguvariian feathers, and I wouldn't have been able to sense Rayna anyway. As I peeled back layer after layer of the palace, I realized I could sense something extra. I shivered at the feeling, but I knew without a doubt that this was the same strange presence I had first felt long ago.

"It's here," I breathed as I opened my eyes again. "It's...stronger, I think. In the past, I could only sense it if I was alone, without any distractions, and even then, it was barely a whisper."

"It spoke to you?" Arii asked nervously.

"N-No." I shook my head. "That's just what its presence felt like back then. It was so weak, barely there. Like a whisper."

Arii remained quiet, thinking, his eyes melting through the color spectrum into a dark yellow of anxiety.

"Rhydin told us that he was the First Archimage right after he killed Dathian. Couldn't the mist be his?" I asked, confusedly.

Arii sighed, "I do not think so. There was no mist at all after Dathian's death, or even five years ago the last time I sent a scouting party to check on things here. Not until I came a few days ago."

"But if Rhydin is supposedly the First Archimage, he *would* conjure a mist, right? Since he didn't, could that mean that the Rhydin we know is an imposter? I mean, *something* isn't right about him," I stated, my words flowing faster and faster. "Remember when Sam wounded him with the dagger? When he was trying to stop Rhydin from murdering Dathian? The gash didn't bleed. It was like a crack in marble. It happened again just a month ago."

Arii continued to appear perplexed. He tapped his long, tan fingers against his chin rhythmically. The old Ranguvariian spoke slowly, "I have been trying to study that. I have not found much, but my research has led me to a certain controversial topic."

"What's that?" I asked tiredly.

"What it is that truly happens when someone's magic is stolen. Stolen completely to the point where there is nothing but a few drops left," Arii answered grimly.

My eyes widened. My heart stumbled. My voice quivered. "Evan told me once that magic can only be stolen in the exact right circumstances, like when-…"

"When making an Einanhi is about the only circumstance because it provides another organism with your exact magic. Magic can only steal itself," Arii explained, his eyes getting darker every second. "There are some instances of it in immediate family members, but neither of Rhydin's parents were mages and he was an only child."

"So, what are you saying?" I asked, becoming frustrated. "That Rhydin created an Einanhi in the last five years and it stole his magic, so now there's a mist here? This isn't making any sense! He definitely wasn't lacking any magic when I saw him last." I suddenly added as my mind whirled, "If Rhydin created the mist, is it a trap for us? Did he lure us here to attack us and that's how Rayna's magic is activated here?!"

I jumped to my feet, ready to sprint back to the throne room, and began taking a deep breath to scream for Rayna since I couldn't sense where she was in this giant palace. Arii, however, leaped forward and caught my hand, saying, "Lina, this isn't a trap. Rhydin hasn't been here since the last time you were here. He abhors this place. I truly do not think this is Rhydin's doing."

My arm went limp in his grasp. I whimpered, "Then why is it here?"

"I think that we should spend some more time studying. Here, in the Archimage Library. Of all places, I truly believe that the answer is here somewhere," Arii answered quietly.

I groaned. I didn't have the reading ability or the patience to look through the thousands, if not millions, of books in this library.

Nonetheless, we got busy. Being well over three hundred years old, I learned quickly that Arii was a speed-reader. I guess it made sense; he'd probably read more books than the last three generations of Royals combined. As the hours passed, he grabbed stack after stack of tomes from the library shelves and skimmed them faster than I could get through a single volume. These books were written for Royals and nobles, people who could afford an upscale, private education. Certainly not farm kids like me who went to the city schoolhouse until they could manage the simplest of reading, writing, and arithmetic.

Angrily, I slapped my book shut and started wandering around the library. I wasn't going to get anywhere if I tried to do what Arii was doing. *Okay, Mr. Presence that has been helpful in the past*, I thought to myself, using my magic to project it a little in kind of a reverse process to sensing presences, *if you want to help us figure out what your deal is with this mist, show me the book I need.*

Instantaneously, a rush of balmy air came from behind me, whipping my shoulder-length brown hair over my shoulder and brushing my cloak and tunic. *Yep, it's still here*, I thought, trembling slightly. *And much stronger than last time, too.*

I barely kept myself from screaming when my hand was suddenly taken by a warm grip, and when I looked, there was nothing there. The invisible hand didn't seem threatening, but it took all of my willpower to not wrench my hand out of its grip and hightail it out of this awful palace.

To my surprise, the strange presence didn't lead me to any of the bookshelves, but instead toward a writing desk tucked in the corner of the room next to a dead fireplace. The cover was rolled up already, and hundreds of parchment sheets had been tossed to the floor around it in crumpled piles. I convinced myself that these were old, from when Dathian was still alive.

A violet, feather quill with a gold nib lifted on its own from the desk and began to write on a new piece of parchment in delicate, boyish handwriting. My eyebrows probably leapt into my hairline at the sight of the first words that the mysterious presence scratched out:

> *The throne of sand*
> *must meet its end*
> *to break the curse*
> *that shrouds the First.*

It was the riddle that I had gotten from that Auklian noblewoman just a couple months ago. The one I'd held onto but had to let lie since it made no sense. With glee, I realized I was right that it was only the first half as the floating quill kept writing:

> *But do hear me this:*
> *should the curse remain,*
> *for all Nerahdis,*
> *just death can be gained.*

Well, that certainly sounded menacing. I threaded my hands through my hair, squeezing my temples. Why did it have to be a riddle? Why couldn't it just be straightforward?

I grumbled louder than I intended, "But what does it mean? What is the throne of sand? Neither Auklia nor the Great Desert make sense!"

The quill suddenly scratched more writing into existence further down the paper:

> *What are nothing more than sand?*

"I don't know!" I shouted, feeling half crazy. "I don't understand any of this! Why are you invisible? *What* are you? *Who* are you?"

The quill began to write slowly this time.

"Lina?" Arii called.

Instantly, the quill fell to the parchment with a smack, spattering ink everywhere. The presence disappeared altogether.

My hands covered my eyes. Arii was going to think I was a lunatic. "Yes?"

Arii sauntered around the corner to find me tucked in the back of the library with the writing desk. He had a concerned expression on his face. Rightly so. "Are you alright?"

"Yeah. Sure." I pinched the bridge of my nose.

Rather than turning back to his mountain of books, Arii halted and scratched the back of his neck. "Lina...I must tell you that I did not come here just for a change in scenery. I came here for a certain book I thought Dathian may have possessed. A book on healing."

I was nodding along to everything he said, utterly fed up with our whole little excursion here, until the last part. "Healing? Why healing? I thought Ranguvariians had the best healers in Nerahdis."

"Well, we like to think so," Arii chuckled uncomfortably, "but we've been presented with a new infliction that our powers have proved worthless against."

I thought for a moment. "The poison, right? The new poison that Rhydin's Einanhis are using. The one that killed June and the others. Don't worry, Arii, I have full confidence in you that you'll come up with an antidote soon."

"Actually, we can't," Arii admitted, his eyes turning a deep ocean blue. "We have tried for weeks. This poison is linked to Rhydin's magic, which erodes ours as you remember from our lesson. We cannot heal it. Ever."

My shoulders slumped, taking in the weight of that information. "Then, we'll be more careful. We'll start wearing more armor. If we can avoid getting cut by these poisoned blades, then that won't matter."

"Lina," Arii sighed. Whatever he was thinking about was truly paining him. "He told me not to, but I truly think you should know that-…"

A scream echoed through the dead palace walls, making the hairs on the back of my neck stand on end. I knew inherently that only one person could make that sound.

"Rayna," I breathed, my mind losing all other tracks.

It was happening. Why hadn't I kept her closer?

Arii snapped to attention and drew his blade, and the two of us rushed out of the library, toppling precarious stacks of books and spreading loose leaflets of parchment in our wake. My mind whirled through a thousand different scenarios that could cause my daughter to scream like that, and I hoped that Chelsea, James, and Conriin were closer to her than we were.

On the parchment that I left in the dust, the new words "I am the true" remained interrupted and unread.

Chapter Thirteen

Rayna

"Taisyn, this place is amazing!" I sang. "I mean, just look at all this history!"

We had already explored the first few floors of the Archimage Palace, which were all fascinating regardless of their disheveled appearances. Each floor had a different theme, and I suspected this was due to all the important guests the Archimage would entertain. After all, he couldn't leave in order to keep his position a secret. There was a floor dedicated to each of the old Three Kingdoms: Mineraltir, Auklia, and Lunaka.

Shamelessly, we spent the most time on the Lunakan floor, desperate as I was to get to know my parents' homeland. What little décor was left included a painting of a dark-haired king with a goatee called Adam, some wall art made of twisted and braided wheat stalks, and a tapestry depicting a city at the bottom of a canyon that looked like it had coal stains on it.

"Don't you think we should head back?" Taisyn asked uncertainly. "We haven't seen any of the others since we lost Chelsea and Conriin on the Auklian floor."

"Nah." I waved him off. "Who knows how long my mother and Arii are going to talk? Plus, if we head back now, we'll never see the rest of the palace!"

Taisyn groaned, but he continued to follow me nonetheless. We went back out to the spiral, marble staircase, which included the whole grayscale from its midnight black bottom to its snowy white top. *This* was definitely something I could translate into my sketchbook later. We ended up skipping the next floor, which looked like it had gold wallpaper from afar, and went right to the top. The top floor was always where all the important things were, right?

The top floor looked just like the throne room and stair case. Black on bottom, which melted into gray and became pure white at the top. This floor was thoroughly torn apart. Tapestries lay in shreds, and other furniture had been bashed. The dust was overwhelming, though, so this damage was done a much longer time ago than the other things we'd seen. The only aspect of this hallway that hadn't been upset was a long line of portraits on each wall. I walked past each one, trying to summarize each for Taisyn, and as I did, I realized there was a cycle. Mineraltin, Auklian, Lunakan. Mineraltin, Auklian, Lunakan. It was easy to tell by their clothing style and appearance.

These were all the old Archimages!

I had never much appreciated history – or any other subject – in school, but my heart squealed with delight at the sight of all these portraits. Nerahdis was becoming a place I understood more and more all the time, and it helped me feel like I was a part of it. Not a little outcast from Caark checked out of everything my parents had been fighting for their whole lives.

"Wow, look at them all! There has to be, like, twenty of them, Taisyn!" I exclaimed.

Taisyn raised his pale hand to his chin. "Nerahdis has only had an Archimage for a little over three hundred years. Being an Archimage must be a hazardous occupation if there's been twenty of them."

I shrugged. Math still wasn't my strong suit. "It's still cool," I insisted stubbornly as I hurried to the end of the line of portraits, describing everything I was seeing out loud. "Huh, that's weird. All these portraits are totally untouched except this one. There's one just sitting on the floor under the last portrait like it was put there purposefully. It's not broken or anything."

"Who's it of?" Taisyn asked.

I rubbed the dust away from the silver plate at the top of the frame. "'Minndosia.' She looks Mineraltin, I think."

This thin woman didn't appear particularly important. My gaze shifted upward to the final portrait in the hallway of a young, black-haired man with violet eyes. He didn't seem like anyone special until I rubbed his plate to reveal the name.

"*Rhydin?*" I gasped loudly. "Taisyn, Rhydin was an Archimage?!"

"Yeah," Taisyn responded like it was obvious. "He was the First Archimage. All the Royals know that now. I guess most people still don't though. Sorry."

I began to ramble, "But how-…?"

Rayna.

I looked from side to side. I could have sworn I'd just heard someone whisper my name. I asked quietly, "Did you hear that?"

"Hear what?"

Rayna.

It was coming from the end of the hallway. I immediately started following it like a bug to light.

"Rayna, I think I can sense something," Taisyn stated slowly, his hand reaching for his head. "A presence…a vague one."

I ignored him. I didn't have the luxury of a built-in, magical compass. We passed a small office on the left and arrived at a set of double doors at the end of the hallway. I shoved them open with a cascade of dust and the smell of mildew, which was quickly replaced by the overwhelming stench of salt. A thrill spread through me at the sight of the ocean opening up in all directions out to a flat horizon. I hadn't realized how much I'd missed this sight until this moment. Homesickness bloomed within me.

"It's the ocean," I said happily, moving closer to the edge of the balcony. "It's dark blue with frothy, white waves. It stretches out as far as I can see with nothing on the horizon. Just a thin line where the dark blue meets the light blue of the sky."

"Sounds nice," Taisyn replied, a small smile on his face that vanished rapidly. "I think we should go back. Something isn't right."

I was just in the middle of saying everything was fine when I suddenly felt something under my arms, like hands on either side, and my feet left the ground.

"*Taisyn!*" I screamed, but it was too late. I was hurtling over the side of the balcony and down toward my beloved ocean. My vision was going black. Wind rippled all around me, deafeningly. Right before I lost consciousness, there was a burst of golden light all around me and then a second flash of fiery light before it all went dark.

My head throbbed. There was a chaos of whispers around me. There was something soft underneath me. My eyes remained closed, the darkness less painful, but I could tell there was light.

That's not all there was.

There was a sea around me. A sea of thoughts and feelings, sights and smells, even though my eyes were shut, and my ears only heard whispers. My head buzzed with all the activity. I could feel fire and light and concern and ferocity and all the things in between. There was another sensation, of something old and strange but overwhelmingly good.

Sensation. Sensing.

Was I sensing presences?!

I shot up out of what turned out to be a bed, my chest heaving. All of my companions were here in this small bedroom, and I looked at each of them in succession, feeling an entirely different slew of emotions, sights, and smells as I did. At Taisyn, I sensed his fire, his hard exterior but kindness buried deep within. My mother was a warm, glowing light that I could tell cared deeply about me. The Ranguvariians and Chelsea gave off vague auras, but there was too much going on in my head for me to hone in on them.

"Rayna? Rayna, are you okay?" my mother's voice lilted in as if it were miles away. "What happened?"

It was then that I realized I was sopping wet. Taisyn, too, as my gaze shifted back to him and I tried to remember, was soaked with his red hair plastered to his skull. I stammered, my mind still coming back to me, "I...I can sense you. All of you."

My mother's face went slack, and Clariion Arii cracked a grin. "Your magic has awakened. Well done, young Allyen."

"You can sense us all?" my mother exclaimed, shocked. She reached for the vibrant, purple feather that hung around her neck. "I guess these don't work as well in such close proximity anymore. But still, I didn't start sensing presences for a couple of weeks after my magic activated."

"Perhaps, she is more powerful," James joked, jabbing my mother's ribs with his elbow.

My pride made me smile. An Allyen with magic, at last! I had waited so long for this moment, and now here it was! Confusion, however, crept into me as I tried to remember what happened. "I remember being on the top floor...and the balcony. Then, I'm not sure. It was like someone picked me up and threw me over, but there was no one there."

My mother's face turned dark.

"It's true," Taisyn said with a hint of a shiver. "One moment we were standing there talking, and the next, she was suddenly hurled over the edge of the balcony. There was a strange presence there with us, but it didn't seem like there was another person there. I know I can't see, and my powers are limited." Taisyn sighed, "My magic helps me see outlines when I use it. She just lifted up out of nowhere. Then her magic exploded out from her, slowing her so the fall wouldn't kill her. I jumped over and used my fire to jet to her and keep her from drowning once we landed."

"Thank you, Taisyn." My mother looked like she had been weeping.

I felt shaken by what Taisyn had done. Would I have done the same for him in that situation? "Thank you," I whispered and put my hand over his.

I looked around at everyone again, now thankful to be alive. When I did, I realized there was an extra person huddled in the corner behind everyone else. The Ranguvariians and Chelsea turned to leave the room, going back to whatever they had been doing before I nearly died, which gave me a better look at him. He was short, young, and pale with black hair, dressed in an old-fashioned tunic with an unbuttoned, lace collar and a pair of simple trousers, no shoes on his feet.

I was in the middle of sensing that he had the same strange presence I had sensed back on the balcony when suddenly the world melted away around me. There was no flash of light like in transportation, just all the colors of the world bled away and reshaped into an entirely different environment.

The bedroom of the Archimage Palace and all my friends transformed seamlessly into an open sky and boundless prairie. The grasses tickled my skin until boots and trousers abruptly covered my formerly bare legs. My hands lifted on their own to brush some hair out of my face, and I realized I now wore guards on my arms. I was also much taller with longer, browner hair than I'd ever had in my whole life.

"Nora? What's wrong?" a female voice asked. "I'm sure he'll be here soon, I promise!"

My eyes shifted automatically to find a young woman standing next to me. Her hair was a gorgeous ocean-blue, and her eyes were pools of the same color. She wore a simple, green-colored frock, the likes of which I had never seen before. A delicate, violet flower was tucked behind her ear.

I found my mouth answering on its own, a deeper, feminine voice resounding, "Nothing, Amelia. I hope you are right. It is a long journey from Soläna to Diagalo."

"Look, there he is!" Amelia exclaimed excitedly as she pointed to our left.

Sure enough, a figure appeared on the horizon, growing steadily closer. For some reason, I began to feel stern and distrustful, although this figure had obviously not done anything to me. As he grew closer, I could see that he was a young man, no more than seventeen or so. He had neat, dark hair and was dressed in the finery of a well-off family.

Must be the son of a noble, a thought entered my mind, unbidden. It didn't originate from my mind. *So, this is Amelia's new beau.*

The boy smiled as he approached us, a nice smile. He had piercing amethyst eyes, but they looked kind. He grinned at Amelia, the ocean-haired young woman, and then held his hand out to me, saying, "I am pleased to finally meet you, Madam Soreta. My name is Rhydin Caldwell."

What? My mind whirled. *What is this? Where am I? Why can't I move or talk?*

"Likewise," the voice that was not my own responded shortly, and my hand shifted on its own to the hilt of a sword slung around my hips. "I must tell you, Rhydin Caldwell, that if you break Amelia's heart, I will end you."

Rhydin's face paled, and he stammered boyishly, "Th-That will not be necessary. I-I have no intention of doing that."

"Good," Nora's voice sprung from my throat again, my lips moving on their own.

The outdoor scene in the prairie rapidly began to melt away again. Young Rhydin and Amelia dissolved like snow in front of me, and the bedroom at the Archimage Palace returned once more. However, it was back to being chaotic.

"Rayna! Rayna, wake up!" Mama shouted, her hands fluttering over me, feeling my forehead and such.

"Wh-What happened?" I slurred, my head throbbing again.

"You passed out," Taisyn answered simply. "We couldn't wake you."

I shot upward, tired of everyone fussing over me. Arii was just re-entering the room, after all of the hub-bub that he had likely heard down the hall, when I asked, "Who in Nerahdis is Nora Soreta?"

"The First Allyen."

I looked to my mother, but she hadn't said a word. Instead, she looked flabbergasted. Taisyn hadn't said anything either; he was waiting for the same answer. Arii looked poised to answer, but it hadn't been his voice I heard. My eyes returned to the corner I'd looked at upon...*whatever* it was I had just experienced, and I realized I knew who it was now.

Rhydin Caldwell. The same boy I'd just met in some sort of dream, except maybe a couple of years older. He looked at me warily with his purple eyes, like he was afraid of me.

Afraid of *me*.

"Rhydin," I breathed, watching the specter in the corner. When my mother and Arii looked around in all directions and returned to me looking utterly confused, I asked slowly, "You can't see him? Standing in the corner?"

Both my mother and Arii turned toward the exact corner I pointed at. Taisyn, even, used just enough of his fire magic to make his fingers glow to try and "see."

Nothing.

"Okay, Rayna," my mother sighed worriedly, "I think maybe you should get some rest."

"No!" I shouted, my voice rising, "R-Rhydin is standing right there! It's not Emperor Rhydin, he looks different! Younger! I just met him in a dream!"

My mother pushed me back into the bed, my head slumping into the feather pillow. She pulled up the covers and tucked them in all around me, as effective as tying me up with rope. "Just…please rest. You've been through a lot today. We'll come back and check on you soon."

With that, my mother turned the oil lamp down and wheeled Taisyn out of the room. Arii dawdled a moment, studying both me and the supposedly empty corner of the room, before he left, too. Effectively leaving me alone in a dark bedroom with an apparition of Rhydin Caldwell.

The specter stepped forward just once, and his color pulsated through him, which made me realize he was ever so slightly glowing. He placed a pale hand on his chest as he whispered, "I'm so sorry. I never wanted you to drown. I just knew that if I put your life in danger, your magic would awaken and save you. You are the only one I can speak to, so I had to wake your magic."

"I-It's okay," I replied, trying not to tremble. I mean, really, he did me a favor. "Why do you want to talk to me? Why am I the only one?"

"We are the only two people in the world with the exact same type of magic," Rhydin explained, his glow continuing to waver. "Both of us were given magic, not born with it. I need to be able to explain what happened myself. Not try to use quill and parchment like last time."

"What about my mother?" I asked, confused. "She also has my magic. And she's been doing it a *lot* longer than I have."

"I know." A small smile appeared on Rhydin Caldwell's thin face very briefly. "I've only recently begun to regain some of my power. Just a few years ago, this wouldn't be possible. I have been able to interact with your mother a little bit because she still possesses some aspect of the original, artificial Allyen magic. But your power is different than hers."

At this point, I just started nodding. I knew absolutely nothing about magic, and I would have to ask a lot of questions later.

Rhydin continued, "For the past three hundred years, I have barely had enough power to pull a book or two off a shelf maybe once a week. As soon as my power began to return, I tried to write a warning in a short riddle for an Auklian woman who traveled here to see if there were any relics left that she could steal. I have no idea what happened with that. Its failure, however, proved that I would need to be able to *tell* my story, and *you*, Rayna Greene, are the only one to whom I can tell it."

"Okay," I said hesitantly, pulling myself up and out of the tight sheets, "but I need to know one thing first. If you're Rhydin Caldwell, who's the evil Rhydin out there that's hunted my parents their whole lives?"

The apparition swallowed hard. He tried to clear his throat. His voice was beginning to fade in and out. "Sorry, I, uh...I have just waited so long for this moment."

Rhydin was just about to speak again when suddenly the door to the room opened, shining a ray of light inside. The strange, ghostly Rhydin vanished. My mother walked into the room with something in her hands. After a quick, skeptical glance at the corner, she said softly, "You're supposed to be resting."

"I'm not tired," I answered stubbornly, crossing my arms.

My mother chuckled slightly, "You get that from your father."

I grinned. Anything I got from him was good.

"I have something for you." She handed me something wrapped in leather as she used her other fingers to stroke the smooth, satin comforter.

I unwrapped it one little piece at a time, and a silver disc was cradled in the leather. It was small and round with a hinge at the top, like it used to be a locket, but the other side was gone. Its face was decorated with a circular, looping design with circles within them instead of the tiny amber studs embedded in my mother's portion which was around her neck. I rubbed its warm metal with my thumb, touched the leather cord attached to it. Even though I already knew the answer, I asked gently, "What is it?"

My mother gave a short laugh, pushing her brown hair behind her ear. "It's a piece of the Allyen locket. Your piece. The locket was designed for the First Allyen to be an amplifier for her magic, to strengthen it. Your uncle and I have pieces too." She tapped on her necklace, which was threaded with a sturdy chain around her neck. "I have the front half of the exterior while Evan has the interior piece. It was broken into two when Evan and I were born Allyens at the same time, and we broke it into three for you. To perform the death spell together."

"Wow," I breathed. Just holding it made me feel all warm inside. I reached out and gave her a one-armed hug, probably the first one I'd ever initiated. "Thank you, Mama."

"You're welcome." Mama smiled big, showing all her teeth. I hadn't seen many of those smiles from her. Then, she stood again and placed her hand on the door knob. "Now, seriously. Get some rest."

"Okay," I sighed, but I couldn't wipe the smile off my face.

Mama shut the door, and the darkness resumed. I looped my piece of the Allyen locket over my head, and before I knew it, Rhydin the specter was back and brighter than ever before. I jumped when he did, somewhat expecting it to all be a hallucination. It certainly wasn't now.

"Why are you brighter?" I asked, gripping my new necklace tightly.

"You have an amplifier now. It strengthens your magic and therefore your ability to see and hear me," Rhydin clarified, his voice louder.

"Alright." That made sense. "So, what are you? If you're Rhydin Caldwell, who's off being an evil emperor?"

Rhydin took a deep breath yet again. "I am the true Rhydin Caldwell. Nearly every drop of magic was stolen from me about three hundred years ago by an Einanhi I accidentally created, which reduced me to what you see before you. Frozen in time, unable to live or die."

My brow furrowed. Aunt Rachel hadn't been lying that the consequences of making an out-of-control Einanhi were dire. "Okay. So why didn't someone destroy the Einanhi so you could get your magic back? How does Emperor Rhydin fit into this?"

"People have been trying to destroy my errant Einanhi for over three centuries. He has almost every drop of power I was given as Archimage," Rhydin replied, fixing me in a fiercely miserable gaze. "The Rhydin you all know *is* the Einanhi."

CHAPTER FOURTEEN

LINA

"Oh, Arii," I groaned as I slowly dropped myself into a cushy chair back in the library. "I'm not sure whether to be thankful or not that you warned me her magic would activate here."

"Hmm. We only saw the location, not the means. Your helpful presence seems to have an agenda," Arii replied in a smooth voice, his fingers folded together.

"Arii. It dropped my daughter off a balcony. I'm not so sure it's 'helpful' anymore," I grumbled.

"Over the ocean, not a mountain. With Prince Taisyn there and a good understanding of how the Allyen magic would spring forth to save her life. It could have been worse." Arii shrugged.

I glared daggers at him. Didn't make a difference to me. "But what about her outburst? About Nora and Rhydin standing in the corner?"

"I am not sure," Arii answered, his eyes becoming yellow and going to the floor. "We can only hope that in time the answer will be made clear."

I dwelled upon that for a moment. It was like she had *seen* something. But what? She had just stared at the wall open-mouthed for a minute or two before she suddenly came back to herself. I didn't even remotely want to consider that the strange presence was influencing her, just as it had begun to physically interact with me.

The Ranguvariian leader was just turning back to his pile of dusty tomes when I dragged myself out of my chair and back toward the writing desk in the corner. My "helpful presence" wasn't present, but the parchment it had been writing upon still remained. I read over both halves of the riddle again, as well as the "I am the true" at the bottom which had been interrupted. Then, I stalked back toward Arii and dropped the page right on top of what he was reading. "I got this. Earlier. From our favorite ghost."

Arii took a few seconds to read the eight lines. "This doesn't really have anything to do with our Archimage mist dilemma."

"I know, but I still think it's important. An Auklian noblewoman died to get the first half of this to me, and now our helpful presence has the rest? It doesn't make sense," I replied, still studying the riddle upside down. "Her fear was palpable as she wrote it, Arii, like she had seen a ghost-..."

"*Mama!*"

Arii and I snapped to attention. Rayna burst through the double doors of the library, dressed but with her shoes missing, and one of her hands seemed to drag something along behind her that I couldn't see.

I stammered, "Wh-What is it? Have you seen something again?"

"Mama, I know this is going to sound crazy," Rayna said between breaths as her chest heaved, her third of the Allyen locket moving up and down. She must have run all the way here from the upstairs bedroom. "But I can see Rhydin Caldwell. The *real* Rhydin Caldwell. He's been trapped here all this time!"

"Rayna, that is ridiculous!" I exclaimed. "We all know that Rhydin Caldwell is a sorcerer that has tried to take over

Nerahdis for the past three hundred years, and eleven years ago, he succeeded!"

"No, you have to listen!" Rayna shouted angrily, stomping her foot.

I opened my mouth to rebuke her again, but Arii held up his hand. "Let her speak."

Rayna steadied herself, trying to regain control of her breathing. Then, she spoke firmly, "The Rhydin you know is an Einanhi. He was created accidentally, took every last drop of his creator's magic, which cursed his creator, the true Rhydin, to become invisible and frozen. He's not a ghost like you think! He's as real as you and me. His power is just gone, but it's starting to return!"

"The magic of the original Rhydin Caldwell is returning. That could be why the mist has returned to the Archimage Palace," Arii mused, stroking his chin.

"Arii, you are not *seriously* entertaining this idea, are you?" I asked incredulously. "It's impossible! Rayna could have a concussion for all we know, and she only *thinks* she's seeing this apparition of Rhydin! The presence could be tricking her."

"Rare. *Extremely* rare. But not completely impossible," Arii replied, the gears in his ancient mind whirring uncontrollably. "She portrays no symptoms of a concussion-…"

"Wait," Rayna said abruptly, which cut Arii and I off. She actually turned and *looked* at whatever thing she was pretending to hold behind her for a few minutes and then returned to us. "Rhydin says that he tried to tell you on that parchment you have there. He was trying to write 'I am the true Rhydin Caldwell' at the bottom. He wrote the riddle, too."

My breath hitched. It couldn't all be true…could it? All these years of fighting the sorcerer I thought I was beginning to know. The way he had cracked like stone both times I'd ever seen him wounded. There was no blood. My father,

Robert, had said that something wasn't right about him. And now, his mind and his magic were dangerously unhinged – and his Einanhi soldiers looking less human every year – just as this presence was beginning to regain his power? I'd slain hundreds if not thousands of Einanhis in the last couple of decades.

Could the Rhydin I knew be nothing more than a manmade creation? When we killed him, would he be reduced to nothing but sand?

Throne of sand.

"If he wrote the riddle, have him explain it," I said defensively. "And how the first half of it was relayed to me by an Auklian woman."

"Oh, he told me that part already," Rayna answered as if it was the most normal thing in the world. "He said an Auklian woman came here to steal things, so he left the riddle for her on a note and made some stuff fall to freak her out. That's how he decided he'd need to be able to talk to someone in order to really tell people what happened, and I guess I'm the only one he can talk to."

"Because your magics are the same. Artificially-created, not hereditary," Arii continued, a sly smile coming to his face. His theory was proving correct.

I looked at Rayna fearfully. Had she discovered that she was not truly born an Allyen?

"Yeah, something like that, I guess." Rayna appeared confused, so I hoped she hadn't. I wasn't ready to tackle that quite yet.

She turned and listened to the invisible presence a little while longer before answering my other question. "Rhydin says the throne of sand represents Emperor Rhydin's reign. He must be destroyed to break the curse that shrouds the First Archimage, to allow the stolen magic to return and let Rhydin Caldwell be normal again. He says that as Emperor Rhydin declines, he grows stronger. But if this doesn't happen, if the curse upon him remains, then Emperor Rhydin will only stay in control of Nerahdis forever and we'll all die."

I reeled. How could it all be true? I thought of all the little instances that my helpful presence had dropped a book off a shelf or warned me that Emperor Rhydin was coming. All this time, it had been a cursed Rhydin Caldwell, the teenage sorcerer I'd read about in that history book. The history book to which *he* had guided me in the hideaway in Dathian's office.

He had been trying to get us to discover him all along. For hundreds of years. And when we left after the battle here, when Dathian had died and we left the palace utterly empty, there was that overwhelming wail of sadness.

How lonely must he have been all this time?

"Okay," I said slowly, beginning to wrap my mind around all this. "This is starting to make sense. However, how was Emperor Rhydin created in the first place? Why in Nerahdis would you try to create an Einanhi that looks just like you-...?" I stopped myself. I was no Einanhi master, but I had created a weak Einanhi of myself to leave in Rhydin's dungeon when my father broke me out. I guess, sometimes, it was necessary.

I reiterated, "How did this all even happen in the first place? Why did the Rhydin we know curse his creator, and why was he given the task to usurp Nerahdis from the Royals? A task he's followed maliciously?"

Rayna turned toward a Rhydin I was starting to really wish I could see for myself, beginning to transcribe the words, "When he became Archimage," when someone else suddenly flew through the library doors.

James was fierce as he looped around the high ceiling of the library and declared, "The Dome is being attacked!!"

My heart fell straight through to my toes. How could this be? Was today the day for impossibilities?

"By who?" I asked in a shrill voice, unbelievingly. Surely, it had to be only a small group of Einanhis.

"Rhydin himself!" James shouted as he landed.

Chelsea, Conriin, and Taisyn came sprinting through the doors, not fast enough to keep up with James. Those words almost made me forget all of our revelations, but now we knew that Emperor Rhydin was not "Rhydin himself." He might be an Einanhi, a magically-creating being, but his destruction was very much real.

Rachel's younger brother yelled again, "Why are you just standing there? We need to go, *now!*"

I glanced at Arii, his expression grim. Then Rayna, who looked torn and like she was clinging to an invisible tree.

If we left, we could not take the cursed, boy sorcerer with us.

But what choice did we have?

"Rayna, I'm sorry, but we have to go," I stated, reaching for her to come to me. "We have to help the Dome. They're not prepared for battle."

Rayna stood there, devastation written plainly on her face. "I don't want to leave him. He's been alone for so long."

"I promise, we will come back as soon as we can." I tucked the parchment with the riddle into my pocket and withdrew my sword from my sash. When she didn't move, I looked squarely at the invisible space next to her, at what I hoped was remotely near Rhydin Caldwell's eyes, and vowed again even though I couldn't bring myself to say his name, "I promise. We will come back. We will help you."

James, Chelsea, and Conriin looked at me like I'd lost my marbles. Instantly, the presence in my mind that I'd known for so long became abundantly thankful. It was enough to bring tears to my eyes.

"Let's go!" I declared, and Rayna begrudgingly released her hold on her new friend. Chelsea and Conriin shuttled Rayna and Taisyn out the doors, likely back out of the palace to the nearest gathering of water. Good, that would give James and I a head start before the children arrived.

James grabbed me in the blink of an eye and unceremoniously took off, speeding through the winding hallways of the Archimage Palace. We passed right over the others' heads with Arii close on our tail, his wings larger and grander than any other Ranguvariian's.

As soon as we were outdoors, the world burst into white, remained void for a few seconds, and then reappeared into a scene that had been the stuff of my nightmares for over a decade.

The city within the Dome had been annihilated.

My chest throbbed as if it had been punched. Everything we ever built lay in ruins. Smoke was filling the underground cavity from hundreds of fires littered throughout the levelled city. As James circled the city for a second time, I desperately searched for any sort of life. The whole place was eerily empty.

James let me down at the fountain, the one thing that seemed to be intact. This was where the children would pop up with Chelsea and Conriin. As I took in the burning Council chamber, the possessions strewn in the road, and the blasted walls of every ramshackle dwelling around me, I found it hard to breathe. "What happened here? I thought you said Rhydin was attacking."

"The messenger said he attacked," James answered wearily as he surveyed the damage with glassy eyes. "She must have meant he attacked earlier, not currently. I'm sorry, I should have clarified."

"It's okay, that doesn't matter. Where is everyone? I don't see any dead," I said as I continued to scan what I could see of the city. No bodies, no blood. Even if our people had been able to get away, there would have been at least a few casualties due to the surprise attack. It was like the Dome had been empty, and it had never once been empty in all eleven years of its operation.

"I think the real question is how did Rhydin find the Dome?" Arii said as he walked about. He looked straight up at the cluster of Ranguvariian feathers that still tried to shine its blue-green light down upon the smoky wreckage. "I will have to get some people to move that. I am surprised Rhydin left it when he is known to experiment on everything of ours."

Arii was just spreading his shard-like wings once again, ready to transport to the Ranguvariian Camp to gather help, when the sound of running footsteps suddenly reached our ears. We all drew our weapons, expecting the worst. I eyed the fountain once, wondering why Chelsea and Conriin had not appeared with Rayna and Taisyn yet.

Around the bend came running none other than Bartholomiiu, my old friend. Relieved, I let my sword fall, and James laughed and hugged his childhood buddy. Bartholomiiu smiled too, his eyes a pastel green, but while he didn't look like he'd been in battle, his limbs seemed weary. At that very moment, a streak of green light came from the fountain, and our four missing companions popped up out of the water, soaking wet.

"Ugh," Rayna groaned as she wrung water out of her clothes, "I am definitely listing Ranguvariian as my preferred mode of transport from now on!"

I fought the urge to chuckle and instead walked closer to Bartholomiiu, my voice quivering. "Where is everyone? Was the Dome empty when Rhydin attacked?"

"They go to Lunaka Castle," Bartholomiiu replied in his broken, albeit better than ever, Nerahdian. "Everyone left. Lunaka Castle will be new base."

"New base?!" I repeated disbelievingly. "Lunaka Castle was a target for its supplies and disrupting Rhydin's access to Soläna's coal, *not* to replace the Dome!" My head spun just thinking about it. *All* the hundreds of people who had lived down here now living in Lunaka Castle. Would we all even fit?

Bartholomiiu shrugged. "I do not know. But dead, anyone left here if not."

I groaned. Frederick was in charge of this mission. I tried to quell the anger I felt by trusting that, for whatever reason, he had decided this was best. "So, they're just going to attack Lunaka Castle? Do we even have the numbers to take it? We were going to gather all the pockets of rebellion across Nerahdis to take on this mission, and on this short of notice, I doubt anyone came!"

"They did not," Bartholomiiu responded. "Right now, decoy Rhydin there. Everyone hoping for best. They travel now. Arrive tomorrow."

Great. Just great. I leave for a day, and everything implodes.

Arii began to talk to Bartholomiiu about getting help to remove the crystal cluster above our heads as soon as possible, especially now that it appeared no one would be coming back. I racked my head for any sort of idea as to how to help, and I only had a day, if that, to do it. How could Sam have gone with them and not waited for me?

Rayna was describing the destruction around us to Taisyn, who actually looked worried for the first time in his life. His family wasn't here either, obviously. My eyes wandered to the northern wall, and all the apartments were dark. It was strange, seeing them that way. There was always light in them, even at night.

Once again, Rhydin had destroyed my home. First, my childhood home, the farm in the Canyonlands. Then the Rounan Compound. Now, the Dome. When would it end?

Not Rhydin. Emperor Rhydin. The Einanhi. And it would end when we destroyed him and restored the true Rhydin Caldwell. We knew that now.

Bartholomiiu soon left to follow Arii's orders, and the rest of us did the best we could to bed down for the night by the fountain. James took the first watch, and Chelsea and Conriin slept on the opposite side. I lay closer to Rayna than she would have probably preferred, and Taisyn was a few feet away opposite to her.

The feather cluster above dimmed as it always did at night, and I found myself wondering if somehow the rebellion discovered that they'd been betrayed. That they left to save themselves and decided to go ahead toward Lunaka Castle because there was nowhere else to go. It certainly made more sense than leaving on a mission early for no reason before your reinforcements arrive.

At some point, I must have fallen asleep. I awoke groggy with a sore back from sleeping on the cobblestones, a sour reminder that I was not the young Allyen that I used to be. As my mind slowly absorbed the morning, I saw Arii and James talking quietly off to the side. I rolled onto my back to see a dozen Ranguvariians hovering like bees around the crystal at the zenith of the Dome, and I swallowed hard. Something that had been a mainstay in my life was about to disappear forever.

Rayna stirred in her sleep, but she evidently was not ready to wake. Taisyn, too, still slumbered. I leaned forward and caught a glimpse of Chelsea washing something in the fountain water, her features barely hinting at her true impish form. It was then that I realized the only thing left that could help the rebellion.

I stood and walked over to her. She mumbled a bleary "good morning," her blonde hair looking akin to a bird's nest. I returned the greeting, and then said, "I have to get more numbers for the rebellion. I need you to take me to your mother."

Chelsea's eyes widened into saucers, and she dropped the tin cup she had been washing, which clanged loudly on the uneven cobblestones. "You *what?* Are you crazy? I can't do that!"

"Yes, you can. If I can just talk to Chieftess Jaana again, I can try to convince her that we're worthy of her help," I explained, crossing my arms over my chest. "If I don't, the rebellion is going to fail."

"No, I mean, I *really* can't do that. When my mother banished me, she took away my ability to transport to the

Aatarilec Grotto, so I can never go home," Chelsea replied sadly. "And you might be able to steal a ship, but it would take hours to get to the bottom of Auklia's basin and you wouldn't be able to breathe without an Aatarilec's help. It's impossible."

"Hmm." I thought for a moment. I hadn't expected that answer. Chelsea was the only Aatarilec I knew now that Sonya was dead. My eyes wandered toward the rest of our crew, most of them awake and staring at us now. My gaze landed on Conriin, Rachel and Chelsea's cousin who was human, Ranguvariian, and Aatarilec all in one. "What about Conriin? His transportation magic works in the Aatarilec way."

"Uh...I don't know, actually," Chelsea answered, scratching her head. "His mother left the grotto when she fell in love with that human-looking Ranguvariian, and she died having him. He was never actually banished."

"Hey, Conriin," I called loudly. The mute, young man looked up, scratching one of his pointed ears as he licked something off one of his fangs, and then hurried over to us. "Are you able to transport us to the Aatarilec Grotto?"

Conriin eyed us both fearfully with his human eyes. He nodded ever so slowly, but his reluctance was obvious.

"Good. I need you to take me there right now," I said determinedly.

"Take you where?" Rayna asked, suddenly behind me. "Wherever you're going, I'm going too!"

I sighed heavily and placed my hand on her shoulder. "Not this time, sweetheart. Sorry."

"But-...!" Rayna tried to fight me.

"The best thing you can do for me right now is to get some magic lessons in before the battle. I'm afraid you might need them," I interrupted her begrudgingly, "even if it's just to protect yourself." My daughter's shoulders slumped, but I knew I couldn't waste any more time. "Conriin. If you please."

Conriin hesitantly walked to the fountain and stretched out his hand. I moved to join him, bracing myself for an underwater transport, when Chelsea abruptly rushed up to him. "I want to come!"

My brow furrowed. "I thought you said you were banished and can't transport to the grotto?"

"Yes, but if I ride Conriin's magic, I can go. With the help of my own of course, so he can still transport you," Chelsea explained, and then her eyes turned dark. "It's time for me to face my mother, once and for all."

"Well, your help certainly wouldn't hurt," I replied, taking Conriin's hand. I didn't know him personally, very few did, but the Owenses doted upon him. I said breathlessly, "Let's go."

Chelsea took Conriin's other hand, and the three of us waded into the fountain, the chilly water seeping into my boots. With a burst of green light, I was sucked into the darkness of a watery void, the utter opposite of the white, airy void of Ranguvariian transportation.

When we appeared at our destination, a dark, coral-ridden cave who knew how far underneath the sea, my lungs beginning to burn, I wondered if I had made the wrong choice.

CHAPTER FIFTEEN

RAYNA

M y mother, Conriin, and Chelsea were gone in the blink of an eye. I clutched my arms as they vanished in the green flash, and then took a quick look around the Dome. This place hadn't been my home for very long at all, but my heart hurt at the sight of it. Books and chairs and anything else people happened to have brought with them littered the roads. Even a doll lay abandoned on the cobblestones.

I touched my new necklace, my third of the locket, reassured by its warmth and the presences of those around me. In spite of everything I'd been through in the last twenty-four hours, excitement brimmed forth inside of me.

I could start learning magic!

"Alright, everybody," I announced loudly, trying to sound in charge, "I think we should catch up with the other rebels! Taisyn and I need as many magic lessons as possible before this battle. Let's go!"

"Oi," James groaned, rubbing his neck, and then whispered to Arii, "she sounds just like her mother."

"She does, indeed," I heard Arii chuckle. "It seems that all the Allyens are like this."

To my dismay, Arii stalled us for another hour until the big cluster of Ranguvariian feathers over our heads was dismantled and taken away. He looked relieved when the task was accomplished, but I didn't know exactly why aside from the fact that he seemed to think Rhydin would come back for it. Emperor Rhydin. The Einanhi. Not the true Rhydin Caldwell, whom we'd heartlessly left alone in the Archimage Palace. Again.

I barely knew him, but something about Rhydin Caldwell resonated with me. No one knew that his Einanhi stole all his magic, rendering him an invisible fraction of what he used to be, spending his days alone and forgotten for hundreds of years. I could tell by looking at him that severe loneliness had done its damage to him, and I wanted to keep him from being alone ever again. After all, as a child secreted away to Caark, was I really all that different? I couldn't imagine being in Caark all alone on top of it all. I vowed right then and there that I would return to the Archimage Palace as soon as possible, to both help Rhydin Caldwell and to discover the rest of his story. There was a lot more behind this accidental creation of an Einanhi that stole all his power. I just knew it.

"It is time," Arii declared suddenly, bringing me from my thoughts. "Take one last look around, children," Arii said, "you will likely never see this place again."

In spite of myself, I did look around again. The fires were finally dying. This was the place my parents dedicated themselves to for practically my whole life, and the place where we became a family again. Nonetheless, I didn't think I would miss it much. Taisyn closed his eyes and breathed the musty, underground scent deep into his lungs. He told me once that he was brought here when he was ten and Lyla eight, so he'd lived here a few years.

I turned to Arii impatiently. "Let's go. We need to catch up before they reach Lunaka Castle if we have any chance of some magic lessons."

The Clariion nodded and offered me his arm, which I took. Arii got a better hold on me, and James took Taisyn while Bartholomiiu began to fly toward the exit tunnel. The Ranguvariians launched into the air, circling the Dome just once more to make sure we weren't leaving behind anything important, and flew toward the exit. Then, the world disintegrated into nothing but white.

I watched the process more than I ever had the other few times I'd transported. I'd transported with both Ranguvariians and Aatarilecs, and both involved a bright burst of light, albeit different colors, as well as an emptiness between locations. Our departure site and destination didn't just blend into each other like an artist mixing colors. The scene blinked into light, became empty, and then rapidly reappeared in seconds.

What I'd experienced in the Archimage Palace was something entirely different. The world had slowly melted from one scene to the other, no in-betweens. If Nora was the First Allyen, she existed hundreds of years in the past. Not now. It was like I saw something she experienced firsthand since I couldn't move or talk in any way. But why? I saw her meeting Rhydin Caldwell for the first time, but what did it mean? Had I seen a memory, or did my befuddled mind make it all up upon seeing Rhydin Caldwell for the first time after being thrown into the ocean?

The world re-materialized. James, Arii, and Bartholomiiu landed in the middle of a trail of people, several of whom jumped back with fright when we appeared out of nowhere. The Ranguvariians issued a few apologies while I looked up at the sky. The sun was climbing high, almost noon. I wondered what time we would reach Lunaka Castle, which was so close to the city of my parents' births.

"Where are we?" Taisyn whispered to me as the sea of people parted around us to continue their journey.

"We're following a dirt path. On the left is a small forest. All the leaves are starting to die and fall off. To be honest, it looks rather awful. Autumn used to be pretty, but now it's just death. Why do people like autumn so much?" I shudder. "On the right is an empty field. Looks like maybe it used to be a crop field, but there're weeds everywhere. Things are beginning to flatten out on the horizon into just prairie. Definitely in Lunaka."

"I hear people all around us. Do you see our parents?" Taisyn asked, his fingers beginning to glow as he sensed the shapes all around him.

I glanced around for a few seconds. The people around me had sour faces. Some of them, men and women alike, wore chainmail and armor, obviously ready for the battle ahead of us, but several others looked no different than they had in the Dome. Elderly people and children walked in groups within the masses. There had to be nearly a thousand people on this road. Every single person who had lived in the Dome, not just the fighters.

What happened in the Dome after we left? How did they all know to leave before Emperor Rhydin's arrival? Bringing *everyone* was never the plan.

"No," I answered. "I imagine they are probably at the front, leading everyone. Or else at the back, making sure no one falls behind."

Arii finally spoke up. "I will take you two to the front of the traveling party. James and Bartholomiiu will go to the back to do as you have said. It is best that I speak to the Royals when we stop for lunch."

I nodded slowly. I had seen the expression on my mother's face when I told her what Rhydin Caldwell had revealed to me. It shattered everything she thought she knew. Taisyn's parents and the other Royals would be no different. My mother was willing to listen and ask questions. While I had no worries about the calm-minded King Frederick, I could only hope that the hothead King Xavier and iron-fisted Queen Sabine would do the same.

Arii picked each of us up like one would a toddler – although to be honest, between our not quite adult heights and his gargantuan height, the proportions of that simile are about right – and jumped into flight. We soared right over the heads of the entire rebellion, many of them looking up when our shadows crossed their path. The new, magical compass in my head was going absolutely crazy with so many people around. Was this what mages felt like all the time? Gornish and Rounans alike, as I saw them, I sensed a little bit of who they were. It was staggering. It was a few minutes before we reached the front of the mob, and looking back, the dark line of people stretched as far as I could see.

It was then that I realized the true importance of taking Lunaka Castle. The Dome was compromised. If we failed, there would be nowhere left to run for so many hundreds of people.

"Rayna!"

I'd know that voice anywhere. As Arii landed, Ky ran up to me and gave me a big hug. I patted his shoulder awkwardly, but I was glad to see him alright. I chuckled, "Glad to see you still have your head."

Ky groaned, "You always have to ruin the moment, don't you?"

I grinned. "Well, of course."

My brother studied Taisyn and I, and then glanced over our shoulders. "Where's Mother?"

"She went to try and get help from the Aatarilecs. She wouldn't let me go with her," I answered, deflating. "We saw what happened to the Dome."

Ky nodded a couple times, and his face grew longer. He asked a few questions about the state of the Dome, meaning that the rebellion had definitely left before the destruction happened. By now, Aron and Lyla had come up to us, and the latter greeted Taisyn, relieved her brother was also okay.

"When will we reach Lunaka Castle?" I asked, my nerves beginning to act up.

"By evening," Aron responded, his teal eyes fierce. "I hope Aunt Lina will make it in time."

"Me, too," I said more to myself than anyone else. But then I had to ask, "What happened at the Dome? You all obviously got out before Emperor Rhydin arrived. How'd you know he was coming?"

Ky, Aron, and Lyla each looked down in turn. Even Dominick, eavesdropping as he rode on the back of his father's horse just ahead of us, began to look sheepish. Nathia was soundly ignoring us from ahead. Chretien and Willian slowed their paces to fall back with us. Willian wouldn't meet my eyes as I glanced from person to person.

"Wait," I murmured, gazing at each of them again, faces that had become very familiar in the last several weeks, "where's Erikin?"

Now, nobody would meet my eyes.

"Did he not make it out of the Dome? Come on, guys, say something!" I began to plead, worrying for my newfound cousin.

"He's the reason we had to leave," Willian spat. "I found him outside the Dome maybe an hour after you left using his ring to summon purple-hued magic, which we all know is only used by Rhydin's Followers. It was easy to figure out what he was doing. We evacuated immediately."

My eyes narrowed. "I don't believe you. Why would he do that?"

"Does it matter why? He used Rhydin's magic, end of story!" Chretien declared, the oldest of us all, even if by only three minutes as Willian's twin.

My brother sighed. "Don't forget, Rayna. Someone ratted out Conriin's pocket right after we got there, too."

My skin bristled. Erikin had claimed someone had followed us from Canis, even though it seemed impossible at the time. My mind brought back the last time I'd seen Erikin just yesterday, the look of guilt written plainly on his face, as well as that black-studded ring he'd always worn. He couldn't have betrayed us all...could he?

All of a sudden, the horses leading the sea of people came to a halt. No words were said, but people everywhere sank to the ground exhausted after a day and a half of marching. Bread was soon broken, and the spicy smell of jerky reached my nose. Even the Royal children were withdrawing the same from their pouches. I hoped Lunaka Castle truly had all the food and supplies that it was rumored to have, or we weren't going to last very long with winter coming.

"Rayna?"

I turned at the sound of my papa's voice. He had just dismounted his horse, realizing I had appeared behind him. He looked weary, dark circles under his eyes. "When did you get here? Where's your mother?"

I repeated everything I had told Ky. Papa's face fell when I said Mama wasn't here, and he became anxious when I said she would be here as soon as possible, hopefully with help from the Aatarilecs. My stomach growled loudly, and his warm eyes went directly to my empty hands. He started to offer me his meager meal, and I lifted my hands to stop him when King Frederick beat me to it.

"Here, allow me," King Frederick said softly, giving my father a knowing look. They had been riding next to each other. The King of Lunaka tore his bread in half and divided his jerky as he stepped forward to give me the larger pieces. I hesitated, before he added, "Please, eat. I do not need it."

Nathia eyed me suspiciously as I accepted the food from King Frederick and took a huge bite of bread, working it down my throat in a big lump. We hadn't gotten to eat breakfast this morning in the Dome since the dozens of rebel chickens and their eggs had vanished, so my stomach was roaring. Taisyn's mother, Queen Mira, proffered up most of her food for her son, and he ate, too.

"Your Majesties," Arii announced, his hands folded neatly at his center, "there is something of which I must inform you as soon as possible. Privately."

The kings and queens all looked a bit surprised, but they moved off the road into the woods a bit where they would not be overheard. Arii herded my father with them, and Papa walked as if he had a hundred-pound weight around his neck. Uncle Evan looked at him funny as he followed, and I began to wonder if there was something more than the abrupt move bothering him.

I sat on the ground and positioned myself so I could watch the Council react to the news of Rhydin Caldwell. My sweet and earthy bread was gone almost instantly, so I started to nibble on my jerky, which had been salted a mite too much. I watched each of the Royals' faces as Arii said the words. I expected them all to react a bit differently, but interestingly, each of them reacted in the exact same way. Wide eyes, gaping mouths. Soon, arguing followed. I couldn't say I blamed them. We were challenging a widely-held belief that was a few hundred years old.

"What are they talking about?" Willian asked, his mouth full of bread.

Ky, Aron, and the other Royal children looked to Taisyn and I. I decided to just go for it. "Emperor Rhydin is an Einanhi. He stole all his power from the real Rhydin Caldwell, and with all his magic gone, he's been stuck invisible in the Archimage Palace all this time."

They all blinked at me. Chretien mumbled skeptically, "Surely you're joking."

"Nope," I said as I popped the last of my jerky in my mouth and licked my fingers. "I saw him. Once my magic activated. He talked to me."

"You got your magic!" Dominick smiled happily, dimples appearing in his cheeks. "Congratulations. Your training can begin now."

Nathia rolled her eyes dramatically.

"Thanks," I grinned, making sure Nathia could see it. "I'm hoping my uncle can teach me a few things before this battle. I want to be able to protect myself."

"Speaking of which," Lyla suddenly piped up as she tied back her copper tresses and turned to Taisyn, "I've got some stuff I want to teach you. I'm not letting you walk into this with nothing, no matter what Father says."

Taisyn's fingers glowed briefly, and he patted his little sister's shoulder in thanks.

The Royals were coming back from their private meeting. All of us kids watched them, knowing our parents better than anyone else. Some of their expressions were unreadable. Even King Xavier had lost his usual fire and seemed stumped more than anything else. Papa looked lost, and Uncle Evan walked past him, looking more determined than ever, and right up to me. He said, "Let's go into the woods. We'll be stopped for less than an hour, and you have a lot to learn."

I nodded numbly and jumped to my feet. We walked pretty much to the same spot where all the adults had just been, and Uncle Evan eyed the piece of the Allyen locket visible around my neck. "I see Lina gave you your piece of the locket. Did she tell you how it works?"

"U-Uh," I stammered uncomfortably, "it's an amplifier. It helps focus my magic and make it stronger."

"Good," Uncle Evan replied, his golden Allyen eyes fierce. "I'll warn you now, my magic training was conducted for the most part by King Daniel of Auklia, Sabine's cousin who died in the same battle Archimage Dathian did. His teaching method was intense, but it allowed me to learn quickly. We do not have much time."

My brow furrowed. What did he mean?

"Do you feel the warmth in the center of your chest beneath your locket?" Uncle Evan asked as he spread his legs shoulder-width apart and let his arms hang by his side.

I searched for it mentally, and sure enough, there it was. A small feeling of heat radiating under my sternum. "Yes."

"You will want to focus on that whenever you muster your power in the beginning. It makes it easier until you get the hang of it," Uncle Evan explained, still in the odd position. "Try to focus that warmth into your hand."

I did as I was told, although I wasn't sure what he meant. My unease meant that nothing happened, so I tried to picture my mother with a golden orb of light magic in her hand. I just wanted to see it, to know that it was real.

After a few minutes of focusing and trying not to think about all the Royal children just a short distance away likely watching, the tiniest of sparks appeared in the palm of my hand and grew into the size of an apple. Heat pulsed through my whole body from head to toe now, and I felt ecstatic.

"I did it!" I exclaimed exuberantly, cupping my precious orb, but the moment was cut short when another ball of golden energy whizzed past my shoulder, a long tail of light trailing after it.

There was another orb in Uncle Evan's hand by the time I looked up, and I suddenly realized what he meant about the intense introduction to magic. He chucked it at my head, and I ducked, flinging my own weak charge at him. It didn't quite make it to him, but I found that my next spell appeared in my hand faster than the first one had. I focused more on this one, building it larger until it was the size of a crabapple, and I threw it harder. This time, it did make it all the way to my uncle, but he crossed his arms in front of him into a glowing "x" shape. My spell bounced right off his arms with a blast of light.

The edges of my mouth turned upward. Now I knew how to block.

The rest of the lunch hour went by rapidly. I was flinging attack spells left and right at my uncle and also blocking his advances by the end of what time we had. While I doubted that battle would be as neat as just the two of us going back and forth, I felt a lot more ready than I had this morning. I could actually help my family fight now rather than be a burden. My anxiety was replaced by relief.

I was sweating and breathing hard as we walked back to the road and the rebels, wading through inches of dead and browning leaves. Uncle Evan acted like maybe he'd power-walked for a mile, nothing more, while I felt like I'd just run a marathon. He chuckled at the sight of me, "When we have more time, I'll start teaching you how to use a sword and magic at the same time. For now, though, here's this."

Uncle Evan strutted up to his horse and withdrew not the sword I was hoping for but a shiny dagger. It had a decent length to it, but nothing remotely what I'd imagined wielding in my first battle. The handle was curved with a beautiful swirling design as Uncle Evan handed it to me, its hilt wrapped in red like my mother's sword, I remembered.

My uncle said quietly, the two of us hidden behind his horse from other eyes, "This is only for an emergency. During this battle, I expect you to aid from a distance. No one-on-one combat. Battles are messy, though, so this is only for if you're close enough to use it."

"To...to kill?" I asked, my fingers holding the dagger starting to feel numb.

"Anymore, seventy to eighty percent of Rhydin's armies are Einanhis. It's not really killing. They'll just turn into sand if you deliver a mortal blow. Nothing to worry about," Uncle Evan explained calmly. It sounded like he'd given this speech before. "They don't even look very human anymore."

My eyes traveled to my toes. Everyone around us was packing up and getting ready to march again. Uncle Evan hoisted his short, stocky frame into his saddle and was about to rejoin his wife and the other adults when I asked again, trying to keep my voice from shaking, "Uncle Evan...? What about the death spell? We didn't practice that. I've practiced it without magic, but-..."

Uncle Evan held up a hand to interrupt me. "I know. We do not anticipate Rhydin's showing up at this battle. *Emperor* Rhydin, that is." His face soured. He was struggling with the new truth, but I could also tell that having to use the title made him angry. "We'll practice the death spell more later, after the battle and when Lina returns."

I nodded uncertainly, but even if he had said yes to practicing that, our time was up. The rebellion was on the move again. Papa's chestnut stallion paced over to me, snorting in my bewildered face, and he reached toward me without a word. Last time I was nose to nose with one of these creatures, I almost died. However, I accepted Papa's hand and hauled myself up into his saddle, tired from the intense magic training. I sat in front of him where I could see, and he wrapped his lanky arms around me.

I'd never been on a horse before, but within an hour, the horse's long strides no longer felt jarring. There were a few other horses spread throughout the moving mass of people, but the majority of them were definitely carrying Royals or other leaders. Most of the other Royal children rode with their parents now after marching all morning. Even Taisyn sat behind his father in his Mineraltin green saddle. Ky seemed content to walk, but after another hour went by, he clambered onto the back of Papa's horse.

Feeling the two of them behind me, I ardently hoped that I had gotten just enough of a hold on my magic to be able to help them. They were both powerful Rounans, but I certainly didn't want to be a burden.

I quickly lost track of time, the rocking of the horse's steps lulling me to something between waking and sleeping, but my father abruptly stiffened to rock behind me. His reaction brought me forward, and I blinked my eyes several times to clear them. We had left the safety of the forest for the openness of the Lunakan prairie. We were the tallest things as far as the eye could see as our horses waded through grasses nearly up to their bellies.

Well, almost.

To our east was a gigantic canyon unlike anything I'd ever seen. Several plumes of smoke in variable sizes slowly lifted out of the canyon, telling me there was a city down there. One tower of smoke was significantly larger than the rest, and I had heard people talk of the mines of Solăna so I could only assume it was from those. Papa was staring south toward the opposite side of the canyon, and I wondered where his childhood home was. When I turned back toward where we were headed, my eyes found none other than Lunaka Castle.

It looked different than I expected, although I'd never seen a castle so I wasn't sure what to expect. It seemed that Rhydin's Followers had built an extra wall around the castle and its moat, and that wall was darker in color with several purple banners decorated with Emperor Rhydin's insignia. A gold flame with red in the center. Only Rhydin's flags flew, no Lunakan flags to be seen.

My eyes drifted to King Frederick momentarily. His face was like pale stone; his eyes glued to his former home. Queen Mira and Princess Cornflower, his sisters, looked like they might weep. I didn't know how long it had been since they'd been there last, but I could only guess it'd been a while.

The rest of the long trail of rebels gathered around us as we came to a stop directly west of the castle. It was a longer walk, since we'd approached from the southwest, but I imagined we didn't want to get pinned between the fortress and the canyon. We stayed a healthy distance away from the exterior castle wall, well out of reach of any bows. The Royals were silent as they studied the castle and how many dozens of glinting helmets shone upon the ramparts in the afternoon sun, representing so many more inside.

As they did so, the people began to prepare. The soldiers made sure that their armor was belted on and snug, their swords and other weapons sharp and in place. The elderly and the children started to gather at the back of our mob, and yet again, I wondered what would happen if we lost. There were dozens of Ranguvariians within our group, the ones that stayed in the Dome at all times. It was now that I realized that Arii was no longer with us, and I hoped he was bringing reinforcements from the Ranguvariian Camp.

Papa let Ky and I down from his horse, and he slid off with a bit of effort. He pulled us both in to his chest, smothering us. He whispered as he clutched us close, "Stay back here until your mother arrives with help. If she doesn't, this isn't a battle to be part of."

Both Ky and I pushed against him, our eyes pleading. Ky said, "I want to help! I'm fourteen, I'm not a child! I can fight!"

"I know you can." Papa smiled sadly. "If we fail today, I am counting on you to fight tomorrow." Papa suddenly swallowed hard, like his throat was bothering him. "You will make a great Kidek, Ky, if I fall today. I know you will make me proud."

Ky may have been fourteen, but even he couldn't keep it together after that.

"You're not going to die," I said firmly, my grip tightening on his sleeve. "You are the Kidek. You are the most powerful Rounan ever. Therefore, you *can't* die."

Papa touched my shoulder. "I wish that were true, Rayna." He pulled me in for a second hug, just me. "I am so glad you are my daughter. I am honored to have been your father, young Allyen."

"Papa, stop," I begged him, blinking the tears away from my eyes. "We will all see each other again *soon*."

"I hope so," Papa replied, flashing me a smile that I couldn't read. It was then that horns began to sound. Papa tightened his breastplate and the guards on his arms, tucking in his chainmail. I eyed the hilt of his sword as he strapped it to his waist, ensuring that he did so securely.

Ky and I were ushered away from the adults too soon. Papa waved at us before he turned to join the ranks of the other soldiers, heading to the frontline where the kings and queens were. The other Royal children created a wave around us, flowing against the grain of the flood of soldiers where we found James and Mathiian. I understood that we were all the future if this went south, but I would have given anything to be up there with the rest of them.

King Frederick turned around to give a speech I could not hear, his voice carried away by the Lunakan wind. Papa was atop his horse again, saying other words to the Rounans of the rebellion. Separate speeches to separate peoples. It seemed dumb to me, but that was an issue for another time. The scale of everything in front of my eyes was unbelievable. But as the old flags of the Three Kingdoms raised and the soldiers suddenly thundered toward Lunaka Castle in a gigantic herd, my rapid breathing was all I could hear.

CHAPTER SIXTEEN

LINA

P anic set in. We hadn't even passed the Aatarilecs' threshold, and I desperately needed air. Dark waters surrounded me on all sides, and the light above was much too far away. I tore at Conriin desperately, barely able to see him, when Chelsea suddenly swam forward, transformed into her true, Aatarilec form. She speedily summoned a green orb of magic with her clawed fingers, which looked more like goop than anything else, and then she threw her hand over my nose and mouth almost like she was going to smother me.

The sticky, magical blob clung to my face like a mask and just in time, too. My lungs gave out, expelling whatever air I had left, which blew the green goop out into a small bubble. Magic glowed within the goop like the veins of a leaf, and when I inhaled out of extinct, fresh air entered my lungs. It smelled moldy and sour, but I'd never appreciated oxygen more. I took several deep breaths until I felt normal again, mumbling a mostly coherent "thank you" to Chelsea.

"We need to go," Chelsea said, her words distorted by the water. Obviously, she and Conriin didn't require any assistance to breathe underwater. "The longer we linger here, the more attention we will attract."

For a split second, the three of us looked around at each other. Which one of us should lead – the human, the banished heiress, or the guy that looked more like their worst enemies than them?

"Follow me," Chelsea announced, her mint-green hair floating high above her head. "Try not to start a fight until we get inside."

The Aatarilec turned, the vaguest amount of light flashing along her lavender skin, and began to swim into the coral-lined cave. I followed her, performing the very best swimming strokes I could muster after my limited lessons in the pond back home, and Conriin covered our rear, kicking off his boots to swim better.

The first half of the tunnel was completely dark and empty. It was as twisted as I imagined the tunnels of an ant hill were, and I just kept swimming after the brief glimpses I sometimes got of Chelsea's clawed feet. The Aatarilec goop over my nose and mouth kept doing the trick, its magic filtering my used air over and over. Every kid at some point in their lives dreamed of being able to breathe underwater, but I had to kick my exhilaration to the curb with the reminder that we were about to enter a snake nest.

Slowly, I realized that there was more and more light. Then, at the next corner, the previously black, plain tunnel was laden with glowing crystals of every color along the rounded walls. It was the most beautiful thing I had ever seen, and I fought the urge to swim up to one and touch it.

As if reading my thoughts, Chelsea warned, "Don't touch those. They suck the life out of intruders."

My arms and legs immediately tucked closer to my body. I was just hoping that we wouldn't run into anyone in this stretch of tunnel when Chelsea suddenly swam forward much faster, her claws locking with those of another Aatarilec. I tried to straighten myself within the tunnel, my toes touching earth between the death crystals, and I drew my sword. My arms were heavy in the water, and my sword was slow to move. It abruptly made sense why Aatarilecs didn't use weapons, because they didn't help Conriin, who was clawless, or I any at all.

Chelsea rapidly knocked out the Aatarilec ahead of us and waved us forward, faster now. However, it wasn't long before we ran into more opponents. I relied more upon my magic than I usually would, which thankfully operated mostly the same underwater. The real trick was trying not to kill any of them. We wanted to work together, not annihilate them.

Chelsea seemed to know something that we didn't know, so she kept pushing forward, flinging Aatarilec after Aatarilec against the sides of the tunnels where the crystals seemed to only stun them since they weren't invaders. Conriin and I started doing the same, but Conriin was having a terrible time continuing to swim forward with dazed Aatarilec warriors scrambling to catch up to him. I was wondering how long this could possibly continue until before I knew it, there was light at the end of the tunnel.

We all suddenly burst through water into open air. We were instantly on our feet, and I scraped the goop off my face before my blade caught an Aatarilec's claws. I swung and parried for a second blow before catching the Aatarilec on the back of her head with the flat of my sword. She fell over, woozy, before several other miniature imps took her place.

Here, however, in the air, I was in my element. The weight of my sword was familiar to me again, and I seamlessly knocked warrior after warrior out of commission with a blow to the head or by tripping them up. Conriin and Chelsea, too, fought Aatarilec after Aatarilec, doing their best not to seriously hurt them if at all possible. All the while, I tried to keep my amazement to myself. I had simply never *seen* so many Aatarilecs! However, this only lasted so long, and it was all too soon before we were surrounded by hundreds of the little water creatures.

"Stop."

The single word was spoken calmly and quietly, yet every one of the hundreds of Aatarilecs ceased herding us into a smaller circle. An orange-haired male snorted in my face, trying to hold himself back, golden rings in his nose. My attention shifted to the back of the room where dozens of colored, silk curtains stringed with gold hung from an extremely high ceiling. Green plant life was all around, thriving in the sticky warmth of this strange air bubble under the sea.

Plopped upon a large, stone pedestal was none other than Chieftess Jaana herself, and her wicked eyes narrowed at the sight of Chelsea, her daughter. As the Aatarilec warriors around us didn't give up a single inch, she asked annoyedly, "What do you want, human? What makes you think you can enter our sacred grotto?"

"We need your help!" I declared from across the room, my voice echoing. "The rebellion is getting ready to attack Lunaka Castle as we speak, and we will not succeed without help from you. Our numbers are not enough, but with your support, this could be our greatest victory against Rhydin in years!"

Chieftess Jaana rocked her head back and forth as I spoke, her spiky, green hair bobbing, like she had heard it all before and didn't care. She rasped, "But what makes you humans *worthy* of my help? My people lie tucked away from Rhydin's influence and have no blood in your battles."

I hesitated. Again, the question I didn't really know how to answer. Chelsea found my eyes, and she gave a reassuring nod. I took a deep breath and answered the best I knew how, my words gaining momentum as I did. "I am Allyen Linaria Greene of Lunaka. I am the one who slayed Duunzer, Rhydin's Einanhi dragon, that threatened to consume all of Nerahdis almost two decades ago. If I had not, the Aatarilecs would still be lost in its Darkness, which took hold of all Nerahdis and made everyone sleep. I can show you the scar on my leg where Duunzer's entire talon pierced through if you do not believe me."

Chieftess Jaana sat back on her pedestal. Several of the older Aatarilecs gazed at me with wide eyes, obviously remembering those dark days.

"After Duunzer came the war," I said, unable to stop telling my own history, "the unprecedented War of the Three Kingdoms. Your daughter told me you have an overfishing problem, and I'm sure Auklia's war effort drained the seas more than any other era. I helped bring that war to an end, but not in the way I ever wished. I regret not seeing Rhydin as the Liberator, turning the people to his cause so that he could become emperor after the war, but it was me and my friends who showed the people his true colors. Now, we have a real chance of taking something big back from him: Lunaka Castle. The beginning of the end."

"So, I should send all my warriors with you because you defeated Duunzer years ago and allowed Rhydin to become emperor?" Chieftess Jaana asked snidely.

Anger rose in my chest. I squashed my hesitancy to speak of the amazing things I had done. "You should help us because I not only freed you all from certain death in the Darkness, but also because I am the first human to ever set foot inside this place without killing a single one of you. If anyone is worthy of your help, it is me."

The chieftess remained silent. All the Aatarilecs fidgeted around me, and several lowered their claws a few inches. Chelsea beamed with pride.

"The new queen of Auklia is my friend," I continued on. "I can promise you that the overfishing of Auklia's basin and the other oceans will cease in return for one thing."

"You are begging for my help, and now you dare to ask for a request?" Chieftess Jaana hissed, rising from her pedestal in an angry tizzy.

"I am worthy of your help on my own merit," I barked, finally sheathing my sword. "I promise you the compliance of

Queen Sabine in exchange for the un-banishment of your daughter."

Chelsea gaped at me, her golden eyes round with fear. Nevertheless, she turned in the direction of her mother, anxiously awaiting her answer.

Chieftess Jaana glared at me fiercely for a few seconds, then a smile curled across her impish face. "You strike a hard bargain, Allyen Linaria. I accept both terms."

Euphoria flooded me. *I did it!* Not only had I secured the numbers needed to help my cause, but I had fulfilled an eleven-year-old promise to help Chelsea return to her home in exchange for helping protect my children in Caark. Chelsea looked so happy she could cry, especially as Aatarilecs around her welcomed her home, calling her "Onna" again. I couldn't stop smiling as I gushed, "Thank you, Chieftess Jaana!"

The chieftess nodded, a nice smile gracing her lips for once, her various beads clinking. Then, she started bellowing orders in a screeching language I couldn't understand, and the Aatarilecs around us scurried away, readying for war on land. They reappeared wearing more armor made of thick leather with a few spears and daggers, the first time I'd seen Aatarilecs with real weapons. They all began to line up, the hair colors on their short heads like a rainbow as they rushed forward to the submerged stairs we had come up, disappearing line by line into a myriad of green flashes of light.

Chelsea worked her way toward me, her eyes brimming with gratitude. "Go with Conriin! I will follow soon once I have talked to my mother."

"I understand. See you soon!" I replied, and before I knew it, Conriin was rushing me forward into the line of Aatarilecs waiting to depart. He grabbed my arm and pulled me back into the water, and thankfully we weren't there long because my green, water-breathing goop was long gone. The dark void of transportation was only with us briefly before Conriin suddenly shot out of the Lunakan river to which we'd transported, his small, Ranguvariian wings taking over.

I sputtered and wiped the water out of my eyes, still not used to underwater transportation, but then the earthy, grassy scent of Lunaka entered my lungs. The smell of my home. I instantly felt rejuvenated. Underneath us, hundreds of Aatarilecs were making their way up the winding river, swimming like horses running at top speed. This river would curve to the west and eventually hook up with the moat surrounding Lunaka Castle.

We rapidly left the leaf-less forest behind, its trees reaching toward us like dead fingers, and I briefly caught a glimpse of the canyon where Soläna lay, my childhood home. All my dreams of being able to return and restart the farm with Sam and our children suddenly felt within my grasp. But then, Lunaka Castle appeared over the hill, and my heart clenched with fear.

The battle had begun. The rebels had rushed up to a new exterior wall that hadn't been there the last time I was here, trying to break down the wooden doors with a battering ram they must have brought with them from the forest. Casualties lay around them as they rammed the gate again, and to my horror, the Followers above them on the rampart began to dump cauldrons of hot coals down over their heads. The rebels tried to hold their shields over their heads, withdrawing with their thick log for another go.

"Hurry!" I shouted to the Aatarilecs beneath us, and they responded in a frenzy, speedily turning the river into something like a tidal wave out on the ocean. They raced up the river, the waters rising up out of their channel as they did. When they finally reached the castle moat, the waters were tall enough to reach the ramparts, dousing all the coals and washing away many of Rhydin's soldiers.

The rebels gave out a deafening cheer, and when the wave had passed, they sped forward with their battering ram and busted the exterior doors open. I smiled as I realized that the old, iron gate of the original castle wall was still open, and only seconds passed before hundreds of rebels were pouring inside of Lunaka Castle. The courtyard was quickly a mess, and Conriin circled it for a few moments as I scanned the chaos for Sam. The rebels had caught all of Rhydin's people inside by surprise, and the Aatarilecs were now entering the courtyard, doubling our numbers. I could barely make sense of what was going on, but when my eyes caught a flash of gold, I told Conriin to take me down.

Conriin dropped me into the thick of it, maybe halfway between the iron gate and the courtyard doors leading inside. I rolled with the momentum and drew my sword, immediately reducing two Einanhis in prim, black uniforms to sand. I fiercely fought my way over toward the gold I had seen from above, Frederick's hair, while also trying to look around for Sam the best I could. The courtyard was total bedlam. No sense could be made of the sea of bodies, half in black and half in a hodge-podge of colors.

Frederick was surrounded by four Einanhis that were slowly cutting him off from the rest of the fighting, despite his best efforts. He charged gale after gale of wind magic, but they blocked every blast. I summoned a golden orb of light magic into each hand and chucked them at the two Einanhis on either side of him. Then, I seamlessly halved the one between us, sand spilling forth. With my help, Frederick was able to spin and tuck his sword under his arm, stabbing the last Einanhi behind him. He bellowed over the roar of battle, the silver crown of wheat shining bright on his head, "I see you were successful!"

"Surprisingly! Come on, we need to get into that castle!" I shouted back. "If we don't get their leaders, this will never end! There has to be at least one human here leading them."

Frederick nodded in agreement and ran toward the courtyard wall, blocking blows from Einanhis with his sword and gusts of wind as he went. I followed him, and he led me up a side staircase that nobody else seemed to have noticed. Of course, if anyone knew how to get into Lunaka Castle unnoticed, it'd be the prince who grew up here.

Once upon the rampart, we kept our heads low and rushed toward the main body of the castle. Behind the base of one of the spires was a small window with a wooden cover that Frederick speedily kicked in. As he crouched and tried to fit his wiry frame inside, I couldn't help but chuckle, "You're a bit bigger than the last time you snuck out, huh?"

"Oh, stop it," Frederick groaned as he ultimately pulled himself through by practically lying down. "I haven't used this since I was a boy!"

I ducked and scurried through after him. A strange, empty echo entered my ears now that we were inside, the sounds from the battle muffled. We stood in an upstairs hallway that was cool and dark, none of the usual lanterns or chandeliers lit. Frederick's sword pointed to the floor as he looked around his old home, and I began to feel probably only half as sick as Frederick did.

The portraits and tapestries were slashed, the furniture broken into kindling, and anything else that once was precious to the Lunakan Royals was destroyed beyond recognition. Frederick's boyhood home, the castle I once defended tooth and nail against Duunzer, had become a place of horrors I didn't recognize.

"Frederick," I whispered, feeling the tick of time as the battle raged on outside. "Frederick, we need to go."

He continued to stand there, horrorstruck. The King of Lunaka surveying the destruction of the castle to which he'd always vowed to return

"Frederick, I *promise* we'll fix it, okay? But we need to take it back first," I said again, more firmly this time. I reached out and touched his arm, right at the crook of his elbow. "Come on."

The king finally looked me with those blue eyes of his, and he nodded. Then, he hurried off down the hallway with me fast on his trail. As we approached the center of the fortress, the hallways began to be lined with crates. Box after box of supplies, nonperishable food, and weapons. All the rumors we had ever heard about Lunaka Castle's supply had not only been true, but they existed in such number that it was nauseating.

These, too, we would put to right, I promised myself. No one in the rebellion or in Soläna would ever go hungry again.

We combed hallway after hallway, room after room, for anybody at all. The magical compass in my head was coming up empty for so long that it felt like hours until finally three little pings appeared as we neared the throne room. Frederick glanced at me, and I could tell that he sensed them too. I took a deep breath as we neared the large door between us and the throne room, adjusting my hands upon the hilt of my sword. Frederick eyed me, his hand on the handle. My teacher, my friend. Unlike every other battle I'd been in, I didn't know who all stood behind this door.

Frederick shoved the door open rapidly, his sword outstretched, ready for anything. Once he had a foot inside the door, I moved to his flank. The room was difficult to scan; it was so dark. The great, iron chandelier with weary, white candlesticks was extinguished. Some light came in through the lead windows toward the ceiling, but the sun was beginning to go down outside. I almost thought that this room was unchanged before I saw the upended thrones, their gold frames fallen down the stairs of the dais.

For a brief moment, I remembered King Adam, Frederick's father and my first foe, as well as his poor wife, Queen Gloria. They had both been killed during the Crushing of the Thrones, the day Rhydin executed all the remaining Royals, even the ones working for him like King Adam. I had hated King Adam and everything he stood for so much. But those thrones were Frederick's now, and it was my job to right them.

I was just about to think that my senses were wrong when suddenly the chandelier above our heads was lit with a few blasts of purple magic that came from beyond the toppled thrones. With the new wave of light, I could see the dust and grime covering every surface, a far cry from the last time I'd seen this place as a young woman, decorated to the nines with flowers for the spring festival.

Frederick gave a small gasp, and I turned my eyes in the same direction as his. Standing upon the dais, their weapons drawn, were two men and a woman. While one of them I immediately realized was Emperor Rhydin's Einanhi decoy, its magical signature in my head only a tiny fraction of what I knew the actual Emperor Rhydin's to be, the other two instantly ignited an old hatred I couldn't quench.

Kino, the woman who murdered my father, hadn't aged well in the last decade. Whenever we went on any mission, some part of me always kept my eyes peeled for her. The scene played over in my mind all the time. Her spear killing my father before we could complete the death spell the last time there were three Allyens. I had vowed to avenge him, but it looked like more than one serving of justice would come today.

Standing next to her and the decoy was none other than Mikael, whom I hadn't seen for far longer. He was only a teenager when he kidnapped my sister, Rosetta, tricking me into thinking she had died along with Keera, our cousin. Rosetta helped Sam and I escape Rhydin's prison tower during the war, determined to save her lost love, which obviously hadn't happened. For all I cared, he had tricked her into loving him. He stood before us now a fully-grown man, although still with a freckled face. He was tall, and his brown hair was shaved close to his skull.

I no longer knew which of them I hated most.

Anger flaring, I dug around in my belt for a throwing knife and chucked it hard at the speed of lightning. Kino and Mikael both raised their blades, only to be surprised when the small dagger embedded itself into the chest of the Rhydin decoy. The Einanhi instantly dissolved into sand, leaving only the two humans left.

Now, it was two against two.

"What a wonderful day!" I exclaimed furiously, pointing my sword in two of my worst enemies' direction. "Two of the people I hate most will finally get what they deserve. Too bad Rhydin isn't here, then you'd all be in one place!"

"He will be here soon!" Kino cackled, her ombre hair now thinning. "He would never allow one of his strongholds to fall!"

"I wouldn't be too sure about that," Frederick answered calmly, his hands holding his sword tightly. "With the Aatarilecs here, any reinforcements he sends in will just get destroyed. We've won."

"Not yet," Kino crooned, glancing at her nails momentarily before she swiftly threw a blade in my direction and rushed toward me.

My sword clashed with hers, an ugly, screeching sound echoing through the throne room. We hit and parried multiple times, my anger threatening to implode with every strike. We danced the dance of warfare, both of us quiet as we focused. I took every opening I could, and I managed to wound her shoulder within minutes.

"You're half the fighter you used to be, Kino," I galled her as she jumped away from me. I charged a golden orb into my hand and fired several shots at her flanks, keeping her from running away. "What's wrong? You don't think I'm fighting fair, do you?"

Kino's one, visible eye beyond her greasy bangs widened. Frederick and Mikael had begun to spar on the opposite side of the throne room, appearing to be pretty evenly matched.

"Because you certainly didn't fight fair with my father when you drove a *spear* into his chest when he wasn't even near you!" I shouted, beginning to lose control. I rushed toward her, clipping her on either side to keep her in one place, and she backed into the stone wall.

"He was a traitor!" Kino cried, her back pressed tightly against the wall now. "He deserved it!"

Just as I reached her, a gigantic gust of wind flooded the throne room, and Mikael was sent flying off his feet. Frederick went after him, and I crouched down to keep from sliding. Kino saw it as an opportunity to run, dashing along the wall toward the hallway that led deeper into the labyrinthine castle.

No. I thought instantly. Panic made my ribs hot. My chance to avenge my father was rapidly disappearing. Before I could think another thought, I sprinted after her, firing all kinds of magic at her back. The few that happened to make contact only left little burning circles in her cloak.

As Kino turned the first corner, I desperately dug around for any daggers I had left and flung them with all my might once I also made the turn. One of them clipped her shoulder. One of them missed entirely. And the last one dived deep into her ribs.

Kino shrieked, and her run fell apart, her legs staggering until she finally fell in the middle of the hallway. I hurried up to her, suddenly mortified at what I had done. I had fired at a fleeing opponent's back.

Blood seeped from my old enemy's mouth, and she sputtered bitterly, "A-Are you happy now?"

She quit moving. Breath left her. After it did, I answered, "No."

I paused for a moment, staring at her. Did I really accomplish anything? Was I any better than her now?

"*Lina!*" Frederick's voice bellowed down the hallway in echoes, which finally stirred me from being frozen in place. I left all my knives where they lay and snatched up my sword, hoping something could redeem me from what I had done.

When I reached the throne room, Mikael had Frederick flat on the ground. He knelt upon the king, his hand in Frederick's golden hair wrenching his head upward with his blade at his throat. I ran as close as I dared until Mikael snarled, "Don't come any closer!"

This. This was an opportunity to do things differently. I said softly, "Mikael, please don't do this. You have a choice.

Let Frederick go, and I will make sure that you can live in peace."

"There is no peace with you rebels!" Mikael scowled, hefting Frederick's neck higher off the ground and closer to his blade. "Nerahdis will never have peace until *all* the Royals are gone! I must finish what Emperor Rhydin started at the Crushing of the Thrones."

Mikael's sword pressed against Frederick's pale neck, and my friend cringed and struggled to get away from it. I reached out with my sword-less hand, carefully creeping forward inch by inch. "Mikael, stop! Please! Your son is with my children. He is safe! You can get away from the rebellion and Rhydin. You, Rosetta, and Erikin. Don't you want that?" I pleaded.

There was absolutely no wavering in his dark eyes, and I saw his murderous intent deep within them. There was no fear, as there had been in Kino's eyes. He drew in a breath, about to respond and likely finish the deed upon Frederick's neck.

Before a single word could escape his mouth, I darted forward, charging one magical shot at the arm that held his sword and another at his opposite shoulder, meaning to knock him off of Frederick. His sword dropped harmlessly away as I had intended, but with the loss of that weight, his body shifted, which caused my second attack to go straight through his unguarded heart.

Mikael fell slowly to the smooth, dusty floor, his life instantly gone.

I'd killed my own brother-in-law. I fell backwards, the fight knocked out of me. First, I'd killed someone who was fleeing, and now I'd killed the man my sister loved? I started to lose control of my breathing, my sword dropping to the floor with a *clang*.

What had I done?

Frederick coughed, touching his intact throat gingerly. He crawled over to me, placing a shaking hand on my shoulder. "Lina…it's okay," he croaked, "you did what you had to do. He didn't give you any choice."

"B-But how will I explain to my s-sister that I killed her husband? To Erikin that I killed his f-father?" I stammered breathily, clutching my knees tightly.

"If you hadn't, I would be dead, Lina," Frederick pleaded, placing both hands on my shoulders now. "There was no mercy in him. Regardless of what happens, you did the right thing."

"What about Kino?" I asked, a frog developing in my throat. "I killed her as she ran from me."

Frederick gave a large sigh. It was clear he didn't know what to say. Instead, he was the usual Frederick and said, "What's done is done. We can only move forward from this point and do the best we can."

I nodded numbly, slowly realizing that I could hear cheering coming from outside. The last Einanhi must have fallen, which meant the battle had been won. Frederick tried to smile, but it was tainted by exhaustion and the grim reality of his old home. Lunaka Castle was now ours.

We were just getting to our feet and covering Mikael's body with my cloak when the door to the throne room suddenly slammed open, its crash echoing throughout the silent castle.

Rachel stood there, looking ragged from war, but her expression was not victorious. Her pale face was lined with worry and dirt. She shouted from across the room, "Lina! I've been looking everywhere for you! Please, you have to come quickly!"

"Why, what's wrong?" I asked, confused. "Isn't the battle won?"

"Yes, but…" Rachel cried, guilt creeping into her blue eyes. Abruptly appearing like one who hated herself, she sighed fearfully, "It's Sam."

CHAPTER SEVENTEEN

RAYNA

My mouth gaped as my mother arrived at the battle leading hundreds of Aatarilecs. The myriad of colorful, water creatures summoned a gigantic, crested wave within the river that washed away all the obstacles facing our people at the gate.

The second the rebels' battering ram split the wooden door of Lunaka Castle's exterior wall, I propelled myself forward to the dismay of James and Mathiian, who had been watching the Royal children. I sprinted back through the camp the rebels had hastily made before the battle, leaping over rucksacks and pots. A small, cracked shield made of wood lay in the grass on the edge of the camp, and I snatched it up as I passed.

The rebels were all inside the courtyard when I reached it, battling hundreds of blank humanoids in black. Uncle Evan was right, very few of the Einanhis actually looked human anymore. I held my shield up defensively as I entered the chaotic space between the exterior wall and the front gate of the castle, keeping my back close to the wall and away from the dozens of duels going on nearby.

Conriin dropped my mother off inside the courtyard, a stone barrier between us, and soon she and King Frederick were rushing around up on the rampart likely to go do something important. Instead of trying to catch up with her, I continued to scan the ruckus for my father, desperate to help him. I would have never dreamed just a couple months ago that my parents' fight could turn into a battle of this scale. All of the presences in my head made me feel like I was drowning.

"What are you doing?"

I nearly jumped out of my skin and turned to see Taisyn, who had followed me. "I need to help my father! He was talking like he might not come back! Get out of here, Taisyn, you don't have to be here!"

"If you're here, then I do," Taisyn answered simply, loudly over the roar of swords. His unseeing eyes felt like they were staring right at me.

I found myself blushing. What did that mean?

Shaking that thought of my head, I asked quickly, "Can you find my father in this mess? With your magic? I can't weed out all these people in my head, I haven't had enough practice."

Without a word, Taisyn's fingers began to glow the usual warm, red color, and it was only a few moments before he took my hand and said, "This way!"

The blind, Mineraltin prince guided me through the battlefield, between all the different clusters of people fighting for their lives, toward the bridge that somehow hadn't been wiped out by the Aatarilecs' massive wave. We crossed the now nearly dry moat and squeezed through the iron, second gate into the courtyard. As people continued to fight and shout, my ears roaring, I was beginning to wonder how long this battle would last.

"There!" Taisyn shouted, pointing toward the back corner of the courtyard, just to the left of Lunaka Castle's main entrance.

Sure enough, I saw my father there fighting three Einanhis. I felt relief upon seeing him alive, but that feeling instantly died. His face was bloodless and he was huffing, struggling to keep up. If I didn't get over there quick, there was no telling what might happen.

I tried to pick the shortest path from me to him, ducking under swinging swords. My fingers found the hilt of the dagger Uncle Evan had given me, just in case. Once I was close enough, I charged a magical blast just as Uncle Evan had taught me and flung it at the nearest Einanhi's head. It successfully collided, and the created being was reduced to sand, right before my eyes. I'd never seen an Einanhi die before, but Uncle Evan was sure right. It didn't really feel like I'd done something bad.

Papa panicked at the sight of me, but instead of moving toward me, he fell backward. I ran to him as Taisyn launched a blaze of fire at the other two Einanhis. I crouched over his head, my hand on his chest, and asked anxiously, "Papa? Papa, what's wrong?"

"Get out of here," Papa whispered fiercely, like he couldn't muster anything more. His breaths sounded like they were scraping up and down his throat.

"Rayna!" Taisyn yelled urgently. "Rayna, I need help!"

Not another second to spare, I stood over my fallen father, placing my little, wooden shield over his chest, and started summoning attack spells with both hands, firing them left and right at the two Einanhis between Taisyn and I. Soon, however, more Einanhis began to approach our corner, and my limited understanding of my magic was fading. My powers shifted toward automatic as my life became endangered, and willpower alone seemed to be keeping us all alive.

Suddenly, another figure jumped between me and the nearest Einanhi, a blast of purple power demolishing it into sand before it could even hit the ground. I was sure my eyes deceived me when I recognized my dirty-blond-haired cousin. "Erikin?! What are you doing here?"

"The rebellion left me tied to a tree outside the Dome! It took everything I had just to catch up!" Erikin shouted, and when he turned to face me briefly, his hazel eyes were filled with remorse. "Listen, Rayna, I have to tell you something!"

"Don't bother!" I replied angrily as I chucked another orb of magic at an approaching Einanhi. "Willian told me that *you* were the one who led Emperor Rhydin to the Dome! And Conriin's poor pocket, too! How could you after everything we did for you? And I see you lied about not having any magic! That's Rhydin's magic, isn't it?"

"Rayna, it wasn't what you think!" Erikin tried to argue as he shot a blast of purple magic right through the abdomen of another Einanhi, using only the hand that wore his usual black ring. Then, in a short lull, he faced me and declared, "Yes, it's true. My father sent me to infiltrate a rebel pocket on Emperor Rhydin's orders to find the Dome, and yes, I'm the one who compromised it. He would have *killed* me if I hadn't! But then you all were so nice to me and you saved my life...I never knew you all were *family!* My father gave me this ring so that I could use magic, but I was trying to get *rid* of it when Willian came upon me. Then to make matters worse, my trying to destroy this horrible ring only sent off a signal to my location-...!"

"The Dome," I murmured, finishing his sentence. Then I asked hatefully, "And why should I believe you? It's an awfully tall tale after all the lies you've told!"

"Because I'm your blood, just as you are mine," Erikin answered, huffing with exertion.

Suddenly, the sky above us dimmed. My gaze shot upward, fearful, but it was Clariion Arii whooshing over our heads, leading at least a hundred more Ranguvariians into the fray. The courtyard was filled with a squall as hundreds of wings circled overhead in order to land, and I couldn't help but smile at the sight of their rainbow of colors. The Aatarilecs had tipped the scales in our favor, and now the Ranguvariians had arrived just in time to finish things for good. The remaining Einanhis were being struck down left and right.

Erikin begged again, "Please, Rayna. You're my only hope for the rebellion to believe me. I *never* wanted this!"

In the midst of this turmoil, the sound of cheering jarred me. My gaze shot around the courtyard, and all of the black-clad Einanhis were gone. Piles of sand covered every inch of the dying grass in the courtyard as if we'd all be transported to the Great Desert. Ranguvariians and Aatarilecs, Gornish and Rounan, all celebrated alike.

"Taisyn," I breathed, trying to describe the scene for my blind friend, "the battle is over. There's sand everywhere from all the destroyed Einanhis."

Taisyn sighed in relief several feet away from me, panting as he leaned against his knees. "That's good. I don't know how much longer I would have held out! Do you see my parents?"

"Rayna!" Erikin shouted, aggravated that I hadn't answered him.

I scanned the courtyard-turned-battlefield. "King Xavier is hurrying towards us. He has a bloody shoulder, but he looks fine. Your mother, Queen Mira, is giving instructions to the rebels outside now that we've won."

"I'm probably about to get an earful," Taisyn groaned. "What about your father?"

In fear, I immediately dropped back down to his side. He was still lying on the ground, his breaths rattling, and his hand no longer clutching his sword. I pleaded, "Papa? Papa, wake up! Papa, we won! Are you hurt?"

"R-Rayna," he struggled to say, almost like his throat was gurgling.

"What's going on here?" King Xavier demanded, his icy gaze darting from his son to me and Papa. At the sight of my pale, weakening father, the king dropped to the ground, touching his head and pulling back his eyelids.

"I-Is there anything I can do?" Erikin stammered, his hands fidgeting in front of him.

King Xavier snapped up, suddenly recognizing my cousin. "Guards! Arrest this traitor and take him to the dungeon!"

"W-Wait!" I tried to say, but it was too late. Several soldiers sprinted across the sandy lawn and grabbed onto the boy, wrenching his ring from his finger. Before I could say another word, they were hauling him off toward the castle, fear and desperation written all over his face.

"Sam, what have you done?" King Xavier spat, his hand now on my father's chest. Then he turned and bellowed the exact words I didn't want to hear. "Help! I need a healer *now!*"

"What's wrong with him?" I cried, as Aunt Rachel suddenly appeared around a corner and darted over to us. Her armor was dirty, and her red hair was slick with sweat.

She shook her head at the Mineraltin king, eyeing me warily. "Take him upstairs. Make him comfortable. I need to find Lina."

King Xavier's face fell, and he looked back at Papa's nearly unconscious face, the awful sound of his breathing all I could hear. He moved to pick him up, putting his bloody shoulder to Papa's chest, struggling to lift his six-foot frame.

I began to gasp for air. "I don't understand! He isn't wounded! Why aren't you healing him, Aunt Rachel?!"

"Because he cannot be healed. We've already tried," Aunt Rachel answered, her throat full and her eyes remorseful. I tried to ask her what she could possibly mean by that, but she was already backing away from me, heading toward the front door of the castle. I screamed after her, but it was no use.

King Xavier was now jogging away from us, and my heart tugged toward him, needing to be close to my father like a magnet. I snatched Taisyn's hand and dragged him after me, following the king up a flight of stairs.

Ever so briefly, as we hurried to keep up, the castle hallway shifted. It melted into a different castle hallway, moonlight pouring through the windows, and the décor centuries older.

A different woman's breathing echoed in my ears, but just as quickly as it had appeared, the hallway phased back into the one at Lunaka Castle. I paused briefly, suddenly dizzy.

"Are you okay?" Taisyn asked, concern written all over his face. He reached out in all directions, unable to see why we had stopped.

"I don't know," I answered truthfully, fighting to catch my breath before breaking into a run again.

King Xavier ducked into the first bedroom that wasn't torn apart. We followed, and I watched as the king yanked back the dusty, immaculate covers of the big, four-poster bed and delicately laid my father out upon it, who was covered with the grime of battle. My eyes glued themselves to my father's sweaty, dirt-streaked face, his eyes half-open now, and I threw myself half over the bed to grasp his limp hand.

"Taisyn, come along," King Xavier whispered to his son, holding his hand out to him.

"No, Father. Please let me stay with her," Taisyn replied so softly I hardly heard it.

King Xavier hesitated for a moment, and I didn't see the warring emotions cross his face. "Fine. But once her mother gets here, you need to step outside."

Taisyn must have agreed because I heard the click of the door shutting, and he was the one who came to kneel beside me. He didn't say a word. He didn't touch me. He only stayed right beside me, and that was everything I needed.

Papa's bandana was falling off his head. I tried to fix it, but to my surprise, his other hand struggled upward and dragged it the rest of the way off. I didn't dare think the words that were inching upon my consciousness until they forced themselves in.

I had just found my father, and he was dying.

Emperor Rhydin stood upon the southern Canyonlands, opposite Lunaka Castle. The dying prairie grasses billowed around him in the fierce, Lunakan wind as he watched his purple, imperial banners be stripped from the castle ramparts. The heavy, exterior wall his soldiers had constructed was burned and soaked simultaneously, and Rhydin could only ponder what had happened here. He had been at Mineraltir Castle when word reached him that this stronghold was under attack.

While Rhydin could have easily appeared with hundreds of Einanhi troops to take back Lunaka Castle and squash the rebellion once and for all, he chose not to. The rebellion was gaining sympathizers all over Nerahdis. Rhydin had no clue why. After all, he was in charge of Nerahdis, and therefore all problems should cease to exist. That was exactly what he had been sent out to do, and he had succeeded. Plus, Kino and Mikael had been in charge of protecting this fortress, and their total failure deserved whatever fate had befallen them.

Yes, Rhydin thought, let them think they've won a major battle. Let them grow a little in their power, and let all their sympathizers come out of hiding and join them. *Then* Rhydin would destroy them once and for all, in one fell swoop.

Only then would Nerahdis be at peace, his centuries-old purpose fulfilled.

Rhydin turned away from the smoldering and drenched battlefield across the canyon and toward the abandoned farmstead behind him. The house was blown open, its innards uncannily preserved, its wood scorched and rotting. Gigantic holes were blown into the barn roof, and the entire thing looked ready to collapse in upon itself. Some goats bleated in the distance, somehow still alive after all this time.

This was where every Allyen had ever been born – aside from Nora of course, who had begun her life in the city before what happened to her. The newest one hadn't been born here either, the one they forcibly created, Rhydin reminded himself. This was also the place where Rhydin turned Allyen

Robert to his side. Several of the Allyens had died here, too, as evidenced by the family graveyard on the hill behind the barn. Allyen Saarah's marker was still legible, and Rhydin smirked in remembrance of the day he killed her, when Allyen Linaria's journey was just beginning.

This place, where Allyen Linaria had grown up, had been abandoned for nearly two decades now, and its depravity gave Rhydin a cold joy that not much could match. He didn't know who else happened to lie in this graveyard. Once he had some extra time, he would have to raze the property completely. Wipe the Allyens off the map for good.

Emperor Rhydin used his dark magic to transport away. It was time to make his plans for retaliation.

CHAPTER EIGHTEEN

LINA

Without thinking a single thought, I sprinted out of the throne room and up the stairs, hot on Rachel's heels. I could hear Frederick's paces behind me, but they sounded like they were a million miles away. Rachel shot down the first hallway that branched off from the stairs, and after poking her head into several doors, she finally stopped in front of one, holding her hands up against me. "Now, Lina, I need to talk to you first-…"

"What's wrong with him?" I demanded, trying to push past her, "Was he wounded in the battle?"

"Uh…kind of…? Not really," Rachel sputtered, her hand on the back of her neck as she desperately tried to remain between me and the door. "Sam was supposed to tell you, but the exertion of this surprise battle must have been too much."

"Tell. Me. What?" I shouted, not caring how loud I was. The cacophonous cheering outside was about to break me.

Rachel's blue eyes squeezed shut for a brief moment, like she would have given anything at all to not have to be here in this moment. Then, she answered matter-of-factly, "He was poisoned. A couple months ago. During that skirmish where he was cut-…"

225

"Along his ribs," I finished for her, my eyes growing wide as saucers. I glanced at Frederick, who didn't look very surprised, only concerned. I glared at him, anger beginning to lick my very bones. "You knew, didn't you?"

"W-Well," Frederick stammered, "y-yes, but I haven't known long. He told me on the trip here. I had *no* idea that this would happen if he fought!"

"But you *knew* he was dying and allowed him to fight anyway?!" I became hysterical. "Frederick, how could you do this? I trusted you! *Both* of you!" I added as I glanced between him and Rachel.

"Now, wait a minute!" the king argued, but I was done listening.

"Let me through," I declared to Rachel and tried to push past her. When Rachel continued to stand in my way, my hand automatically found the handle of my blade. I growled, "*Move.*"

Rachel sighed, relinquishing her post, and I blew through the door away from them both. Inside was a dusty bedroom looking mostly untouched. Sam appeared out of place in the large, Royal bed, his colorless face smeared with the dirt of the battlefield, but there at least wasn't any blood that I could see. Rayna was huddled at his side with Taisyn next to her, and I could feel my fury beginning to implode.

"Rayna," I said shortly, trying to keep it together for a few moments more, "go find your brother please. Bring him back, quickly."

My daughter's eyes appeared to beg me otherwise, but she understood. She wrenched herself away from Sam's side and ran out the door with Taisyn as her shadow. Rachel, too, placed her hand on the door knob and drew it closed.

When I heard the click, my gaze shifted back to Sam. My husband of nearly sixteen years. His head was propped on a feather pillow with golden thread, his fading red-brown hair slick with sweat. Most of his body was hidden by the blankets of the bed, so I stalked forward, threw the blankets off his chest and wrenched his tunic up out of his pants. I hadn't seen him without a shirt since the day of his injury; we'd been so busy adapting to life with teenagers in our tent.

That thin, red line over a handful of his ribs I'd seen months ago had bloomed into an ugly, white scar, surrounded by blackened flesh that stretched in every direction along his veins. It almost reminded me of the Epidemic, and nausea overtook me. I threw his shirt back down. I couldn't bear to look at it. I replaced the blankets to where they'd been, but Sam's hand remained uncovered, clutching the bandana that marked him as Kidek. The fact that he had already taken off just made me angrier. How could he just give up?

When his eyes opened halfway, their brown color duller than I'd ever seen, my voice twisted with pain and tears into a scream. *"How could you not tell me?* After *everything* we've been through, all this time?"

Sam's throat bobbed a few times before he spoke, his voice dry and weak, "I-...I couldn't bear to tell you. B-*Because* of everything we've been through...knowing that this time, the battle was already lost."

Whatever control I had left shattered. I threw myself to my knees at his bedside and wailed, "Wh-Why didn't you have the Ranguvariians heal you? There had to have been *something* we could have done! I-I didn't even get a chance to s-save you!"

"I did," Sam whispered, his eyes closing as he took my hand, "The Ranguvariians tried everything they could when we were at the camp. That was the whole reason either of us was invited to the camp. We have done everything imaginable to try to cure it. There is nothing that could be done for this poison. Just like June."

I shook my head furiously. I remembered Arii saying that now. How could I have been so blind? "This isn't fair!" I shouted furiously, hot tears streaking down my cheeks. "Back during the war, I had a vision that you would die in a battle,

227

and we were able to change the future! Why didn't that happen this time?"

"I-I don't know, Lina," Sam coughed, his brittle fingers clutching mine with the strength of a mouse. "I made my choice. I wanted to enjoy the rest of my time with you, getting to know Ky and Rayna. Not fearing something I couldn't fix."

"Then why did you fight today?" I cried, beginning to shake. "You could have had *more* time if you hadn't drained yourself!"

"Because I needed to make sure you were okay with the Dome gone. That you would be safe," he mumbled, "you and the kids."

My head sank against the plush covers of the bed. I just couldn't, anymore. Sam's familiar, warm presence that smelled of freshly-tilled soil was flickering in my head, and it broke me to know that soon I would never sense him again. I left wet patches in the quilt when Sam's hand clumsily brushed my hair, and I looked up to see him looking at me. I tried to memorize it, right then and there. What it looked like and felt like when his eyes met mine.

"I love you, Lina," Sam whispered, his voice cracking. "I've loved you through every trial we've faced. Duunzer, the war, going to Caark, creating the Dome…through everything Rhydin has ever thrown at us. You're still the farm girl I fell in love with."

My breathing hitched as I took a deep breath, my tears falling freely. "I have always loved you, and I always will. In plenty and drought, in plague and blessing, until my coal goes out."

Sam smiled weakly, his cheeks becoming wet. "Even after my coal goes out."

I was about to dissolve into sobs when the door burst open again. But when I looked, I sobbed anyway because there stood our two children. Fourteen and thirteen. The picture of Sam and I together. They had just gotten their father back, and now he had to leave them.

Rayna's eyes were glassy while Ky's expression was riddled with disbelief. I could see the moment the atmosphere of the room hit him, and I hated it. The two of them rushed to Sam's other side, and Ky sputtered the word "how" over and over.

I cleared my throat, trying to hold it together for my children. "Your father was poisoned a couple months ago. That poison has finally run its course, and it cannot be healed."

Both Ky and Rayna began to weep, and the elder began to shout how it didn't make sense and it wasn't fair, exactly how I'd reacted. I opened my mouth to try and help him when Sam surprisingly overpowered me.

"When you two were brought from Caark, it wasn't because Rachel changed her mind. It was because I'd asked her to bring you, once we figured out the gravity of my injury. If this hadn't happened, you two would likely still be in Caark or in another pocket somewhere after the invasion," Sam said softly. "Everything happens for a reason. But I wish I could have been with you two longer."

I tried to hide my shock but failed. How had I not seen? Why had I not questioned that Rachel had suddenly changed her mind after over a decade of fighting her for our children?

Sam weakly lifted his other hand, which held his bandana, into Ky's. Ky's eyes tripled in size at the sight of the navy swatch of fabric with its purple borders and golden stars that signified the Kidek, leader of the Rounans.

Sam mumbled, his voice growing quieter, "I am so proud of you, Kyler Thomas. You've excelled in every lesson Nathia and I have given you, my son. As I said before, you will make a truly great Kidek, even if I wish I could have kept this burden from you longer. Your mother will be there for you every step of the way, just as she has for me."

Ky's expression crumpled as he gripped the bandana, but then Sam turned to Rayna. However, before he could speak, Rayna shook her head and held up her hand. It seemed Sam had spoken to them both before the battle, and Rayna did not desire a repeat. It was just too much. So, Sam kept it short. "You...you will always be my daughter...and I think you may end up being an even more powerful Allyen than your mother. I know you'll keep her and Ky in line."

I eyed Sam warily. The last thing we needed right now was for the truth about Rayna to come out.

Rayna blubbered, "I will, Papa."

"T-Tell...Frederick to come in," Sam breathed. He was becoming weaker.

Sure enough, I could sense Frederick's cool-headed, windy presence still beyond the door. I called his name, and only a beat passed before the door gently opened, revealing the king's wiry frame. He inched into the room cautiously, but while the rest of our people were outside celebrating, he looked as worn with sadness as ever.

"P-Promise me..." Sam said before he could not continue. He tried to swallow several times, his breathing ragged, but nothing more came.

"I know," Frederick answered, swallowing his emotion, his gaze glued to Sam's limp form. "Lina, Ky, and Rayna will want for nothing as long as I am king."

Sam barely nodded in response, his eyes finding Frederick across the room only once. Frederick covered his mouth with a wiry hand, hiding his disbelief that all this was actually happening, and I could see the gears moving through his mind. Suddenly, Sam's statement made sense. Who could possibly care more about Rayna, and therefore her family, than the man she was originally born to?

After a few moments of silence passed, aside from the sputtering sounds of Sam's labored breathing, I ordered everyone out of the room. Frederick instantly made himself scarce, a loud noise coming from the hallway soon after, but the teenage children dawdled.

Both of them, in their own way, both verbal and nonverbal, tried to steady themselves in this last moment with their father. Ky backed away slowly, tying his father's bandana around his head, which nearly broke me yet again. Rayna clung to Sam's hand, and then leaned forward to whisper something into his ear that I couldn't hear. Then, the two of them were gone, leaving me alone.

I stood and wandered to the door, numbly rotating the skeleton key that had remained forgotten in the lock for who knew how many years. The death rattle had settled into Sam's throat, the sound that encompassed my entire world at the moment. I drew the light drapes at the window, choosing to ignore the happy campfires below in the courtyard where people and mythical creatures would celebrate long into the night. Pyromages were launching their magic into the air, and each time one of them burst, the bedroom was briefly flooded with a red flash before growing dimmer and dimmer in between. The sun was going down on Sam's last day.

He didn't appear to be conscious anymore, but his ragged breaths went on, each a little shallower than the last. I didn't light the glass lamp sitting on the fine-wood, bedside table. Instead, I kicked my filthy boots off and crept underneath the covers, scooting close to Sam's familiar frame. I wrapped my arms around his stomach, trying not to hinder the weary rise of his ribcage, and nestled my head into the crook of his neck. Sam moved just barely in response, rotating his head so that his jaw rested upon my forehead, and I let my tears fall.

My mind traipsed backwards in time. Over the last eleven years spent in the Dome. The hundreds, if not thousands, of missions we led together fighting for a cause we believed in. Back to our first mission, so to speak, of taking Ky and Rayna to Caark where they could grow up in safety. The rocky patch in our marriage over that decision, which came out only stronger than ever. Our newlywed years in the Rounan Compound, and the nightmare so long ago of his death that spurred our search for him during the war. The nightmare I now realized was a blessing because I got to work against it. All his help during my first year as an Allyen. When he caught me after I leaped through the air, firing my arrow through Duunzer's shadowy heart. When he found me as a child in the middle of the forest, Rhydin's kidnapping attempt thwarted by Ranguvariians I wouldn't know existed for another decade. That was when we'd met for the first time, at nine and ten years of age. Back when I thought my entire future was nothing more than taking over the family farm when my mother, and who I now knew to be my step-father, retired.

Sam was the only constant through it all. Through the loss of my parents in the Epidemic and the rest of my family to Rhydin. Through becoming an Allyen and Duunzer. Through the war and losing control of Nerahdis to Rhydin. Through our fleeing from Lunaka and establishing the Dome and now our return to our home country. Through *everything*.

Time became irrelevant. The clock on the wallpapered wall, an item only Royals could afford, hadn't been wound in years, and it showed a preposterous time which somehow went along with everything I was feeling. My mind played memories over and over again rather than be present in this moment from my worst nightmare. I tried to find something positive. That Sam got to die in a real bed in a real bedroom in our hometown rather than our shabby, temporary tent in a hole in the ground. That was about it.

At some point, late in the night when the rebels downstairs had finally worn themselves out, the breaths ceased. The rising and falling of his ribcage came to a stop so subtly that at first, I didn't notice. It just...stopped. I squeezed him tighter, his head heavy on mine, the fact of his death still unreal. I fought the internal begging that he would wake up because I knew it wasn't possible.

Samton Greene, Kidek of the Rounans, the only man I'd ever loved, was dead.

Frederick exited the room in a hurry. He felt he had no place in there, but that didn't keep him from throwing a punch into the nearest suit of armor, the only one in the hallway that was still upright. He stalked back down the hallway, unable to remain still. All this time, he had maintained some level of hope that this fight would be finished in their lifetimes. *All* of their lifetimes. That he, Sabine, and Xavier would reclaim their thrones, and people like Sam, Lina, Evan, Cayce – their whole generation really – could return to the lives they knew before Rhydin arose from anonymity with Duunzer.

His wind magic licked his fingers in torrents, the anger within him was so fierce. Of all the people to die on that battlefield, Sam was the least deserving. He didn't deserve to be slain by nothing more than Einanhis, Rhydin's empty shells of magic. Not when the real battle for Nerahdis was still to come. Lina had often told him over the years of her whimsical dreams for the future. Of being able to return to the Canyonlands, the home buried deep in their blood, to begin their farm anew. Where was that dream now that Sam wouldn't see tomorrow?

As Frederick meandered down the staircase, lost in thought, he caught sight of the situation outside. The rebels were ecstatic with their victory. It had come just when they needed it most. The sun was rapidly closing in on the horizon, but Frederick knew the celebrations wouldn't end with the coming darkness. He wished he could silence them all for Lina's sake, but he knew more that they needed this. The people needed a morale-boost. Let them all rejoice while they could. For perhaps a third of them, news of their leader's death tomorrow would shake them to their very core. At least, with winter coming, they were now all stationed at a stronghold filled to the brim with supplies.

When Frederick reached the bottom of the stairs, the others were waiting for him. The remaining Royals stood huddled in the castle foyer, and most of them had pleasant expressions on their faces. After all, they had just accomplished a major feat.

His sisters, Mira and Cornflower, weren't quite as animated as the others, glancing around at the greatly-changed state of their old, childhood home. Everyone's faces fell at the sight of the Lunakan king, and Frederick steadied himself at the sight of his son, Dominick, standing with the rest of his family.

"Is he...?" Mira asked quietly, barely to be heard over the chorus of cheers outside.

"Not yet," Frederick answered, touching his son's shoulder. Dominick and Ky were the same age, and he couldn't imagine having to say goodbye to his son this young. "But he will be by tomorrow, if not sooner."

Mira stared down at her sandy boots, her porcelain face carefully schooled as she clutched Lyla to her side. Xavier's hand cupped his chin, his blue eyes becoming glassy. Frederick's brother-in-law had spent weeks with Sam during the war when they'd both been drafted. Sabine seemed slightly sad, but she hadn't known Sam and Lina as long as the others.

Taisyn, who had been standing with Xavier and Mira, suddenly took off toward the stairs. Frederick found himself surprised at his agility, but when he noticed the blind boy's fingers glowing, he could only assume that magic was helping him see. Xavier called out after him, but the boy kept running, likely to go find Rayna. Willian, the younger of Sabine's twin wards, speedily followed.

It was then that Frederick felt a tug on his sleeve. Nathia, his adopted daughter, had come to stand next to him, a lock of blond and brown hair falling in front of her green eyes. "Father, who will be Kidek now that Kidek Sam is almost dead?"

"His son," Frederick replied simply, not understanding why she was even asking. The girl may have been a Rounan, but still. When her face soured, Frederick gave her a look that cut her off before she could say anything that might embarrass him. He knew the girl had big ambitions and possessed great prowess, but hoping to be Kidek over Sam's own son was ridiculous.

"What do we do now?" Cornflower, Frederick's youngest sister, asked. Her light fingers threaded through her golden curls that so reminded him of their mother.

"Do not disturb the upstairs hallway. Lina will come down when she is ready," Frederick said, taking a deep breath. Then, he made a big gesture toward the door. "Now, go outside. Mingle with your peoples. They must know that we too celebrate this victory and that we are one of them. The Royals must never be viewed as separate again if our family reigns are to survive in the post-Rhydin world."

Sabine turned on her heel almost instantly like she was desperate for a breath of fresh air, and Chretien followed closely. Xavier, Mira, Cornflower, and Lyla went too, albeit slowly. Nathia gave Frederick a dark glare before she tried to leave, but the king said sternly, "You will show nothing but support for the new Kidek and his mother. Any talk of your being Kidek will not be tolerated."

Nathia scoffed angrily, circling around and dipping into an imaginary curtsy meant to mock him. "*Yes*, Your Majesty."

Skies above. The sixteen-year-old had been his ward for nearly ten years since she showed up at the Dome as an orphan from Stellan, and every time he started to wonder if she was starting to grow into her role as the king's charge, she proved him otherwise.

"Father," Dominick asked, reminding him that he was still there, "are you coming?"

"I have something I need to do. You go ahead." Frederick tried to smile, but it didn't quite reach his eyes.

Dominick nodded, and Frederick's eyes caught on the pieces of him that resembled his mother as he turned to join the festivities. Frederick had never stopped missing Cassandra, even after so many years. Yet, time had done its part. He'd felt like he was drowning in her loss when it first happened, just as Lina likely felt now. But now, the sting of her absence was not as sharp as it used to be. Frederick could only hope that Lina would someday feel the same relief, but he knew it would probably take years. He'd had Cassandra for only a few, short years while Sam and Lina had been something that once seemed to have no beginning and no end.

As he thought, Frederick wandered back into the throne room where he and Lina had just fought for their lives. Their various movements in their respective duels were preserved in the thick layer of dust on the floor, and Mikael's body still lay off to the side underneath Lina's cloak. Frederick walked past him, his focus only on one thing. He approached the dais and the two golden thrones that lay fallen on the two stairs.

He grasped the first one and heaved with all his might, pushing the gold-plated throne up the stairs of the dais so that it rested on all four feet again. Frederick stared at it for a moment, catching his breath. He didn't have good memories of this throne. For most of his life, his father, King Adam, had sat upon it, exacting his iron will. He only barely remembered when his grandfather before him used it. Every Lunakan king back to King Spenser had sat upon this throne. Now, it was Frederick's.

The golden throne looked lonely back in its usual spot between the stone columns and in front of the chocolate-brown, velvet curtains hanging along the back wall. Frederick turned and moved toward the second of the golden thrones, the one his mother had used. Both thrones were pretty much identical, although this one was ever so slightly smaller, which made it easier to heft back to its place. The two thrones looked much more natural together on the dais.

It made Frederick feel sick to think of ruling all of Lunaka alone. Ruling a remnant of the Lunakan people in the Dome was one thing. The entire kingdom was another. He'd always dreamed Cassandra would rule at his side, but that dream was crushed long ago. Whether it was Cornflower or Dominick, Frederick hoped he could talk someone into reigning at his side.

With his job done, Frederick moved to exit the throne room, hoping to find someone to remove the bodies before Lina came back down. Then, he went and made his appearance among the people, trying not to glance up at Lina's window too many times.

CHAPTER NINETEEN

RAYNA

After whispering the words "I love you" in my father's ear for the first and final time, I flew out of the bedroom of death, honoring my mother's wishes. I pulled the door shut behind me, hearing it click like the final nail in a coffin. My hand fell from the knob. I stared at it for a few seconds, feeling torn between barreling back in there to stay with him until he breathed his last and running far, far away from this forsaken place.

"Rayna?" a voice jolted me from my thoughts.

Even though Ky had exited just ahead of me, it wasn't him waiting for me outside the door. I slowly turned to see Willian and Taisyn, two of the princes of Nerahdis. Taisyn still looked like he had just walked off a battlefield while Willian looked mostly untouched in his crimson tunic. I stood there, wordlessly, until one of them decided to speak again.

Willian cleared his throat, his frog-green eyes uncertain. "Do you want to go downstairs? There's a big party outside. It might help get your mind off things?"

While that was probably the kindest thing the Auklian boy had ever said to me in comparison, it still made me balk. "No, thank you," I answered, my voice shaking.

I glanced at Taisyn to see what he had to say, but instead of words, the boy closed the gap between us and just hugged me. It felt like he was trying to squeeze me so hard that maybe all my broken pieces would fit together again. No matter how hard I fought against them, tears leaked down my cheeks.

Willian looked peeved. He glared at the back of Taisyn's head and stomped back towards the stairs. I wasn't in the mood to speculate on what that was about, and my emotions overtook me as I buried my face in Taisyn's shoulder. Maybe, if I couldn't see the world, then the world couldn't see me cry.

It wasn't fair. Why was I only just reunited with my parents for my father to be torn away again? I should have had him for years more, yet that wasn't the case.

Suddenly, I began to feel strange. Taisyn melted away from my arms like he'd never existed. The grays, blacks, and browns of the abandoned castle hallway liquefied and transformed straight into an outdoor setting, no void in between like there was with transportation magic. Many of the same colors re-shaped themselves into a night sky dotted with a thousand, twinkling lights shining down upon a different prairie scene that I didn't recognize. Instead of standing, I was now crouched on the ground, and I couldn't move my own head to check out my surroundings. All I could see was what was in front of me. A gravestone.

My body was racked with sobs, and while my heart welcomed them, they were not my own. Was this another memory of Nora's? Why was I seeing the First Allyen's memories?

"I am so sorry. You were my only friend, and I failed you," choked the deeper, female voice in my own throat.

I studied the stone closer, difficult to see in the dark, and I made out the name Amelia Eason. I gasped, although my mouth, no longer my own, didn't move. Amelia was the blue-haired, young woman I had seen in the previous memory, where she and Nora traveled to meet the real Rhydin. What had happened to her? And what was her relationship to Nora?

"I promise you, Amelia," Nora's voice sprung forth from my mouth again, "I *will* avenge your death. I don't know what happened to Rhydin to change him so, but the Ranguvariians are going to help me create my own magic so that I can stand a chance against him. If I fail, then I vow to you that my descendants will take up this mission for however long it takes to destroy him. So that I can save us all. I just wish I could have saved you."

My hand moved on its own accord to clutch some of the freshly-tilled earth under the gravestone, and then Nora stood, bringing my vision upward. The scene began to shift away as I saw a large, newly-constructed building at the bottom of the hill, but that was all I could make out before the hallway of Lunaka Castle swirled back into existence.

"Rayna!" Taisyn was shouting, his hands gripping my shoulders hard. "Rayna!"

"Taisyn, stop, I'm fine," I replied softly, putting my hands against him to make him let go.

"What happened?" Taisyn asked. "You went limp, and you wouldn't respond to anything I was saying!"

"I…" I hesitated, wondering if he'd think I was crazy. I sighed. "I don't know. I'm beginning to think I'm seeing the memories of Nora Soreta, the First Allyen."

"What makes you say that?" Taisyn scoffed, his old, grumpy attitude making a sudden reappearance.

I took his arm and began walking him further down the hallway, away from the bedroom door. "I don't know, it's the only thing I can think of! The first time it happened in the Archimage Palace, I was suddenly seeing her meeting the real Rhydin for the first time with a girl named Amelia, all through her eyes. Rhydin and Amelia seemed to be beginning a relationship in that memory. But, just now, I was back in Nora's point of view grieving at Amelia's grave! I mean, what else could I be seeing but Nora's memories?"

Taisyn touched his freckled chin. "You were grieving in the memory just now?" He thought for a few moments, and then added, "What happened right before you saw the first memory?"

I shrugged, not sure why this was important. "Well...I guess I'd just seen Rhydin Caldwell for the first time, standing in the corner of the room."

"And then you saw a memory of Nora seeing him for the first time," Taisyn mused. "I think these memories are connected to things you're experiencing in your own life now that your magic is awake."

"Huh. I hadn't thought of that." Seeing Rhydin linked to Nora's seeing Rhydin. My grief for Papa linked to Nora's grief for Amelia. "That makes sense and all, but it doesn't explain why it's happening."

"True," Taisyn admitted. "My father told me about Rhydin. How the emperor we know is an Einanhi. It's so hard to believe. What is the real Rhydin Caldwell like?"

"He's really nice, actually," I replied as I dragged him into another room down the hallway that had a huge bay window. I made him sit on the window seat, and then I sat on the opposite side, staring out the glass. "In this last memory, I don't think Nora knew what really happened to Rhydin. I mean, she said he 'changed,' but nothing about being an Einanhi."

"Well, of course she didn't. If she had known there were two Rhydins, then she would have told Clariion Arii, and all this wouldn't be such a surprise," Taisyn responded like a know-it-all.

"Alright, alright, you have a point," I said defensively. "It's just crazy to think that the Allyen magic was created and passed down to so many people in my family all because Nora wanted vengeance for Amelia."

"Vengeance for Amelia?" Taisyn repeated, confused. "Why? How did she die? Did someone kill her?"

My jaw dropped. I hadn't put it together until he said that. "Rhydin killed her," I breathed. "The Einanhi one, I think.

But, why would he do that if the real Rhydin Caldwell loved her?"

"I don't know," Taisyn replied quietly, shaking his head. "I think Rhydin Caldwell is the only one who can tell us now."

My gaze returned to the window where my parents' homeland stretched out like a giant scroll of prairie grass running all the way up to the mountains in the distance. The huge canyon lay off to the left, and the plumes of smoke were getting smaller as the night approached. I wondered what it would be like to grow up at the bottom of a canyon, its rocky walls as a frame to every part of the town. We were quiet for a few minutes before I quickly gave Taisyn a run-down of everything I could see outside. Lunaka wasn't his home, but it was his mother's childhood home so he was still interested.

After a couple more moments of silence, I murmured, "I want to go back to the Archimage Palace, Taisyn. The real Rhydin is trapped there by himself. He can't leave because he has so little magic left that he's invisible."

"That sounds awful," Taisyn said, still facing me even if he couldn't see me. "I'll go with you if you want."

"That'd be great," I tried to chuckle, my tears for Papa beginning to return. "I'm going to save him, Taisyn. I'm going to fulfill Nora's vow to destroy the false Rhydin and save the real one with the magic she's passed down to me. Only then will my father's home be safe."

"That's a big job, but I think that if anyone can do it, you can," the Mineraltin prince replied.

"Thanks," I croaked, rested my cheek against my knees. We stopped talking then. Taisyn stayed in his corner of the bay window, and I stayed in mine. He let me weep in peace without making me feel like a poor, little weakling. It was the best thing anyone could do for me at that moment.

At some point, both of us must have fallen asleep. When my eyes opened, the pink light of dawn shone through the dusty window into the abandoned sitting room we'd found. I stretched, trying to fix the crick in my neck, but Taisyn was still snoring slightly.

I fished through my cloak pockets, looking for my sketchbook. When I found it, I delicately placed it on my lap, just staring at the cracked, leather cover for a moment. It seemed like a century since I snuck out of the shack in Caark with nothing but the clothes on my back and this sketchbook, off to the city of Calitia to see if I could throw myself in some danger to activate my magic. I hadn't known at the time that I would never see my childhood home again. That Ky, Aron, and I would board a ship that would bring us to this point.

On a blank page, I whipped out my charcoal and started to sketch. The billowing prairie with imaginary paths that seemed to appear and vanish depending on the wind. The rocky canyon nearby with its signs of life churning underneath. The few remaining farms on the opposite side of the canyon, the partially-harvested fields like a patchwork quilt. The steep slopes of the mountains in the distance, somewhat obscured by some morning fog, their bald heads white with snow. The twin moons hanging low in the sky, their faces large and full. Lunaka was truly beautiful.

When I found myself moaning about colors for the millionth time, my eyes wandered from the page and landed on Taisyn, still slumbering away even as the rays of the morning sun crept closer to his face. How spoiled had I been to whine for colored pencils when my best friend could never see them? I did my best to describe things to him, but how did one describe the color red? Or the color blue? It was impossible, and he would never know it.

Once my landscape was finished, I flipped through all the pages of my sketchbook, looking at all my old drawings. The portrait of Mathiian's sleeping face that I'd done on the boat ride from Caark. Another landscape of the cliffs up by my old school, the dark, roaring ocean below. One of my favorite plants in the jungle, a large bush with wide, smooth leaves, each with a purple heart ringed in green. Aunt Rachel reading

Aron a bedtime story on his little cot in the boys' room of the shack I'd grown up in several years ago.

Finally, I reached the page near the middle that had been dog-eared long ago. A drawing of my parents when I'd tried to imagine what they looked like, a hodge-podge of all the different little things our caretakers used to say about them. They were still face-less, since nobody had ever really said what their faces looked like, and I'd been too busy spending time with them and practicing the moves of the death spell to draw.

I went to work. Papa's face was still clear in my memory, but I knew that one day it would not be so. A long, dark stroke for his nose. Soft lines for the rims of his eyes, the windows to the soul. Full pupils and irises, like he was happy to see me. A lopsided grin for his mouth, and angled lines for his brows. I adjusted the light shape of the scar I'd drawn long ago to better fit his new face, and then a few minutes later, I found myself absent-mindedly fixing several other things I'd sketched long ago. The length of his hair and how the bandana had sat upon it, the shape of his ears, the clothes he was wearing in the drawing.

I moved seamlessly from his portrait to my mother's next to him. I re-did the clothes she was wearing as well, using firm, black strokes to fill in the short, black dress with gold trim she usually wore, and then moved to her face. Large, round eyes, but a petite nose and mouth. I committed everything in my mind to this one drawing. Then, I sat back and admired my work. It really looked like the two of them staring back at me in black and white. Then, I shut the book and clutched it to my chest, wishing that I didn't feel like I'd just closed a chapter of my life.

Taisyn suddenly stretched, his long arms brushing the top of the bay window, and groaned quietly. He scratched his copper-colored head and rubbed his tired eyes. "Rayna? Are you awake?"

"Yeah," I answered sadly, still hugging my sketchbook. "How did you know I was still here?"

"I can sense you, silly." Taisyn smiled. "Ever since your magic awoke, I've been able to sense you. Your warm, light magic."

"Oh, yeah." I'd forgotten about that. I had become so accustomed to Taisyn's fiery presence being in my head that I didn't notice it anymore. "I guess I still have a lot to learn."

"You'll get there," Taisyn reassured me.

I nodded, lost to my thoughts. I had to practice my magic as much as possible if I even hoped to help Rhydin Caldwell.

"Are you ready?" Taisyn asked hesitantly, "To go downstairs? Face the day?"

I took a deep breath and exhaled loudly. "As ready as I'll ever be."

We both stood. Taisyn adjusted his clothes and ran his fingers through his hair, trying to ascertain that he looked put together and not like he'd slept on a window seat. I helped him smooth down a red sprig on the back of his head that looked like a cow had licked it. I decided I didn't care what I looked like. My fingers were stained black with coal, and some of that dust had migrated to my cheeks. My hair was revolting against yesterday's braid, and my clothes were heavy with sweat. But Taisyn couldn't see it, so I didn't care. For now, my scrubby exterior matched my chaotic interior.

We walked back down the hallway slowly, passing the bedroom I'd left yesterday evening. I could sense my mother's presence in there. Her magic beckoned to mine like twin magnets. But hers was the only one I sensed in that cold, shut-off room, so I knew it was true.

My father was dead.

CHAPTER TWENTY

LINA

Nothing was the same. My heart begged for something familiar. My eyes ravaged every nook and cranny of what used to be a place I could have walked around blindfolded. Winter's first, crisp breaths huffed down my neck, and I pulled the hood of my borrowed, black cloak higher over my head. Ky and Rayna stumbled after me, one lost in his own little world while the other soaked up the world like a sponge. It felt odd to be back here with them, but I couldn't stay away.

We had walked over a small, rickety bridge that crossed a deep offshoot from the canyon, but that sense of home didn't feel as warm as it once did when we entered Harvey land. This was where I'd grown up, where I'd spent the first nineteen years of my life, and yet I couldn't recognize it.

The old, oak tree at the end of the tree row marking our property line was felled and rotting on the ground, likely due to lightning. Dirt and dust swallowed up the foot of every remaining building, years' worth of dust storms left to their own devices. The barn was still standing in the distance, the one my grandfather raised up on the same footprint as the original barn, but its roof was riddled with huge holes, burnt along the rims. Those were from magic, my memory reminded me, from the battle that took place right in my front yard on my last day here. When Rhydin murdered Grandma Saarah.

Rayna jumped when a billy goat suddenly popped its head out a sagging, barn window and bleated at her loudly, its long, white beard stained yellow which meant there were some female goats somewhere. I shook my head in disbelief. I'd had to abandon them after that battle, yet those stubborn things had lived long enough to reproduce, obviously. My mother used to laugh and say that goats had a knack for trying to get themselves killed. Of course, that always went the other way, too, where they just wouldn't die.

Before continuing toward the barn, I left my invisible path and headed toward the house, which was leaning to the side like it was exhausted of standing. The door was gone, and all the windows were broken. I steeled myself and entered the home I last shared with Rosetta and Keera, both of whom I'd thought died with Grandma Saarah.

The floor was covered in dust, but everything inside was surprisingly preserved. The wobbly table still stood in the center of the front room by the fireplace, tin dishes and utensils still sitting in their places like we were all coming back. A pot sat in the fireplace, but its inside was clean, likely eaten by some animal years ago. Even in the back room, there were still three straw ticks lying on the floor, half-covered in dirt. The back window was the only one that wasn't broken, still open from where Keera and Rosetta had tried to make their escape.

"Mama?" Rayna asked, breaking me from my thoughts. "Where are we?"

I turned on my heel and left the room before I could think too much more. "This was where I was born. I grew up here with my mother, step-father, and my sister, Rosetta. Later, my cousin Keera came too."

"Oh. What happened to all of them?" Rayna asked again, innocently.

"My parents died in the Epidemic," I said slowly, a phrase that I used to say all the time but never did anymore. "It was a disease engineered by Rhydin to kill Evan and I. Keera was killed by Rhydin's Followers, and I thought Rosetta was too. She might still be alive somewhere. She's Erikin's mother."

For once, Rayna didn't ask another question. She and Ky silently followed me back out of the house and around the corner of the barn. The grove of trees was overgrown back here, far taller, darker, and denser that it'd been the last time I was here nearly two decades ago. Dozens of stone markers stared back at me, all of them discolored and covered in moss to varying degrees depending on how old they were. The oldest ones in the back were barely legible while the one in front, its spot dark with fresh earth, was clear as day.

Samton Thomas Greene. Born 323, died 359.

He never even reached forty.

It'd been a few days since his death now. Frederick had orchestrated his burial while I remained sequestered in my room until I could figure out how to function without my other half. It had taken me far too long to journey out here and see the grave for myself.

For humans, our calendar began when Emperor Caden and the original Gornish and Rounan inhabitants landed in Nerahdis, but we only wrote birth and death dates that way. For every other purpose, such as letter writing, we used the years of our respective king's reign – although that was probably the old Royals' way of reminding everyone constantly of who was in charge. That was also probably why it was so easy for people to forget that Rhydin ever existed, even after he was emperor three centuries ago before Nora made him disappear. As far as I knew, Ranguvariians and Aatarilecs, the indigenous peoples, didn't number their years like we did.

Frederick had offered to bury Sam in Lunaka Castle's cemetery, but I didn't want him over there. This was where he belonged. With the rest of my family, and in the soil we both had grown up tilling and had always dreamed of returning to.

Just not like this.

I still couldn't believe he was gone. Seeing the grave with my own eyes didn't make it any more real. It had to be a delusion. My husband couldn't be dead. He had been a force to be reckoned with, a powerful Rounan, and now he lay beneath the earth like none of that mattered. My mind played tricks on me constantly, like he would walk through the door any second and things would return to normal.

I didn't want to do this life without him.

"Lina?" a voice floated over to my children and I on the wind.

Ky and Rayna turned around to look for who was there, but I numbly continued to stare at my husband's marker. The two of them glanced at each other and walked away, deeper into the graveyard and up the hill behind the barn.

"What do you want, Frederick?" I murmured, still not moving to face him.

"I...I just wanted to make sure you were alright," Frederick stammered. He walked to my side where I could barely see him out of the corner of my eye.

"You allowed my poisoned husband to fight in a battle, knowing that it would exhaust him. Now, he is dead. Am I supposed to be alright?" I asked tersely, trying to contain myself.

"Lina, it was *his* choice," Frederick replied firmly, touching my elbow. "We both knew the same Sam. You can't tell me the man didn't have a stubborn temper."

I tried to shake him off, but it didn't work. Hot tears were leaking from my eyes no matter how hard I tried to keep them in. "You still could have done something! You at least *knew!*"

"Sometimes, people make decisions we don't like! Sometimes-..." Frederick's voice broke, and that was what finally made me look at him. His face was thin and pale, lined with worry. He looked like he hadn't slept in days. "Sometimes, people make decisions that are best for the people they love. Not themselves."

"This isn't the same as Cassandra!" I bellowed, losing all hold on myself, "Absolutely nobody else knew what she was planning! For all we know, we could have kept her from dying and *still* gotten Rayna! She kept *everyone* in the dark about her illness and pregnancy, even *you!*"

"I *know!*" Frederick snapped. Something had shifted. The ever cool-headed Lunakan king who mediated literally every meeting had vanished, and I paused in uncertainty, wiping away my traitorous tears. "I know, I was in Auklia helping Daniel when I should have stayed with my own wife. I know, if I had been there it could have all turned out differently. Perhaps, Cassandra would be alive. Perhaps, I could have fended off Robert, and Taisyn, my nephew, would not be blind. Perhaps, my *daughter* would know who I am, even if she is no longer my blood. Trust me, I *know*. It is a decision that haunts me every day, and Daniel was still killed alongside Dathian."

A sob escaped me. After so much tragedy, how could we still breathe?

"I'm sorry, Frederick," I blubbered, "but you still could have stopped Sam."

"Could I?" the king shouted, "His death sentence was written regardless, Lina. If not now, then in another month, if that. Let the man die with honor on the battlefield or a slow, painful death withering away in bed? I let him make the choice. He thanked me for that, so I hope you can find it within yourself to forgive me for something that is not my fault!"

I squeezed my eyes shut, and more hot tears spilled over my cheeks. I knew he was speaking the truth, but it hurt too much to admit that he was right. Sam was headstrong and stubborn, and he never let anyone stand in his way. My pain kept my mouth glued shut because, however foolishly, I still believed that having Sam for another month was better than this. Regardless of the fact that I would still feel this same way, just postponed for however long and without blaming Frederick.

I was about to open my mouth to say something more when suddenly Rayna and Ky came flying down the hill, yelling. I reached for my sword, fearing the worst, but there didn't seem to be anyone following them. Sniffling and rubbing the evidence of tears off my face, I called to them, "What is it?"

My two teenagers rushed right up to us, panting. Rayna's eyes met mine, and she said between gasps, "There's something...up there...that I need...you to come see...right now."

I eyed Frederick, but he seemed as perplexed as I did. We agreed, and we followed Ky and Rayna back around the barn and up the hill, trotting between graves as we went back in time. The stones became more and more worn with age as we went until we finally reached the very back of the graveyard where the trees were thick with gnarly knots and tangled branches. I'd never been this far back before. There were probably around forty graves in total, although one of our bigger fields that we typically planted with corn or wheat wasn't too far behind the graveyard.

By now, Rayna had caught her breath, but she still pointed with a shaking finger toward a cluster of graves under the dim canopy. "G-Go read them," she stammered, pale as if she'd seen a ghost.

Oh, good grief. Nevertheless, I walked forward wordlessly and approached the trio of what had to be the oldest graves here. If the markers hadn't been stone, nobody would even know they were here at this point, and the faces were so mossy they were nearly illegible. My eyes picked out a few portions where it appeared Rayna or Ky had done some scraping in order to read them.

My jaw dropped as I finally made out the one in the middle. "Nora Soreta Rodgers," I breathed, barely audible.

My maiden name was Harvey, but Grandma Saarah's maiden name was Rodgers. I'd never known that name went so far back. "I had no idea she was buried here. Although, this farmstead has been here for over three hundred years, so I guess I should have assumed."

"N-No, the other one," Rayna stuttered. "The one on the right."

Briefly, I glanced at the one on the left. Charles Patrick Rodgers, born 4 – died 59. Must have been Nora's husband, the original Rodgers. My eyes caught on the death year and moved back to Nora's stone. It was the same year as hers. Her dates were 7 – 59. I wondered if there was a connection there.

When Rayna cleared her throat in impatience, I went on to the third stone. This one was a lot harder to read. I did some extra rubbing along the name, trying to get a feel for the letters. The dates were 11 – 32.

"Uh...Amanda?" I asked, almost entirely clueless, turning to face my daughter. This grave might be the absolute oldest one here.

"Amelia Eason," Rayna said, her voice shaking a little.

"How do you know that? The name is all but gone," I asked, staring at the stone again.

"I know because I saw it when it was brand new," Rayna admitted sheepishly. "I had another vision the night Papa died. I was Nora again, and she was weeping at this grave."

My brow furrowed. Frederick, too, looked completely lost. "Amelia. I've heard that name before," I murmured, trying to remember where.

"I think she may have been Rhydin's betrothed. In my first vision, I saw Nora meeting Rhydin Caldwell for the first time because he was Amelia's new beau," Rayna explained. "Then, in my second vision, Nora wanted to avenge Amelia's death. She vowed to destroy Rhydin by creating her own magic, but I think by then, the Einanhi Rhydin had taken over. I think he killed her. But Nora didn't know that there were two Rhydins."

Rhydin's *betrothed?* Now that was a phrase I never thought I'd hear. I felt paralyzed with shock. Suddenly, I realized that was where I'd heard the name before. Emperor Rhydin – Einanhi Rhydin – had mentioned it the last time I'd seen him, when he was rambling about trying to make Nerahdis into "a better place."

"Okay, hang on, back up," Frederick said loudly. "What are these 'visions' you keep talking about?"

My mind went blank. We hadn't exactly had time to talk about it since that revelation came right before the news of the Dome's attack. I suddenly felt like an awful mother.

Rayna jumped right in. "Taisyn and I have decided that I am seeing Nora's memories. I seem to see them when something in my life coincides with something in hers. I saw her meeting Rhydin for the first time when I saw the real Rhydin for the first time, and I saw her grieving Amelia while I was grieving." Rayna seemed confident in her answer, perhaps even proud that she had figured it out on her own. In return, I felt proud of her.

"So Einanhi Rhydin killed the real Rhydin's betrothed, and Nora buried her here before going to the Ranguvariians and becoming an Allyen to avenge her," I mused, trying to keep it straight in my head. "Who was Amelia to Nora? Why would she be buried here and not with her own family? There's no middle name, so Nora must not have been family. And that just shows how much we still don't know about Einanhi Rhydin's creation! Why would he murder the person his creator loved?"

Frederick crouched down and touched his forehead as I stood. Too many questions, not enough answers.

"That's why we need to go back! To learn the rest of the story!" A fire lit in Rayna's eyes; her passion was contagious. "Only Rhydin Caldwell can tell us! Mama, you promised that we would go back."

"You're right, and we will," I vowed again, placing my hand on her shoulder.

"I think you are right," Frederick began as he righted himself, "but you'll need to ask the Council about that. This affects us all."

"Isn't there a meeting this afternoon?" I asked, someone's reminder tugging at my memory.

Frederick nodded blankly, and it was like a silent agreement to head back. The four of us navigated our way back out of the graveyard, and I stopped for a second at the front as the others went on. Robert, my father, was buried near the Dome, but everyone else was here. My mother Elaine, my step-father Liam, Grandma Saarah, Keera, and now Sam.

My eyes clung to Sam's name on his stone, and I felt like I couldn't move another inch. *I can't leave him here. I have to stay with him*, my thoughts rolled all over themselves like crashing waves.

"Mama?"

I turned automatically at the word. Both Ky and Rayna stared back at me. Ky had Sam's face and his eyes. Rayna had his ears and his brown hair laced with some red. They were Sam, and they needed me, which was the only thing that moved my feet from remaining planted before the grave for the rest of my life.

My parents, Grandma Saarah, Keera, Luke, Robert, Sam. The number of people I had to avenge was still growing.

We made our way back to the horses we'd left on the property line. Frederick's white stallion stamped next to them, all of them from the castle stables. I mounted my dapple-gray mare, and the kids both clambered onto their shared gelding, neither of them having ridden before. Rayna never let that horse out of her sight whenever it was near, like she expected it to kill her.

Then, we rode through the Canyonlands, the fields and farms surrounding the canyon that held Soläna in its depths, all the way around to Lunaka Castle, which took about an hour. My eyes soaked in the sight of what little we could see of Soläna from all the way up here, its pulley systems chugging away on either side of the canyon. Yet, my joy of being home was forever numbed. The omnipresent Lunakan wind was eerily calm as we rode, and I couldn't help but wonder if a last-minute, autumn storm was headed our way.

As we approached the castle, I noticed another mass grave had been dug a short distance away from the exterior wall. The first grave housed those who had fallen in the battle itself, while it was too soon to know how many would inhabit the second. All our enemies' blades had been poisoned during the battle, so anyone who dripped more than a drop of blood was succumbing to the same awful poison as Sam and June. The Ranguvariians were doing what they could, trying to learn for the future, too, but it was hopeless. We'd lost more numbers to the poison than the blade at this point. Frederick had been far more than lucky that Mikael never drew blood with his sword at his neck.

Rebels were busy repairing the damage we'd done to both of the castle walls when we rode in. The bridge over the moat had been hastily patched together over the last few days after the Aatarilecs' tidal wave, but something better would have to be built and soon. For all we knew, Emperor Rhydin could arrive with troops any hour.

We went straight to the stables, and the smells of hay and manure assaulted my nose. Yet, they were familiar scents that calmed me far more than the sterile, stony smell of the castle itself. Ky and Rayna half-slipped, half-fell off their horse as I guided my mare into her pen and began the process of taking off the saddle and rubbing her down. When I looked up again, I was surprised to see Arii towering in the doorway leading to the castle keep, his bright orange clariion's robe hard to miss.

"Hello, Arii," I greeted him softly, still not really in the mood for much talking.

The Ranguvariian smiled and nodded in response as Ky and Rayna brushed past him, headed for the new Council chambers within the throne room. He moved in front of

Frederick before he could pass by, and I braced myself out of habit. "I wish to speak to you both."

Frederick glanced at me. The Council meeting was about to start, but something told me that Arii knew that. We followed him wordlessly just inside to a quieter corner, away from the ears of our people working in the stables.

"I imagine that you will likely be asking the Council's permission to return to the Archimage Palace today," Arii began, his voice almost a whisper. "I believe it might be best to not share Rayna's ancestral memories with anyone else."

"Ancestral memories?" I repeated, confusion likely apparent on my face. "Is that what she's seeing? Why? Do you think they're dangerous?"

"It is my understanding that she is seeing them for a reason. It cannot be coincidence that Rayna is the first Allyen since Nora to have truly artificial magic, and she is the only Allyen to have ever seen them. This links her to another as well, and I fear that if the Council were to discover this link, it may put all the Allyens in danger," Arii explained.

"Wait, linked to whom?" Frederick asked, trying to keep up. He crossed his arms over his white suitcoat.

"Rhydin Caldwell," I murmured, although still facing Arii and not Frederick. "The real Rhydin was the son of a nobleman with only the propensity for magic due to a distant Royal relative. His magic was given to him by man when he became Archimage, not by birth. Just like Rayna and Nora. I read it in that history book he gave me."

"If people were to think that what happened to Rhydin could happen to Rayna, or any of the other Allyens, it may incite panic," Arii continued, his eyes melting into a fierce, gold color. "Therefore, do not tell anyone else about these visions. I expect the meeting today may have quite the public audience. People must not think that Rhydin and Rayna are the same."

I nodded slowly. Exactly what I needed while grieving my husband and helping my son take over as Kidek.

"Lina, we are going to be late," Frederick whispered into my ear. I finally faced him and nodded, and the three of us hurried back down the hallway and through the castle labyrinth toward the throne room.

When we entered, I tried to hide my shock. The room had been cleaned to a sparkle. Every speck of dust was gone, and all new candles had been placed along the iron chandelier above our heads. A gigantic, wooden table had been dragged to the very center of the room, directly beneath the chandelier, while the thrones upon the dais were empty but imposing. On top of that, every spare inch of wall and floor space was taken up by nearly every survivor of the Dome. Our Council meetings back in the Dome normally attracted a few onlookers, but never like this. It was the first meeting to be held aboveground and in a castle to boot.

Arii found a space in the back, his seven-foot height ideal for seeing above the crowd, as Frederick and I squeezed through people who smelled like they hadn't bathed in a week to get to the table. Xavier, Mira, Cornflower, Sabine, James, Rachel, and all the Royal children were already there, and I found my place between Evan and Ky. My son sat as straight as if there was a rod bolted to his back, his father's bandana tied tightly around his head and his sister hovering beside him like a bodyguard. It tore my heart in two.

The meeting began slowly with a few simple tasks of establishing some rules, which really, for the most part, were an echo of our practices in the Dome. No leaving without permission, meals served on rations at certain times, we would help assign people rooms, etc. While we read through the list, I saw each of the nervous ticks the other Royals presented. Xavier's nose-rubbing, Sabine's finger-tapping, Cornflower's hair-stroking. The number of eyes on us was stifling, and we hadn't even gotten to the serious conversation yet.

After several minutes of the easy topics, Frederick finally stood and cleared his throat. My anger at him diminished a bit more now that he was leading the argument for returning to the Archimage Palace, for which I simply didn't have the energy. Rayna's eyes gleamed with hope as everyone gave the Lunakan king their attention.

"What I have to say isn't easy," Frederick began, meeting each of our gazes in turn, "but we know it to be true. At one of our previous meetings, as some of you can attest, we discussed the recent changes in Emperor Rhydin's actions. We have come to learn that the Rhydin we know is actually an Einanhi, a magically-created being."

The throne room descended into cacophony. Whispers rapidly degraded into shouting, and fear ruled the room. I knew at once that Arii was right about keeping Rayna's ancestral memories to ourselves. Various statements reached my ears, mostly "that's impossible" and "how do you know?" Yet, overwhelmingly, the roar above all the rest was, "*Who in Nerahdis created him?*"

Frederick raised his hands, trying to regain control over the meeting. Xavier and Sabine stood, too, whirling around to face their respective peoples. Ky must have felt the need to do the same, and I stood instinctively after he did.

When the chaos grew the tiniest of bits quieter, Frederick continued, "I know it is hard to believe! I know I did not think it possible. An Einanhi of his caliber is unbelievable and unprecedented, but I have personally seen him be wounded, only for his skin to crack like stone, no blood in sight. We do not know how or why he was created as a clone of his creator, but the real Rhydin Caldwell is locked within the Archimage Palace, invisible because his clone stole his magical powers. It is my belief that we should travel there to get answers from him as soon as possible."

The boiling fear in the room instantly transformed into rage. Even a few of the Royals looked at Frederick like he'd gone mad. The rebels around us began to shout again until an older woman stepped forth, her brown hair streaked with white like a skunk. She barked, "If the creator of Rhydin is still alive, he needs to be killed before it is too late! What's keeping him from creating another monster to kill us?"

All the color drained from Rayna's face. The words tumbled out of my mouth before I could hardly think them through. "The real Rhydin doesn't have any magic! We don't know how Emperor Rhydin came into existence, and we need to understand that if we ever hope to destroy him!"

"But his power is returning!" Sabine snapped, her hand gripping her blade. "The new mist at the Archimage Palace is proof of that!"

"Rhydin the Einanhi is the worst enemy we've ever faced! The free-thinking human being that created him will only be worse! If he is a clone as you say, he must only be a fragment of his creator's evil heart!" a male voice bellowed from somewhere out in the crowd.

"You don't understand!" I shouted, spinning to face the crowd as a whole, and then I chanted, "'The throne of sand must meet its end to break the curse that shrouds the First. But do hear me this, should the curse remain, for all Nerahdis, just death can be gained!'"

The crowd's clamor quieted upon hearing the riddle. The old fears of magic and anything remotely magic-sounding or ominous immediately grabbed hold. I went on, lying about the words' origin to make the audience listen, "I received this riddle from a very powerful sorceress. If we do not destroy Emperor Rhydin and his reign, we can never break the curse on the First Archimage. If his curse isn't broken, all of Nerahdis is doomed to live under Emperor Rhydin for eternity! This whole thing is a *curse*; Rhydin is not his creator's puppet!"

My words reached a few in the audience. I could see it in their eyes as I looked around. The riddle held a certain weight to it that I didn't quite understand, but even if I hadn't revealed that Rhydin Caldwell gave it to me, I still believed in my core that the words were true. The young sorcerer had befallen some sort of misfortune to get to where he was, trapped far away for over three centuries while a clone of himself wreaked havoc. The only way things would get better was if we broke the sorcerer's curse.

And that meant defeating Rhydin, our goal from the very beginning.

"Everything about the creator aside," I said again in a hoarse voice, trying not to look at Rayna as I did, "our objective has not changed. We must *still* remove Emperor Rhydin from power and destroy him."

A big cheer echoed around perhaps half the room. The other half continued to watch us with wary eyes, their arms crossed defensively over their chests.

"This is why we need a new Archimage," Xavier piped up, leaning against the table with his good arm. "Nothing has ever been decided by a large room of people. We all will never one-hundred-percent agree."

"Hear, hear," both Mira and Sabine replied heartily.

Princess Cornflower shrank in her seat. Frederick declared, "That is a conversation for another day. Perhaps, we will put it to a vote if you all truly believe that we will all never agree."

To my dismay, the mass majority of all the heads around the room and around the Council table nodded. The last thing we needed was to slap another person into the flawed role of Archimage, ruler of the Royals.

Xavier and Sabine speedily took over the meeting from there, salvaging whatever attention spans they could to discuss war strategy and the coming winter. I melted back into my seat, frustrated at the people's fear and lack of understanding. I tried to remember what it had been like to be one of them, long ago before I was an Allyen. I tried to remember the fear that choked me every time magic was mentioned or the powerful Royals were seen around town.

A memory of seeing a Rounan hanging as a child shook me down to my bones because I knew that was the fate for any common mage. For anyone even *suspected* of having magic outside the Royals. That fear had ruled the first nineteen years of my life, so I desperately tried not to hold it against the rebels for their fears now.

Rayna, on the other hand, who had not grown up with a fear of magic, was steaming in her seat. She looked like she was about to blow a gasket. Taisyn had wandered around the table from the Mineraltin quarter just to stand next to her, nothing more, like he could help cool her off just by being near. I would need to decide what I would say to her. If I would offer to help her back to the palace in secret.

Someone had just made the announcement that we would not move against Emperor Rhydin until after the winter – after all, that seemed to be the number one rule of warfare learned from wars past – when another voice from the crowd piped up, "I would like to address the Council."

Well, that was odd. A man waded through the sea of people toward our table, and when he appeared, I couldn't help but think I'd seen him before. He was very tall with dark skin and old enough to be my father. His clothes hung off him a bit, as if he'd lost some weight, but who hadn't in the Dome really. He spoke with a gravelly tenor when he said, "I wish to say something on behalf of all the Rounans here."

Ky's ears perked up, but my jaw dropped. I recognized his voice. I knew who he was, and I fought the urge to hide. During the war long ago, I had served as temporary Kidek after Sam was drafted. A man had ambushed me in the mercantile because a neighbor in the Compound had stolen from him and violated the Rounan Law of *Blutuern*, which forbade the use of magic to control another's actions. He had been so nasty to me when I wouldn't pursue the perpetrator, a kind man with many children and a small wallet, that I'd ended up punching him. This man couldn't accept me because I was Gornish, and now, here he was a decade later, addressing the Council. I gritted my teeth in preparation for his words.

"We all mourn Kidek Sam's passing. He served us honorably during one of the darkest times in Rounan history, and we will never forget that," the man rasped, his brown eyes unreadable. "However, his son is young in this tenuous time, and we have all decided that a regent should be named until he comes of age. Someone who can truly fight for our rights in the new Nerahdis."

Fear and anger gripped my heart. What was he doing?! Was he trying to place the Kidek bandana on his own head? How dare he dishonor Sam's last wishes! Ky looked like he was sitting on pins and needles, his eyes as wide as saucers.

Frederick and Xavier both eyed me, and even Sabine's attention had been drawn back to the table from her twin wards. Since the man was Lunakan, Xavier gestured to Frederick to speak. "Okay," the king said warily, "who do you have in mind?"

"Allyen Linaria," the man answered simply, the edges of his mouth twitching upward. "She did a fine job during the war, and we all believe she will do so again until her son is of age."

I suddenly felt dizzy. I leaned on my chair for support. Nearly a third of the room, all of the Rounans, were now smiling at me. After all these years of fighting for equality between the Gornish and the Rounans and making what seemed like zero headway? And of all the Rounans in the world to make the recommendation? I was speechless. Ky had relaxed in relief, a grin on his face for the first time in days. The rod had been removed from his back, and he gladly stripped the bandana from his head and offered it to me.

"I couldn't agree more." Frederick smiled confidently.

My fingers were numb as I took the worn fabric from my son. I felt comforted for perhaps a millisecond that my son could be carefree for a few more years. But as soon as I wrapped the bandana around my own head for the very first time, all the Rounans around the room lifted their right fists and beat their chests over their hearts, creating a boom of thunder within the throne room.

My breath left me as I realized my biggest challenge yet was just beginning.

Chapter Twenty-One

Rayna

Middle Winter 12th, Year 12 of King Frederick's Reign
(Year 14 of Emperor Rhydin's Reign),

My mother gave me this journal today. Apparently, every Allyen ever has written in its enchanted pages, although I have to admit, writing isn't really my thing. She thinks it is my turn to use it, but I think she's lost her desire to write. Her last entry was the day before Papa died nearly two months ago. She just seems off. Something more than Papa's death. Anger bubbles under her skin almost all the time, no matter how hard King Frederick tries to be there for her, but there's something else there and I'm not sure what.

Winter is so much worse than anything our teacher ever taught us in Caark. The air is thin and dry and stings your lungs with every breath. I mean, your breath comes out in white smoke outside as if your lungs are burning. Why do people live where it is cold? Caark may not have the beauty of autumn, but at least it never tortures you.

I overheard King Frederick mention that this is one of Lunaka's nastier winters. Between the ice storms where the sky flings pellets of frozen water at you and the six feet of fluffy, frozen water that got dumped on us last week, I can only assume that these are the events to which he is referring. Just makes me wonder what in Nerahdis a "nice winter" looks like.

The rebellion has settled into Lunaka Castle somewhat well. We are all stacked on top of each other because while the castle has nearly a hundred rooms, there are several hundred of us, even after all the casualties.

It was a big hullabaloo at the beginning. Gornish people didn't want to share with Rounans, and vice versa. My mother has pretty much been running around like a chicken with her head cut off ever since she was made Kidek in Ky's place, although he's acting as her assistant. As the weeks have gone by, things have gotten a little bit better.

For now, anyway.

Mama, Ky, and I are sharing a smaller bedroom with Uncle Evan, Aunt Cayce, and Aron. It's nearly like living in Caark again, although James and Bartholomiiu are the only Ranguvariians who still live with us. Aunt Rachel, Jaspen, and Mathiian all went back to the Ranguvariian Camp. I'm excited for Mathiian to learn more about how to be a Ranguvariian, but I'll miss him.

These days, I spend all my daylight hours learning how to use my new magic. Uncle Evan is my usual teacher since Mama is so busy, but his teaching style pretty well matches my style: jumping in headfirst. The three of us practice the death spell, *Alytniinaeran*, whenever we can, but the run-throughs are few and far in-between. Everyone keeps saying that we have the whole winter to prepare for the final battle against Emperor Rhydin, but

I hope Mama gets more free time soon. Otherwise, I'm not sure I'll be ready.

I still pop by the Royal children's lessons too, even if I don't practice with them anymore. Taisyn's fighting in the battle proved to King Xavier that he was ready to truly learn how to use his fire magic. I watch their lessons sometimes in the afternoons. In some ways, fire magic is surprisingly similar to my light magic. The light and the heat anyway, the general concept of how it felt; however, the motions are totally different. The movements and spells that Taisyn's father taught him are much bolder and broader. Fire is about strength, while air and water are more flowing motions (I started watching Dominick, Willian, and Chretien's lessons, too). Nathia pretty much ignores me now. Not sure why, but I really don't care.

I visited Erikin in the dungeon yesterday. The dungeons in this castle are really deep underground; I almost thought I wouldn't make it back up all those stairs. I don't know what possessed me to go see him. My so-called cousin. By the time I got down there, I was too angry to even say anything. Intentionally or not, he still essentially brought Emperor Rhydin to the Dome, which forced the rebellion to act upon their plans to conquer Lunaka Castle a lot sooner than they'd thought.

If he hadn't done that, Papa wouldn't have been in that battle. He may have been poisoned, but maybe he could have been around longer. Maybe I could have gotten another month with him, which could have tripled what little time I'd gotten with him. Erikin barely got a word in before I spun on my heel and left.

That word had been "please."

Ugh. I'll have to go see him again and actually let him talk.

Alrighty, let's wrap this up. I haven't had any more ancestral memories since Papa died, and I've drawn out the two I've had a bunch. I have portraits in my sketchbook of both Rhydin Caldwell and Amelia Eason. Mama has looked at them several times; I think they help her wrap her mind around it all.

What we know right now is that Rhydin Caldwell was made Archimage at the young age of eighteen, likely after the first memory I had. He wouldn't have still been living in Diagalo — a small Lunakan town that apparently no longer exists according to a history book I found while Dominick and I were cleaning up the castle library — as an Archimage.

But what happened between the first memory and the second? There could be years in between, especially since the fake Rhydin had appeared by then. When was he created and the old Rhydin cursed? How did it happen? Did Amelia find out there were two of the man she loved, and that's why she was killed? Or for some other nefarious reason? How did Nora and Amelia know each other if they weren't family?

I don't care what everyone else thinks. I *am* going to save Rhydin Caldwell. Their fears that he's worse than Emperor Rhydin are just plain stupid, no matter what Mama says about people fearing magic so much they become illogical. I'm the only one who's truly gotten to talk to him, and I just know there isn't any malice in him. If they could just meet him, they would know, too! I'll get to the Archimage Palace by myself if I have to, once I figure out where exactly it is. Taisyn promised to come with me.

Hopefully, I'll have another ancestral memory soon to help me continue to piece Rhydin Caldwell's story together in the meantime. I have no idea how I'm getting them, but they sure are helping unbury what truly happened to the First Archimage.

It's crazy, really. People thought the story of the First Archimage ended generations ago. Turns out, it's been going on for over three hundred years.

And I'm determined that I'm going to be the one to give it a happy ending.

END OF BOOK FOUR

Acknowledgments

Michaela

I was thirteen when I wrote the very first draft of *The Allyen* in the year 2007. It would be a full decade and hundreds of rewrites before my first book would make it into print as a fully-realized, fantasy novel, and now it is unbelievable to see the fourth book in this series come to life. This story and these characters are near and dear to my heart, and I am eternally grateful to you, my loyal readers, who continue to make this dream possible. Thank you for sticking with me this far; I can't believe this series is almost finished!

Thank you to my husband, Olin. You have always urged me to do what I love, and I am so thankful to have you support my writing. I could never do this without you. Also, thank you to my toddler daughter, Cassidy, for starting to take two-hour naps. Those literally made this book possible.

Thank you to Rachel Evans and Hannah Robinson, who help me create detailed outlines and conquer torturous writer's blocks. I'm so thankful to have other people just as invested in my story as I am!

Thank you to Daphne Olson and Cynthia Riley. You both keep my grammar in check, make sure I don't say "just" too much, and keep the injuries medically-accurate. I don't know what I'd do without you!

Thank you *so much*, Magpie Designs, Ltd. and L.N. Weldon, who continue to create the most gorgeous covers I've ever seen. I'm truly going to be sad when this series is over and I have to stop looking for dozens of arch and castle pictures with which to spam you. Thank you for everything!

Above all, thank you to my Heavenly Father for everything He has given me. I give You all the glory.

Thank you to everyone! I appreciate you all! I can't wait to continue on to Book 5, the *final* installment of The Story of the First Archimage series, so find my author page on Facebook or visit my website to stay in touch on future publications!

Visit my website to learn more!
www.michaelarileykarr.wordpress.com

Made in the USA
Monee, IL
28 February 2023